"Well? Would you h_____
tacked *you?*" she challe_____

"Good God, Georgie!_____
diculous!"

She giggled. "Oh, dear, Gus! I do admit that was a most improper question. I believe I've had too much of this delicious champagne."

"Yes, you have. And I will not be able to help you, if you become too foxed to walk. You must go to bed before you become quite disguised and I decide that you are open to improper suggestions and would be willing to accommodate me."

She opened her eyes wide and stared at him, then laughed merrily as she reached over and rested her hand on his arm. "Oh, you would never really do such a thing!"

"What?"

"Ask me to lie with you?"

"A man, finding himself alone with a woman, and with no other female about, might well do such a thing."

"But of course, *you* would not. With me."

"No. No, I wouldn't," Sedge lied through his teeth. All the thinly veiled talk of amorous dealings and sexual euphemisms had stirred his blood.

"You cannot abide me. And you're afraid I would try to compromise you."

"Georgie. Go to bed!" he ordered.

"Is that a request, an invitation, or an order, my lord viscount?" she asked provocatively, rising from her chair somewhat unsteadily and swaying toward him. . . .

Other Zebra Regency Romances by
Meg-Lynn Roberts

An Alluring Lady

A Perfect Match

A Midnight Masquerade

Christmas Escapade

Love's Gambit
Meg-Lynn Roberts

Zebra Books are published by

Kensington Publishing Corp.
850 Third Avenue
New York, NY 10022

All Kensington titles, imprints, and distributed lines are available at special quantity discounts for bulk purchases for sales promotions, premiums, fund-raising, educational or institutional use.

First Printing: July, 1996

Printed in the United States of America

ZEBRA BOOKS
KENSINGTON PUBLISHING CORP.

ZEBRA BOOKS are published by

Kensington Publishing Corp.
850 Third Avenue
New York, NY 10022

Zebra and the Z logo Reg. U.S. Pat. & TM Off.

First Printing: July, 1995

Printed in the United States of America

Harriet to Dorimant:

"When your love's grown strong enough to make you bear being laughed at, I'll give you leave to trouble me with it: till then, pray forbear, sir."

Sir George Etherege,
The Man of Mode, IV,i

Chapter 1

"Where in blazes is that damned landlord?" the fashionably dressed gentleman muttered between his teeth. He was feeling distinctly out of sorts as he was tired, hungry, and cold on that gloomy February day, despite his many-caped drab greatcoat. But most of all he was impatient. He flicked his coiled driving whip against his leather riding boots in irritation as he stood in the doorway of the common taproom. He was waiting to be shown to a private parlor in the little out-of-the-way inn where he had been forced to stop on the road between Marlborough and London.

His steely gray eyes flickered to a table set against the windows where a young lady was sitting in a pool of watery sunshine that was filtering in through the dusty window panes. She was laughing merrily.

Unbuttoning his greatcoat, he reached into the breast pocket of his jacket and took out his quizzing glass. He studied the back of the girl's head. She was facing away from him, chatting avidly to two roughly dressed young lads, local farm workers, from the look of them.

It was the sound of the small lady's rather exuberant laughter that first drew his attention. It rang most painfully through his head this morning, for he had had a late night, sitting up over cards and a few bottles of wine in the inn where he had put up the previous evening. Then afterward there had been that convenient serving wench ... Really, he had not found her at all desirable, but she had been persistent, and he had drunk more than he had intended. And so he had allowed himself to be persuaded to take her to his room.

And now he was late. Late for the house party where he was expected. Had been expected last night, actually. A group of his intimates was waiting for him to complete their party including one beautiful, coolly reserved lady, who had recently given him some hope that she might not be averse to sharing his company more intimately than heretofore.

One of the prized blacks that drew his sporting curricle had gone lame about half a mile down the road from this inn. It was a damned nuisance. He cursed under his breath. Augustus Sebastian Stanhope St. Regis, fourth Viscount Sedgemoor, did not like having his carefully laid plans thrown out. He did not like it one bit.

Much as he hated to use job horses and leave his acclaimed pair here at this inn, he needed to hire a new team to take him the thirty miles to Grey Towers, the estate of his friend, John Henderson, Baron Leftridge. But the lack-wit ostler he had encountered in the inn yard had been quite vague about the possibility of hiring such a team, saying the one pair of fresh job horses at the King's Head had only just been hired out. "They's already bespoke, yer honor."

The viscount had glanced around and noted the rather dilapidated black curricle with the cracked leather seat that stood to one side of the almost deserted inn yard. Looking bored, he had pulled out a coin, which he flipped to the man. The ostler had tipped his rather dirty cap with a hand that was itself none too clean, winked, and said he would see what he could do.

In the meantime, Sedge had taken himself inside the inn where he decided to order up a quick bite to eat and a pot of coffee. He had left his previous accommodation before dawn, with no food and very little sleep. He was driving himself, as was his custom, and had no servant along to help smooth his way. That circumstance usually presented no problems. Invariably, he found that his rather aloof, aristocratic manner and his deep pockets served him well in seeing that his needs were met with alacrity, whether by eager-to-please landlords, or by accommodating sporting wenches.

However, his lofty manner and deep pockets did him little good if there were no obsequious landlord about to bow low and immediately do his bidding.

The girl sitting across the taproom laughed once more, causing Sedge to wince painfully. He pressed his thumb and forefinger to his closed eyes for a moment before he glanced at the merry female again, noticing for the first time the color of her curls bouncing and glowing red-bronze in the faint light from the window. Those heavy curls, tied back with a gaily-colored ribbon that had become loosened, tumbled riotiously down her back. They looked wanton.

He found the color of the chit's hair offensive. It was quite definitely a bronzed red copper. And the stylish pelisse of bright rose pink braided with heavy black cording she wore clashed appallingly with that frightful red hair!

Red hair had always offended him. Of all the women who had bestowed their favors upon him, only one had had copper-colored hair. And that fiery-tempered woman had defied him quite outrageously. She had been more than pleased to become his mistress, willingly sharing his company and his bed for a week, but finding that he had no intention of marrying her, she had ranted and raved and stormed at him, then gone off and married a duke.

"Oh, I do not for a minute believe such a thing!" the girl was saying to one of her companions. "A mysterious, perfectly round, flattened circle in the midst of the stubble of last year's cornfield formed by fairies or other strange beings in the night? It is some trick one of your neighbors has been playing on you."

"It's one of them corn circles, fer sure. Been known for hundreds of years. Some says it's fairies' meeting places. Come out to t' farm and see fer yerself, miss," one of the boys challenged.

"Oh, I could not possibly do that, you know. I have only Pip, my groom, and Rufus to chaperone me."

Sedge could not believe his ears. The girl's cultured accents proclaimed her gently born, as did her ill-chosen but obviously expensive pelisse and her very fashionable bonnet resting on the seat beside her. She was undoubtedly a member of the gentry, at the very least.

She laughed again, the bright, merry sound ringing round the taproom and setting off a renewed pounding in his head. She was obviously not well acquainted with her roughly dressed companions. Their accents and words proclaimed them low-bred persons. One of the yokels had addressed her as "miss" and was trying to convince her to venture out, alone, with him to his farm.

Good God! She was some runaway schoolgirl, if he were any judge, with no more sense than a swan, about to get herself ruined by some farm workers whose attentions she had most unwisely and improperly attracted.

Sedge looked around hastily, wondering if he could leave before his presence was noticed. He would find it excessively distasteful to become involved in some ridiculous, undoubtedly tearful saga of a runaway schoolgirl. He certainly could not afford the time it would take to return the chit to her home.

"Oh, miss, ye'll be safe enough with Sam and me. And then ye can see the circle fer yerself, and see that I ain't roastin' ye."

"Well, I would truly like to see it, but you see, I haven't time. I am on my way to London and I must make use of what daylight there is to continue my journey."

"Lunnon? What'd ye want to go there fer, miss? None but thievin' rascals there," the young fellow advised her. "Sure to fleece ye afore ye can turn about."

Perhaps the yokels had only robbery in mind, not

seduction, Sedge thought on hearing this last statement. He sighed. It was distressing, but he supposed he would have to rescue the brainless chit from her predicament. The duties of a gentleman could be a great nuisance sometimes, he reflected with a grimace.

He sauntered forward lazily, fixed the two lads with a chilling look through his gold-rimmed quizzing glass, and bowed to the unfortunate red-haired child.

"It would seem that you require some assistance, miss. May I offer my services?" he intoned in a cultivated accent adopted to put pretentious nobodies in their place. "I am the Viscount Sedgemoor," he announced suavely.

Producing a finely wrought gold card case from his pocket, he flicked it open with one long finger, and drew out a gold-edged engraved calling card of heavy vellum which he handed to her.

The girl looked up and smiled sunnily. "Oh, sir. I didn't see you standing there. How impolite we have been. Will you not sit down and join us," she invited graciously, for all the world as though she were a dowager duchess, instead of an ill-favored, badly behaved, runaway girl fresh from the schoolroom. Sedge frowned heavily.

"I am Georgiana Carteret, by the way. But everyone calls me Georgie." She smiled up at him, her sapphire blue eyes twinkling brightly in her freckled face as she gave him her hand.

Sedge was so astonished by her careless acknowledgement of his presence that the quizzing glass fell from his hand to dangle down to his waist on its ribbon. He was left gasping for air for a fraction of a second as he automatically took the small hand stretched out to him. He recovered admirably as he executed a small, stiff bow over that little hand, and trusted that his lapse had gone unnoticed. "Miss Carteret. Charmed," he drawled smoothly.

"Viscount Sedgemoor, you said your name was?" she asked.

"That is correct, ma'am." He lifted his chin so that he could stare down his aristocratic nose at the little upstart.

At his almost imperceptible nod, Georgie continued chattily, "Well, my lord, allow me to introduce you to Sam and Joe Taylor. They are brothers, you know, and they work for Sir Henry Worley at his manor some five miles from here, although sometimes they help out doing odd jobs here at the King's Head. They have been telling me the most amazing story about mysterious circles that appear in the corn fields in the middle of the night to flatten all the leftover stalks of grain into a perfect circle. They think it the work of fairies. Have you ever heard of such a thing, my lord?" Georgie asked with a droll look in her twinkling blue eyes.

How the chit prattled on, ready to tell him the life stories of the country bumpkins, with no thought at all to the impropriety of making the acquaintance of two such low-bred persons, nor of the way she was speaking to *him* so familiarly. Why, she should be thanking him tearfully right now and begging him to convey her back to her father's house.

"*Miss* Carteret," he interrupted her. "Have you no thought to the impropriety of your situation?"

"I beg your pardon, my lord? What situation would that be?"

"Why, you are sitting here alone, unchaperoned, with two persons quite unconnected to you. And you said you were traveling unaccompanied by anyone other than your groom, and some other individual with the unfortunate sobriquet of Rufus."

"*Three* persons."

"I beg your pardon?"

"I am sitting here chatting to three persons quite unconnected to me, my lord. I also do not know you, but you have a look about you that tells me you are no danger to me. Sam and Joe are quite harmless, I assure you." She waved her hand casually at the two lads who were staring goggle-eyed at the imperious viscount.

"Do you always talk to every stranger you encounter?" Sedge asked with silky irony.

"Why, yes. I have never considered it before, but I suppose I do. It only seems polite, you know," she pointed out sweetly. "And Rufus is not a *person*, you know. He is my dog." With that correction, Georgie went off into merry peals of laughter.

At the sound of its name, a large reddish-coated dog emerged from under the table to lick his mistress's hand, then ambled forward, tail wagging, to sniff about Sedge's buckskin driving breeches.

Sedge was outraged. He did not know why he bothered trying to rescue the uncouth chit. Quite vulgar she was, the way she was carrying on with those yokels and speaking to him with so much impertinence. And her appearance was vulgar, too, almost wanton—except that she was a mere child.

Sam and Joe said not a word, but just stared at the viscount with their jaws hanging open, awed that such a great swell of a lord was taking note of their presence at all.

The landlord bustled in just then, wiping his hands on his apron as he came up to the viscount, bowing and scraping, saying that he understood his lordship was desirous of having some victuals fetched from the kitchens immediately.

Sedgemoor thought of denying that such was the case. He wanted to turn on his heel and take a dignified leave before the proceedings got further out of hand. But his stomach growled at the mere mention of food, and he could not deny his hunger.

"Fetch me a beefsteak and a large pot of coffee immediately, my good man." As the landlord turned to do his bidding, Sedge called out, "Wait! Show me to your best private parlor, first."

"Oh, no, Lord Sedgemoor, no need to mew yourself up all alone. Do join us here. There is plenty of room, you see," Georgie invited casually, moving along on the backless wooden bench on which she was seated to make room for him.

"Miss Carteret," he drawled with chilly hauteur. "I can see that you do not require my assistance after all. I prefer to take my meal in a private parlor, not in the *common* taproom, where one is forced to endure the company of low-bred persons."

"I'm as sorry as can be, yer lordship," the landlord interrupted, "but one of the winders in the private parlor is broke, and as it's a mite chilly in there, perhaps yer lordship would be more comfortable in here where there's a nice fire goin'."

Sedge stifled an oath. "Very well, you may serve me in here. Over at this table." He walked over to a small round table set in a dark corner of the taproom at the farthest distance he could get from the outlandish chit and her hayseed companions.

"Now don't be churlish, Lord Sedgemoor," Georgie coaxed him. "We are sitting at the best table, being closest to the fire, with the advantage of a bit of light from this window. You will be all alone in the dark over there in that cold corner."

"I have nothing else whatsoever to say to you, ma'am," the viscount answered at his most dignified. There was nothing he would like more at this moment than to give her the cut direct and march out of this confounded inn.

"Oh, nonsense. Of course you do! I can see that you are dying to ring a peal over my head for my rash, unladylike behavior in traveling to London all alone, with just my groom and dog for company. And I am driving myself, too, you know. Did you ever hear of such a thing? Is that not even more scandalous? Do you not long to know the whole sad story behind my escapade?"

Her sapphire eyes twinkled at him all the way across the room, angering Sedge even more. Why, the chit was teasing him. Him! The highest of high sticklers. One of the most courted—and feared—gentlemen in all of London!

Georgie turned away to conceal her chuckle at the look of pompous outrage on the viscount's face. He looked as though he were about to choke on his own neckcloth.

The ostler stuck his head in the taproom door at

that moment and whistled, making a hand motion that signaled to Georgie's two companions, Sam and Joe, that they were needed out back. They jumped hastily to their feet and took a mumbled leave of Georgie, their eyes shifting worriedly to the stiff-necked nob sitting in the corner glaring at them out of hard, steely gray eyes.

"That there gentry nob's a right cold 'un." Sam said in an undertone to Joe as they left.

"Aye. A right lethal blade 'e has fer a tongue," Joe agreed.

After her two companions left, Georgie continued her story despite the viscount's lack of encouragement. "Yes," she said between dainty bites of a jam tart, "I am on my way to London, driving my own curricle. I had to stop here to change horses. I was fortunate enough to be able to hire the only team they had available here at the King's Head. By the way, you should try some of the jam tarts, Lord Sedgemoor. The pastry is exceptionally flaky and quite delicious. Perhaps it will sweeten your temper, my lord," she said outrageously.

Sedge smiled. It was an unpleasant, brittle smile and the light of triumph showed in his cold gray eyes. "I believe you will find that you are mistaken, Miss Carteret. I am afraid that I have preempted you. I have hired that team. They are at this moment being harnessed to *my* curricle."

"Oh? What makes you think so?" Georgie asked sweetly, surreptitiously peeping out the dirt-streaked window to see that the team was, in fact, being harnessed to *her* curricle by Sam and Joe.

"The power of influence, Miss Carteret, the power

of influence," the viscount answered smugly, then wished he hadn't, for she began to laugh again. Sedge had never in his life met a woman who made him feel so . . . insignificant.

Woman? He reconsidered. No. Miss Georgiana Carteret was a mere chit of a girl. A red-headed, freckle-faced, dab of a female, who seemed to think it her duty in life to turn everything into a joke for her own amusement. First he had been offended by her appearance, now he was outraged by her impertinent manners. She goaded him almost to the point of wishing to do her some violence. He was not used to having his will crossed and his words gainsaid.

"You think to drive a curricle all the way to London, do you, Miss Carteret? I doubt you will last the first stage."

"Do you, Lord Sedgemoor? Well, then I think I shall surprise you when I tell you that I have already driven three stages from Chitterne St. Mary. That's on the southern edge of Salisbury Plain in Wiltshire, you know. From here, driving to London will be a snap." So saying, she snapped her fingers and smiled that merry smile that was beginning to drive him mad.

"I have never met a female yet who could drive more than a one-horse gig without tearing the animal's mouth to shreds and landing herself in the ditch before she had gone a quarter of a mile. Women know nothing about how to drive properly. And they certainly do not drive their own curricles to London," he pronounced with awful finality.

"I do. So I suppose you have met one now."

He gave her a patronizing stare. "I take leave to

doubt that, ma'am," he drawled, giving her a mocking smile while desperately trying not to let her goad him into losing his temper. He was having trouble enough quelling the urge to shout at her until she meekly admitted that he was in the right of it.

"Oh, you have my leave to doubt all you wish," she replied gaily, waving her hand airily. "I saw your pair being led in. Your gelding was limping. A stone under his right front hoof, I should think. Bruised and quite sore now, no doubt. A beautiful pair they are, Sedgemoor. Sleek and high-couraged. I congratulate you on your good eye. You will not want to take a chance on further injury to such a magnificent horse, I am sure, so you will have to rest him for at least a week. I can see that the pair are well matched for size—and beauty, of course. Are they as well matched for action?"

Sedge sat listening to her knowledgeable comments in astonishment. Well-concealed astonishment. "Indeed they are, ma'am," he admitted coldly. "Twould seem someone undertook your education in such matters. Your father or an older brother, perhaps?"

"Oh, no. 'Twas Pip and the stableboy at home. Papa is much too interested in—er—other things to have much concern for me—or his horses."

"Gleaned all you know from a stablehand. Now why does that not surprise me?"

"I do not know. Why does it not?" Georgie asked with a gleam of mischief in her eyes.

"Because only such an unladylike chit of a girl would consort with stable servants," he shot back.

His reprimand would have unnerved most women, but Georgie was made of sterner stuff.

"An unladylike chit of a girl, am I? Hmm. You are not very complimentary, are you, my lord? Are your manners an example of what I am like to encounter from the *gentlemen* in London? T'would hardly seem worth going there, if so."

Sedge was knocked off his pins by her masterly set-down. "You are a madcap scamp of a schoolgirl, running away from home, I don't doubt," he responded heatedly.

"Why, Lord Sedgemoor, do I look like a woman who would leave her own home? Her loving parents? Everything that is familiar and comfortable for an arduous journey to London and the unknown?" Georgie asked demurely, feigning surprise. Her eyelashes swept down over her cheeks as she lowered her eyes modestly. Then she peeped up, adding, "And it has been years since I left the schoolroom, you know." When he said nothing, she continued, "I left home only under the greatest of provocations, I assure you."

"You are enough to provoke a bloody saint," he muttered under his breath.

"What was that, my lord? I could not quite hear you. Was that a prettily phrased request that I tell you the whole sad story?" Georgie asked, then went off into gales of laughter at the look on the viscount's face. It was not anger or disdain so much this time as the astonished look of a wild animal that had been caught unexpectedly in a trap.

"Never mind," she said, wiping away the tears of laughter from her eyes with a corner of her sleeve. "I am afraid you would just put on that haughty look of yours, try to freeze me to death, and lec-lecture me in that arrogant voice about the d-dangers I will encounter and my unladylike behavior. Oh, d-dear, but you are so f-funny." She began to laugh again, merry peals ringing through the taproom as the landlord himself came in to serve the viscount.

"Here ye be, me lord. A tankard of ale and a prime beefsteak, cooked to a turn. Sal's bringin' the coffee and the rest of yer victuals." He turned and spoke to Georgie. "And the fresh team's been hitched up to yer curricle and they's ready to go, Miss Carteret."

"Oh, good! How efficient you have been!"

"I'm afeared, it's comin' on to rain though, miss."

"Never mind, we can put up the folding hood and I have a rain slicker to wear over my pelisse. I am used to being out in all weathers, you know, Mr. Johnson, but thank you for your concern. Pip, my groom, has been fed, too?"

"Aye, miss. In the kitchen. He's holdin' the horses' heads and waitin' for ye in the yard now, miss."

"Thank you, Mr. Johnson. You have been most helpful."

Georgie opened her reticule, took out her purse, and withdrew several coins, then handed them to the pleased-looking landlord.

"And please tell Mrs. Johnson that the meal was excellent. I have recommended her jam tarts to Lord Sedgemoor. I shall certainly stop here again, if I happen to be traveling this way. Good day, Lord Sedgemoor. So *pleasant* to have made your acquaintance," she called over to the glowering viscount as she rearranged her reticule on the sleeve of her pelisse. "It has been a most entertaining half an hour. I hope you do not have too long a wait before the ostler can send to one of the farms for a team for you," she added innocently, opening her large blue eyes wide. "Come, Rufus."

And with that parting shot Miss Georgie Carteret tripped out of the taproom with her large hound at her heels, still wearing that maddening smile on her wide mouth and that bright twinkle in her eyes.

Sedge watched her go, filled with impotent anger.

She left, taking the last of the day's sunshine with her. The room suddenly seemed very cold and dark. The sun had disappeared behind the clouds, leaving only a cold, gray light coming in through the dingy windows where the maddening female had baited him with her lively, impertinent comments. Soon the sound of wind and rain penetrated to Sedge's ears.

"Now her's real quality, if ye don't mind me sayin' so, yer lordship. Not like some females as come in here, all la-de-da posturin's and condescendin' airs. Friendly like. Had Sam 'n Joe eatin' outta her hand in a twinklin'. Not in the common way is Miss Carteret. No, indeed, not in the common way at'all," Johnson said, nodding wisely as he left the room.

No, Miss Carteret was certainly *not* in the common way, Sedge thought, trying to damp down his irritation at the way she had stolen that team from him, after he had bribed that halfwit ostler for them too! He tried to regain some measure of sangfroid after the way she had had her fun at his expense, teasing him to death, making a sizable dent in his amour propre, leaving him to kick his heels at this out-of-the-way inn while she went on her merry way to London.

Try as he would to take no further interest in the matter, Sedge could no more help himself than he could fly. He rose from his seat, went to the window, held back the dingy curtain with one long finger and watched as Miss Carteret, now wearing a dark rainslicker, turned her curricle in the inn yard with perfect precision, flicked her long driving whip out over the horses' heads, and set off at a smart trot down the road to London.

Bested by a small, impertinent female! Who would have believed it? He assured himself that no word of the recent incident could possibly reach any of his cronies and acquaintances in London where he was known as one of the most sophisticated men about town, capable of giving the most cutting of setdowns for the slightest infraction or the mildest foolishness.

Sedge's shoulders slumped from the rigid position in which he had been holding them as the small bundle of mischief disappeared out the door and down the road. He felt as though he had just gone ten rounds with Gentleman Jackson himself.

Yes, he reluctantly admitted, he had just suffered the worst drubbing of his life and at the hands of a red-haired, madcap hoyden. He wished never more to set eyes on the maddening chit. Should he ever again be forced to endure her company, he would certainly let her know who was master in no uncertain terms.

How would his reputation fare, if the *ton* ever got an inkling of how he had been teased unmercifully and beaten to a team of horses by one small scrap of a female? he wondered as he sipped his ale.

He gave a short bark of bitter laughter. No one would credit it. Certainly not the hordes of beautiful women who constantly cast themselves in his way, hoping for a word of favor, a look of interest from him.

Not only was his title an old and honored one and his pockets deep, but with his blond good looks and his tall, well-built form, honed to firm muscle and sinew by his penchant for keeping himself in top athletic trim, he was aware that he was accounted a regular Adonis. Many of the women with whom he had had bedroom dealings had told him so.

One of his favorite mistresses had told him a few years ago he looked more like a choir boy, than a toplofty, arrogant lord when he allowed himself to relax. She had teased him about his seductive, bedroom eyes, too. It was too bad Polly was no longer available. She had been able to relax him. But she had had an offer of marriage from another of her patrons, and she had told Sedge that while she would miss him dreadfully, she could not turn down her chance at a home and family and respectability and some comfort for the rest of her life. He had agreed that she could not miss the chance. But he still missed her occasionally.

After Polly's departure from his life, he had not favored another woman, either of the *haut ton* or the demimonde, with his company for more than a few weeks at a time. Pol had not been beautiful, but she had been a cozy, warm armful with her black curls and huge brown eyes and soft, creamy skin. But mostly it had been her sweet, comfortable manner that had always made him feel relaxed. She was so kind, he sometimes forgot she was being paid to show him every consideration.

Damn it all to hell, he thought, setting down his tankard of ale with a bang on the scarred oaken table. Why was he thinking of lying in a warm bed with a cozy armful of woman when he needed to be on his way to Leftridge's estate?

If they would only hurry with that team, he would be on his way. Completely forgetting his previous fervent wish never to set eyes on her again, he now vowed to teach Miss Georgiana Carteret a much-needed lesson. He would show that impertinent female that he could outdrive her any day. He would overtake her and her brace of ridiculous companions on the road and give her the go-by before she knew what was happening.

Chapter 2

"Eh, Miss Georgie, but ye took'd that corner tight as could be," Pip, Georgie's groom spoke from his place beside his mistress on the curricle seat as they bowled along the turnpike past a succession of well-tilled fields, open grassland where sheep or cattle grazed, and dense hedgerows that grew so tall it was impossible to see what was on the other side.

"Yes, I did, didn't I, Pip?" Georgie answered as she drove along quite happily despite the deteriorating weather conditions. The light was fading to a murky, dingy gray and it was beginning to rain more heavily since they had left the King's Head some half an hour previously. Rufus fidgeted on the floor under the curricle seat, trying to find a more comfortable position, but he didn't disturb Georgie's concentration on her driving.

She had taken the measure of the hired team during the first mile or so and had them well in hand now. They were neither bonesetters nor the most prime bits of horseflesh she had ever driven. But they were strong, steady goers, despite the fact that their

action was not perfectly matched, and Georgie set a
smart pace as she bowled along the well-traveled
road from Marlborough to London.

The light mist falling from the heavy gray February sky didn't bother her for her pelisse and rain
slicker adequately protected her from the wet and
cold. But she was worried that the light would not
hold for many more miles. It was doubtful that she
would reach London and her dear, old autocratic
grandmother, Lady Carteret, tonight.

She thought they would have to stop at the next
decent coaching inn they reached. In the meantime,
she let her mind drift back to her recent encounter
with the haughty Viscount Sedgemoor. What an uncommonly handsome man he was, at least when his
fine, regular features hadn't been marred by that almost ever-present scowl. That thick golden blond hair
and those pale gray eyes of his were arresting
enough, but added to those perfections there had been
his classical features and tall, well-proportioned physique. His High-and-Mightiness was surely wildly
popular with females of all stations, Georgie thought
with a smile curving up her lips.

And he knew it, too. And knew his position. She
had found it irresistible to poke fun at him, so high
in the instep as he had been. She had enjoyed taking
him down a peg or two. To judge by the look on his
face, no one had ever had the temerity to attempt
such a thing before.

Well, he would be the better for it, she thought
with a small satisfied grin. A little humility was always good for the soul. If she were his keeper, she

would give him a healthy dose every day, she decided with a merry laugh.

"'Ere, wot's so funny, miss?" Pip asked from beside her.

"Er, just thinking back over an amusing incident at the inn, Pip. I met a gentleman there who was a proper nob."

"Too 'igh in the instep for you, were he, miss? Hit's my guess, you landed 'im a facer or two afore you was done with 'im."

"Well, I do believe I managed to get the better of him once or twice during the course of our conversation. But, oh, Pip, he was not at all pleased. I wish you could have seen the look on his face!" Georgie went off into peals of laughter and Pip had to urge her to have a caution with the team. She sobered immediately, but her thoughts returned to the viscount.

Imagine! Accosting a complete stranger in an inn and taking her to task for her behavior as he had done! The man certainly did not lack for arrogance.

Perhaps he was married and the father of young daughters, or perhaps he was an elder brother who had sisters about her age, and that explained why he had seen fit to upbraid her as he had for speaking to Sam and Joe. As though he were her grandfather or some stern schoolmaster! It had been an extraordinary incident.

Georgie giggled. Whatever the case, she had certainly paid him back for his interference in her affairs. He had looked ready to strangle her when she left the inn.

It was her friendly nature that had led her into conversation with the two lads in the taproom in the first place. Of course, if she had thought about it, she would have acknowledged that it was not quite proper. But she never did think about these things. Heavens, she had been finishing her meal in the out-of-the-way inn and saw no harm in chatting to the two boys. She had known she was in no danger from Sam and Joe. They were as harmless as lambs.

She could not quite say the same for the viscount.

Another woman would have been in floods of tears, ready to sink through the floor in embarrassed humiliation at such a lecture from an imposing, aristocratic stranger, but Georgie could only see the amusement in it all, as she did in most things. She bit back a smile. Lord Sedgemoor needed someone to stand up to him, to banish that perpetual scowl, to teach him to look at life a little more humorously. Someone to loosen him up and remove that iron rod from his arrogant spine.

Would she encounter him in town, she wondered, once she was ensconced with her grandmother? If he weren't yet married or betrothed, she would have to review her list of acquaintances and see if she could come up with a suitable match for him from her legion of eligible friends. Someone to liven him up. If he were already married, she would be sure to make the acquaintance of his wife and teach her how to counter his arrogance, and not let herself be dictated to or ridden roughshod over.

"There's a ve'icle a comin' up on us fast, Miss Georgie. Got a gent crackin' 'is whip over 'is 'orses' 'eads. Drivin' 'is prads well up to their bits, 'e is. Wants to give us the go-by," Pip warned her.

Georgie was just then negotiating a rather tricky

hill that had turned quite muddy in the rain. There
was a sheer drop on one side, and a steep incline to
a grassy ditch on the other.

"Oh, Lord! It will be difficult for me to pull over
to the side here. Why can't the driver wait until we're
past this hill? Then I will gladly let him pass, if he is
in that much of a hurry."

"Maybe 'e's wishful of provokin' you to a race,
Miss Georgie," Pip offered.

"On this hill? He would have to be in his cups or
dicked in the nob to do such a thing," she replied
scornfully.

Georgie held her team steady with firm hands and
pulled as far to the left-hand side of the road as
she could, one wheel of her curricle running along the
verge of the road above the ditch as she heard the
hooves of the horses close behind her, sloshing
through the mud and coming ever nearer.

Just ahead, Sedge spotted the dilapidated curricle
that surely belonged to the forward chit who had
twitted him in the taproom of the King's Head. He
smiled grimly. Prided herself on her abilities as a
whip, did she? Well, he had known that he would
catch her up, even though he had had a quarter of an
hour's later start. He had driven his team hard, determined that that red-haired fright of a female would
not outdrive him.

Now his team had up a full head of steam as he
crested the steeply curving hill. He would show Miss
Carteret what driving to an inch meant on a hill such
as this, he thought determinedly. He approached the

rear of the vehicle in front of him, measured the amount of room he would need to pass, then saw a spot just ahead that would be admirably suitable for the tricky maneuver.

On the sharp downward slope of the hill, he had his team charging forward at full tilt. He waited until the last second. Then, holding the reins in one hand, he cracked the whip over his horses' heads, urging them to even greater speed and edging them to the right of the other curricle. The hired team responded to his double commands and surged forward.

Sedge's team was almost even with the second vehicle when the offside wheel of his curricle skidded in one of the muddy ruts in the slippery road. The curricle began to slither to one side and its left wheel touched the right one of the other vehicle.

There was a mighty splinter, then his curricle began to topple to one side. After perhaps two seconds, during which Sedge tried to retrieve the situation, he realized that his curricle was going to turn over. He threw his whip away and jumped.

"Gor blimey, Miss Georgie, what a piece of drivin' to bring us off safe!" Pip, gripping the side of his seat with white-knuckled hands, congratulated his mistress as Georgie brought her curricle safely to a stop above the edge of the ditch. "That there gentry cove's dicked in the nob, 'e is. Tryin' to pass you on this 'ill, in all this mud! Cow-handed fool!"

Pip was shaking in his boots, and even Georgie's hands were not quite steady when she passed him the reins as she prepared to jump down and see what had happened to the other driver.

"I must see what has happened to the gentleman. Rufus has already gone to have a look," she said somewhat shakily.

"Ere, Miss Georgie. Oughta let me do that."

"Yes. You can come too, as soon as you can secure these horses. Be quick, Pip. I'm sure I shall need you to help me with the other team, as well as with the driver."

The gentleman had managed to jump clear of the curricle as it crashed onto its side, but he had rolled over and over down the grassy incline. Georgie saw at a brief glance that he had landed awkwardly in the ditch, where he lay unmoving.

She went first to the other team, grabbing the harness of one of the horses that was plunging and kicking, trying to pull itself free of the traces of the overturned curricle. She yanked sharply on the reins, bringing the animal's head down and giving it a low-voiced command. As it steadied, she ran her hand over the horse's velvety nose, uttering soothing noises. The beast rolled its wild eyes at her, but subsided at her authoritative tone and assuring voice.

Pip was beside her in an instant, holding onto the harness of the other horse.

"Don't think these nags is too badly injured," he said, running an expert eye over the two animals. "Ain't nothing broken, I swear."

"Secure them and come help me, Pip," Georgie called, leaving the animals in Pip's capable hands while she hurriedly made her way down into the ditch to see to the fallen driver.

Rufus had raced down the grassy slope ahead of his mistress and was sniffing about the fallen man, poking him with his cold nose and laying a wet paw on the shoulder of the caped greatcoat the gentleman wore.

It was awkward going, encumbered as she was by her pelisse and rain slicker, but Georgie grabbed up her skirts in one hand and managed to clamber down to the injured gentleman.

"Blast these long skirts! I should have worn a pair of Papa's old riding breeches. Would have saved myself a heap of trouble," she grumbled as she lost her balance and slithered the last few feet to where the man lay in the ditch. She was greeted by Rufus, who licked her face. "Down boy. Let me see to the gentleman, there's a good dog."

Georgie crawled over to the injured man on her knees. He lay on his stomach, his head turned to one side against the soggy ground. His hat had fallen off and she saw that his face and very blond hair were liberally spattered with mud, as was his greatcoat. He appeared to be unconscious.

"Oh, good Lord!" Georgie exclaimed, recognizing Viscount Sedgemoor despite the rain and dirt that covered him, obscuring his fine features. "I hope to heaven you aren't dead, Lord Sedgemoor, for that would complicate my journey considerably," Georgie said, wondering how on earth she was to deal with the situation.

Gently, she put her hand on the side of his neck, feeling for a pulse. A moan escaped his lips at her touch and Georgie gave a great sigh of relief. "Thank God! You're alive! Well, we will soon have you right as rain, see if we don't!" she exclaimed optimistically.

"Will you indeed, ma'am? That will be a miracle," Sedge said through gritted teeth, as he tried to raise himself. Realizing that his leg hurt abominably, he ceased his efforts as excruciating pain shot through him.

"Where are you injured?"

"My leg. I believe it must be broken," he got out. He closed his eyes as a nauseating faintness overcame him, hoping that he would wake soon and that this appalling nightmare would have vanished.

"Pip, you'll have to go for help!" Georgie called to her groom who stood on the bank above, peering down. "I think the gentleman has broken his leg. We'll need a board to carry him on and at least two more people to help us move him from here. I will stay with him until you come back."

"Aye, Miss Georgie," Pip answered, straightening up and thankfully spying a farmhouse at no great distance from the road.

"Good God!" Sedge muttered as he came back to consciousness and recognized Georgie's voice speaking quite close to his ear. How he recognized her through the haze of pain that suffused him, he didn't know. "Your groom—he must not reveal my identity," he insisted through gritted teeth.

"Pip, wait!" Georgie called the groom back. "Say nothing of our names or identities. Say only that a lady and a gentleman have had an accident," she instructed her servant.

"Right, Miss Georgie," Pip said before turning on his heel and making for the nearby farmhouse.

"Do not worry, Sedgemoor," Georgie said brightly, patting the injured man on the shoulder in a reassuring fashion, "I will think of something."

"Good God!" Sedge repeated. He closed his eyes again at the sight of Georgie's freckled face. He could not bear to open them and contemplate his companion. Not only was the pain from his injured leg unbearable, but now he was doomed to spend several more hours in the company of the infuriating baggage from the King's Head Inn. He bit down hard on his lips, drawing blood, as he stifled the groan of pain that rose in his throat.

"The accident—all my fault," he muttered breathlessly. "Should never have tried to overtake you on this accursed hill," he added, furious at himself for allowing the need to best her gain the upper hand and supercede his good judgment. How could he have been goaded so far as to do such a foolish thing? Nothing remotely like that had ever happened to him before. He would never live it down.

"Well, I'm sure you would have accomplished the task easily if it had not been so muddy here," she assured him magnanimously. "I could see that you are a first-rate whip. I believe your wheel must have skidded in one of the muddy ruts."

His eyes still closed, he tightened his lips against the pain.

"What can I do for you, my lord?" Georgie asked, her low voice full of kindness and concern. She used both her hands to carefully lift his head from the wet, muddy ground so that it could rest in her lap. She soothed her hand down the side of his cheek, pushing the hair out of his eyes, then took out her handkerchief and gently began to wipe the mud off his face.

"I wish I could tell you to go to the devil, but I needs must . . . ask . . . for your . . . help . . . instead," he gritted out, his breathing labored.

"Well, you are certainly not very polite, Sedgemoor. It was not *my* fault you did such a daft thing as try to pass on a narrow, muddy hill. But, of course, I shall help you. I would do as much for any creature in distress. . . . Does it hurt much?"

He gave a crack of pain-filled laughter. "It hurts like . . . the . . . very . . . devil!" he swore, then mercifully lost consciousness.

"He's sleeping comfortably now, ma'am," the doctor said to Georgie as she stood talking quietly with him outside the door to the room where Sedgemoor had been put to bed. "I must thank you for your help in holding him when I set his leg. I needed two people to help me and while Farmer Thorpe is a strong man, his wife was of no use at all."

"Yes, Mrs. Thorpe did go white as a sheet as soon as we cut off his boot and she saw his poor broken leg, did she not? I'm grateful that she did not swoon before you ordered her to leave the room," Georgie remarked. "However, it was very kind of her to take us in, in the first place. I do not know what we would have done else. . . . What do you wish me to do for him overnight, Doctor Hamilton?"

"Well, I've given him a hefty dose of laudanum, so I believe he will sleep through the afternoon now. When he wakes in the late evening, he should have nothing but water, then another dose of laudanum. I've measured it out for you. That should see him through the night and I will come again in the morning to see how he does."

"Thank you. This is rather difficult, Doctor, but—will he make a full recovery?"

"Oh, no doubt about that, my dear Mrs. Moor. He is young and healthy. Has a strong constitution, I would say. But as his wife, you know that."

"Er—yes. Yes, he does. But I'm sure he will be greatly annoy—ah, upset, if he were to be left with a permanent limp from this accident." Georgie looked at the doctor appealingly, willing him to tell her that such an outcome would definitely *not* be the case.

"As to that, time will tell. He has a slight fracture of the tibia bone in his right leg. It was relatively easy to realign and set perfectly. He must keep quiet these next few days, though. If he tried to move around much, he may disturb the bone as it knits back together. If he were to disturb the setting, then I could not answer for the consequences."

"I shall just have to see to it that he is kept perfectly quiet. Thank you, Doctor Hamilton. You have been very straightforward with me. I will just get my purse and see you to the door," Georgie said, looking worried.

"Buck up, young woman," the doctor advised, patting Georgie heartily on the shoulder. "That strapping young husband of yours will give you a score of sons, aye, and daughters, too, before he's ready to stick his spoon in the wall."

Georgie forced a smile as she went off to get her money purse from her reticule in order to pay the doctor with some of the last of her precious few coins.

After she had seen the doctor to the door, Mrs. Thorpe met her in the hallway.

"Will ye be wantin' some dinner, Mrs. Moor?"

"I do not think I could eat a bite, but I would appreciate it if you would feed my—*our* groom," Georgie replied.

"Oh, dearie, ye must take some food. Keep yer strength up. That comely husband of yourn's gonna need some lookin' after in the next few days."

"Yes, perhaps you are right, Mrs. Thorpe. I shall try to make a good dinner of whatever you can provide. I can't tell you how much your hospitality means to me—us. Poor Lor—my poor husband would have been in much worse case, if we had had to take him farther afield. It was very lucky your house was so near and that Mr. Thorpe was working close to home so that he could help us carry him here. And you've been very generous to give up your best bedroom, too!"

"Yer right welcome, ma'am. Me and Thorpe is right proud to have such quality as yer good husband and yerself that's used to all the best to stay at our humble cottage. I'm sorry as can be that I don't have another room to offer ye for tonight, cause that man of yourn is sure to be amoanin' and agroanin' the night through."

"Oh, that's all right, Mrs. Thorpe. I must stay with him, in case he needs anything, or calls out for me."

"But ye won't want to be lyin' in the same bed, ye'll never get any rest. I'll ask Thorpe to set up the truckle bed in the bedroom, when he finishes his dinner."

"Yes, that will do nicely, Mrs. Thorpe," Georgie said with a winning smile to conceal her inner misgivings.

Seeing the young woman's tender care of the injured gentleman, Farmer Thorpe had jumped to the conclusion that the two young people involved in the accident were husband and wife.

Georgie had not contradicted him.

No, she had confirmed the farmer's conclusion, naming herself and the viscount "Mr. and Mrs. Moor." That would certainly conceal their real identities, she had reasoned, pleased with her own quick thinking. On the spur of the moment she had concocted a tale to explain away the accident, too, saying that she prided herself on her skill with the ribbons and frequently drove her own curricle when she and her husband traveled. They were in the habit of racing one another for brief stretches on their journeys, she explained, and they had dared one another to race their separate curricles along that stretch of road. They had not known about the treacherous hill ahead of them, she had said sorrowfully, that had led to Mr. Moor's breaking his leg. Mrs. Thorpe had clucked her tongue over this sad statement and had told Georgie not to worry, that she and Mr. Moor had landed in good hands.

Explaining away their lack of luggage by saying that it had been sent on ahead, Georgie felt a small pang of guilt at deceiving the friendly Thorpes, but she didn't stop to consider any other consequences of her numerous faradiddles. What the viscount would say when he learned that she had declared them a married couple did not trouble her thoughts.

Sedge was muttering in his sleep, trying to toss and turn, but something was pressing him down, making it impossible for him to move, or to get into a comfortable position. "Wha—who? What?" he cried out, moving his right arm strongly so that he pushed Georgie off his chest as she leaned over, trying to press her hands as hard as she could against his shoulders to stop him from moving about. She was determined that he would do himself no further injury while he was in her charge.

"Now, Lord Sedgemoor, do you hear me? You must cease this struggling and trying to fight me off."

"Why? are you trying to ravish me?" Sedge asked facetiously, coming fully awake in an instant and rising up from the bed slightly, bracing himself with his arms.

"You will do your poor broken leg no good at all, if you thrash about so, you know," Georgie told him, her face only inches from his as she pressed him back down and began to smooth the bedclothes around him.

He grimaced and watched her movements with narrow-eyed suspicion.

Georgie moved to the old oaken dressing table to pour him a glass of water from the serviceable brown earthenware jug resting there. "How are you feeling now, Lord Sedgemoor?" she asked. "I hope the pain is not too bad. The doctor thought you would want water when you finally awoke. Are you thirsty?"

"What are you doing in my bedroom in the middle of the night, ma'am?" he asked, ignoring her solicitous questions and trying, rather unsuccessfully, to ignore the abominable pain in his leg. He looked at his red-headed nemesis, seeing that she stood before him in a dowdy, rumpled gown of a discolored green material. The ugly gown stretched too tightly over her rather well-endowed figure, while her long coppery red hair was in wild disarray about her face. He could almost believe that she had indeed been trying to ravish him, so wild and unkempt did she look, as though she had just risen from a bed that had been put to lusty good use.

She moved forward to the bed again and began to help him sit up so that he could drink the water. "Why, I'm looking after you, what did you think?"

"If you think by this trick to force me into wedding you, I tell you here and now, it will not work. Many women have tried to force me to the altar, with just such devious, ill-judged tricks as this, and I assure you, none has ever succeeded."

"What, you have broken some one or another of your limbs and been rescued by some kind lady several times before now? What a strange habit to cultivate, Lord Sedgemoor!" she teased him. "You must be a physical wreck, yet I didn't notice that you were marred in any way when the doctor was undressing you," she said provocatively.

He frowned at her and said coldly, "I trust that you were not actually present when I was disrobed. But, however it was, I warn you. Be you ever so compromised, I will not marry you! Do you understand me, Miss Carteret?"

"Oh, you are so silly. Your wits must have gone begging in your fall. I would not want to marry *you*. A man who tries to censure my behavior and who thinks he can walk in and order my life for me, when he had never seen me before in his life. Why, I would not marry such an arrogant, bad-tempered man for all the tea in China! Come now, don't gape at me with your mouth open like that. You look just like a fish." She gave a low laugh.

"Here. Drink." She handed him the glass of water and he did indeed raise it to his lips and downed it thirstily.

"I shall get you some more, then you must take the laudanum the doctor left."

"No. I shall not take laudanum. And I meant what I said. You stand warned."

"Do not be so stubbornly foolish, Sedgemoor. I am sure your leg must pain you dreadfully. And you need your rest so that it will heal and you can leave this place in a week or so."

"A week or so!" he exclaimed. "I shall leave tomorrow." Something like panic pulled at him. He must get to Leftridge's soon or likely a search party would be sent out. He could not be found in company with this fright of a schoolgirl!

"Will you, indeed?" Georgie asked, hands on hips. "And how will you accomplish that, I wonder, with a broken leg, a smashed curricle, and no servants to help you?"

He bit his lip and looked uncertain for the first time. "How—how badly is my leg broken?"

Georgie regarded him with an indulgent smile. He was human after all. "The doctor said it was a fracture of the tibia bone and should heal perfectly well, *if* you rest, Sedgemoor, and don't jar it about while it knits."

He grimaced. "The horses?"

"Both shaken but unharmed. Mr. Thorpe will see them returned to the King's Head tomorrow."

"Thank God. And my curricle? There's no salvaging it, is there?" he asked with a frown, thinking of the spanking new vehicle he had recently purchased.

"'Fraid not, Sedgemoor. It was pretty well smashed to smithereens. I believe Mr. Thorpe has already seen to its removal from the road."

He digested this news with another inward curse at his own cow-handed driving. Looking pensive, he held out his glass, indicating that he would like another drink. "I believe you have a groom with you?" he asked as Georgie went to pour more water for him.

"Yes. Pip is his name. Do you require his services in some way?" She surreptitiously dumped the laudanum in his water glass while she had her back to him.

"Yes. I would like to employ him to take a message for me tomorrow to some friends who live not too far off. And I think it would be much better if it were he, rather than you, who, ah, waited on me while I'm tied by the leg here. He can better see to my, ah, needs."

Georgie bit back a smile as she handed him the glass. "Of course, I shall have him see to you for quite a bit of the time. And I believe Mr. and Mrs. Thorpe will look in on you too, when they can spare the time from their farm chores."

"Who the devil are Mr. and Mrs. Thorpe?" he

asked, then made a face as he realized that he had just downed a full glass of water that had been adulterated with the laudanum. "Blast you, you little imp of the devil!"

Georgie ignored his furious curse. "The Thorpes are the people who own this house. They are farmers in these parts—Little Bickton is the name of the small hamlet just along the road, I gather. The Thorpes are wonderfully kind people. You are very fortunate, and owe them a great debt of gratitude for the way they helped carry you here and for their open-handed hospitality.

"They have given us their best bedroom, too, and agreed to let us stay here until your leg is healed enough for you to travel, you know. I hope your purse is full, Sedgemoor, and you can pay them back for all their generosity, for mine is quite empty after paying off the doctor who set your leg."

"You took it upon yourself to pay the doctor for me?" he asked coldly, more aggravated than he could say by her highhanded assumption of authority, and unwarranted interference in his affairs. He wished to give her a tongue lashing she would not soon forget for her presumption, but he was already beginning to feel drowsy from the laudanum and could not take the managing little baggage to task as he wished to do.

"As you were quite unconscious, what else could I do? I'm sure you would not have welcomed a search of your clothing so that I could locate your purse."

"By God, you had better not . . . where are my clothes?" he asked groggily, realizing that he was clad only in a voluminous white nightshirt under the sheet and coverlet.

"I believe Mrs. Thorpe is laundering them for you. Your outer clothing at least was all wet and covered with mud."

"What a damnable coil!" Sedge uttered grimly, but his words were overtaken by a yawn. His eyes were heavy. Try as he would, he could not keep them open.

Georgie leaned over him and gently pushed back a lock of golden hair that had fallen over his forehead with a cool hand, soothing him. "I hope you will be able to sleep now, Sedgemoor."

"Yes. You had better go to your own room now, too. Get some sleep." His eyelids drifted shut.

"Oh, I intend to," Georgie murmured, "get some sleep, that is. But I'm afraid there's only the one room, you see, Sedgemoor."

There was no answer to her provocative statement. The viscount was deeply asleep.

Chapter 3

Sedge woke to bright sunlight streaming in through the bedroom window, spreading over his face. He stirred uncomfortably, aware of a dryness in his mouth and an ache not only in his leg, but in his entire body. His head pounded unmercifully. He groaned.

"Oh, Sedgemoor, you are finally awake!" Georgie exclaimed as she saw him lying on the pillow with his eyes open, though they looked somewhat dazed and unfocused. The bubble of laughter that welled up in her at his expression of horrified shock on seeing her, spilled over and echoed throughout the small chamber.

Seeing Georgie standing across the room from him, Sedge closed his eyes tightly for a second. He looked again, not sure that his eyes had not deceived him at first glance, or that he was still in the grips of the drug he had been tricked into imbibing earlier. But no. There she was, as large as life.

Larger.

He closed his eyes again in disbelief. Quite plain and freckled she was—a decidedly flawed figure, too, dressed in an ugly, hopelessly wrinkled round gown of bottle green Merino wool. With that wild, copper hair—definitely not flaming auburn tresses, but almost carroty red—she looked like something from a comic pantomime. And that merry laugh, assailing his ears again! "Oh God! I thought I was having a particularly realistic nightmare, but it's all too true," he uttered in loathing.

"You look very much better this morning, you know, even if you are still feeling thoroughly out of sorts," she said as she approached the bed and handed him a glass of fresh water, then reached to put an extra pillow at his back so that he could sit up. "You are not so pale as you were yesterday and your eyes have lost that bruised look."

"Remind me to give you a recommendation as a purveyor of fustian."

Georgie laughed merrily. For the first time, he noticed her even little white teeth and the twin dimples that appeared in her cheeks when she smiled.

"What are you doing here? I thought I had made it clear that you were not to come into this room again." Even as immobile as he was, his gray eyes held a distinctly dangerous threat.

"No! Did you?" she answered, taking no notice of his ferocious look. "You may well have *said* such a silly thing, but I'm sure I was too sensible to take any notice."

"Now, see here, Miss Carteret, do you have the impertinence to defy me—" Sedge's outburst was interrupted by a knock on the door, followed by the entrance of the doctor.

"Ah, I'm glad I find you awake, Mr. Moor. How

do you go on today, young man? Leg give you much trouble overnight?" Doctor Hamilton asked.

Sedge's eyes narrowed suspiciously as he heard himself addressed as "Mr. Moor."

Georgie was making hand signals behind the doctor's back, putting her finger to her lips, indicating that he should say nothing. The devious chit had obviously given them all a false name, Sedge realized.

Well, he had to admit, it was as well the people here didn't know they were dealing with a member of the aristocracy. Perhaps word would not leak out and some measure of secrecy about this abominable episode could be maintained. Could he dare allow himself to hope that his foolish accident would *not* become the latest *on-dit* for the *ton* to sneer at?

Sedge cleared his throat, glowered at Georgie and turned to answer the doctor. "I was given so much laudanum that I hardly know what kind of night I had. I'll not have that vile mixture again. Have someone bring me some brandy. That will put me to sleep, if the pain should become unbearable."

"Well, well," Doctor Hamilton was saying as he lifted the sheet to examine Sedge's leg. "Perhaps you could take some brandy instead, young man. But it's not likely these good people will have any about the house. You'll have to send your servant to the Cross and Keys, a hostelry located some two miles farther along down the road in Little Bickton, if you wish to make such an expensive purchase."

"Yes, I will do that," Sedge agreed somewhat breathlessly as he tried to suppress the moan that rose to his lips when the doctor examined his leg. He raised his eyes to the ceiling and clamped his lips together tightly. Then he noticed Georgie standing right beside the doctor.

"Leave the room *now,* if you please, Miss—"

"Oh, now, my dear, don't be so squeamish," Georgie interrupted hastily. "The doctor will be finished in a moment."

Doctor Hamilton finished his examination, pulled the sheet back in place and lowered his brows at Sedge. "I know it hurts like the devil and you are in great discomfort, young man, but that's no reason to bark at your good lady in such an ill-tempered fashion. She has tended you all night, you know. And yesterday, she held your hand and bathed your face while we were getting you ready. Then she and Farmer Thorpe held you most competently while I set this leg for you. You should be thanking her," the doctor lectured him sternly, "not taking out your spleen on your good wife."

"My *wife!*" Sedge almost strangled on the words. "She is *not*—"

Georgie's hand signals became frantic behind the doctor's back as she pulled a comic face at him, indicating he should not contradict the doctor.

"This woman is *not,* ah, this is not what's she's accustomed to," Sedge finished lamely, looking at Georgie with murder in his eyes.

She had to suppress a grin. Looking ready to explode with fury, his face had gone almost purple with rage.

"No, I daresay it's not," Doctor Hamilton agreed. "From the look of you, I would say you are used to being tended by an army of servants, not by this competent little lady." The doctor turned and smiled approvingly at Georgie. "Even though nursing an injured man may not be what you're used to, from the look of your patient this morning, I must say, well done, Mrs. Moor!"

Looking demure with her hands clasped behind her back, Georgie smiled back at him and thanked him for the compliment.

"I shall be sending for my servants without delay, so that my *wife* will be spared the onerous duty of looking after me," Sedge commented, grimacing angrily.

"Well, well, make yourselves as comfortable here as you may," the doctor recommended, saying that he thought it would indeed be wise to send for some help for the sweet little lady, but he warned Sedge not to think of journeying anywhere for at least two weeks, unless he wished to risk permanent damage to his leg, possibly even causing a permanent limp.

Sedgemoor looked grim at this warning.

Georgie wisely left the room with the doctor to see him out and did not return until Pip had been in to see to any of his lordship's as yet unmet needs, and Mrs. Thorpe had taken him a tray of the bland food the doctor had ordered.

When Georgie came back into the room several hours later, she tried unsuccessfully to hide her wide grin of amusement, the smile that always revealed her dimples.

"So. You have finally dared show your face in here again, have you, *Mrs. Moor,*" Sedge ground out angrily, laying aside the book that he had been unable to concentrate on. "Ready to explain your diabolical scheming lie and take your medicine, are you? Your trick will gain you nothing, as I have warned you before."

"Well, Sedgemoor, what would you have had me do?" Georgie asked, her eyes widened guilelessly. "There you were, lying unconscious in a ditch, with a broken leg. Obviously, I could not leave you. And obviously, there is not enough room here to accommodate both of us. And, besides, I did it to protect myself."

"Protect yourself! I have never heard of such an outrageous farrago of fiendish nonsense in my life!"

"Well, I could not use my own real name, you know."

"I know nothing of the sort," he contradicted.

"It would have quite improper for me to have stayed here with you as an unmarried lady. And I suspected that you would not want your identity and title known either."

"But even so, you did not have to say we were married. This is some trick you have concocted to force me to wed you."

She ignored his jibe. "Just the opposite, Sedgemoor. I might be traced. If word got back to my father that I stayed here alone with you, he would be sure to demand that you marry me. Especially when he learned that you are a wealthy lord. He's a high stickler for the proprieties, you know," she told him with an innocent look on her face, while her blue eyes twinkled devilishly.

"How do you know I'm wealthy?" He seized on this.

"Oh, I don't *know,* but I assume with all your talk of servants and privileged living that you must have some blunt concealed about you somewhere."

He gave her a cold look and did not answer. She grinned at him.

"Besides, by giving false names and false identities, I was protecting you too, you know. Don't you see, if everyone thinks we are already married, they can't force us to wed. I thought it a brilliant plan."

"Brilliant? It's the most hairbrained scheme, the most illogical reasoning I have ever encountered in my life!" He glared at her. "You wish to force me to wed you, but as I've sworn to you, I will not do it."

"Oh, you're back to that, are you? I did not even know you were *not* married when I started this charade, so you might as well forget your grievance and concentrate on getting yourself out of this ticklish situation."

"Ah, now that you've gotten me into the fix, it is up to *me* to get us out of it."

"Oh, I shall rescue myself, Lord Sedgemoor, never fear."

"Not with a wedding ring from me, you won't."

"Well, I daresay if I wished to force you to marry me, I could convince enough people that you have compromised me. After all, we spent the night together in the same room."

"What!" He glared at the truckle bed, assuming the servant had slept there. "Why, you, you . . ." Words almost failed him. "Fiendish hussy!" he managed finally.

Georgie laughed again. "Never fear. You are not to my taste, as I've told you before. And I suspect I'm not to yours. Who is Polly, by the way?"

"Polly?" he answered warily, not about to reveal to this little fiend that Polly had been his favorite mistress. "I don't believe I recognize the name. Where did you hear it?"

She grinned widely at him and her eyes danced with mischievous lights. "Oh, you called out for her in your sleep."

Sedge could feel himself flushing, from his neck to his ears. Damn it, he never blushed! The little imp of mischief was wreaking havoc with his self-esteem.

Georgie was pleased with the result of her words. She was succeeding admirably in her plan to distract him from his pain and keep him from becoming too bored and restless as he lay in bed. She didn't mind that perhaps she was agitating his mind in the process.

"Aha! I see that you *do* recognize the name, after all. I'm not surprised. You were most anxious to, er, *speak* with her last night."

"Ah yes, now I recall. Polly was an old friend. I haven't seen her in years. Why I should have called out for her is something of a mystery," he declared mendaciously. "Must have been the laudanum you dosed me with." He glared at Georgie, his jaw clenched. "Did I say anything else?" he couldn't help asking, knowing by the wicked gleam in her eyes that he had. He wished to know the worst of it.

"Why, yes," she replied and his flush deepened to a dull crimson. "But it was mostly gibberish."

Georgie spared him the knowledge that he had called out for Polly so soulfully that she had risen from her own bed to go him and see if she could offer some comfort. She had lit a taper and had guessed that he was in the throes of some dream. When she had touched his face with a cool cloth to soothe him, he had grabbed her hand and held it tightly, begging her to stay with him.

"Oh, Polly, Polly, how I've missed you!"

"Did you, my dear?" Georgie had answered in a soft voice, wondering who Polly was and what she had been to him.

"So warm and sweet. Stay with me, Polly. Don't leave me."

"Yes, I will. I will not leave you," Georgie had promised, holding tightly to his hand as she bent over the bed watching his face. His eyes were closed but kept flickering open from time to time as he moved about restlessly.

"You'll not go and marry Bob, then?"

"No. I will stay with you." Georgie had told him what she thought he wanted to hear.

"Good. Kiss me then."

Georgie had leaned over, puckered her lips, and pressed them softly and briefly to his.

He had chuckled. "That's a bit chaste for you, Polly my girl," he had said, then smiled right into her eyes, his own wide open. It was a particularly beatific smile too, at such variance with his usual cold sneer that for a moment Georgie thought him transformed into an angel, a happy light gleaming in his gray eyes in the semi-darkened room.

She had begun to move away then, but he had taken her by surprise and suddenly grabbed her wrist. With unexpected strength, he had pulled her up over his chest into a kind of embrace so that she lay half across him on the bed, with one of his hard, muscular arms holding her tightly about the waist. Then he had pressed his lips to hers and kissed her warmly, his mouth moving softly over hers. His tongue had flicked out and run over the outline of her full lips, probing gently at their center parting as one of his hands found her breast and caressed it for a few moments.

The sensation was entirely new to Georgie. No one had ever touched her there before. But she decided it was not at all unpleasant and made no move to fight him off or pull away. Then he had drifted into a calmer sleep, leaving her very curious about just who "Polly" was as she carefully lifted herself off him and went back to her own uncomfortable bed on the floor.

Viscount Sedgemoor was not looking at all calm now, however. Nor did he look the least bit angelic. His eyes were half closed and he was looking down his nose at her, like some beaked bird of prey about to attack its dinner. If he thought that by directing such a ferocious stare her way, he could call back all the words of his drugged sleep during the night, he was much mistaken, Georgie thought on an inner chuckle, wondering if he remembered anything of their encounter.

Sedge was furious. He would like nothing better than to put his hands around Miss Carteret's neck and squeeze until she was quite, quite dead. The chit had access to some of his most closely guarded secrets, some of his most private thoughts, it seemed. Yes, and something was teasing at the edges of his mind, something that told him there had been more than words exchanged during the night. He *did* remember dreaming of Polly. He could swear he had felt her all warm and cozy, lying with him in this very bed. The feel of her soft, full breast was still imprinted on his hand. And the sweetness of her lips lingered on his. God damn it all to hell! He hadn't kissed this fiendish red-haired tormenter while he had been in a drugged sleep, had he?

"Oh, stop looking as though you want to murder me, Sedgemoor. However much you may dislike it, you are reliant on my good will for the next few days to see you through this nasty patch. I can send Pip with a message wherever you wish, after he has executed a commission for me, that is."

"Yes. I would like to send a message immediately. It is good of you to remind me of it, Miss Carteret," he allowed grudgingly.

"Call me Georgie. No need to stand on ceremony here." She smiled dazzlingly and gestured at the small, spare room, indicating Sedge's helpless position in the bed. "What shall I call you, anyway?"

"Sedgemoor will do nicely," he informed her in his most haughty manner.

His words and attitude were so at odds with his position in the tumbled bed, his blond hair looking all rumpled against the pillow where he lay in the white nightshirt, that Georgie couldn't help the merry peal of laughter that escaped her. "Oh, you are so stiff. Can you not unbend a little? Really, I am no threat to you," she assured him with a twinkle. "How do you know I am not married already?"

"Are you? If so, then I pity the poor fellow more than I can say. But I don't believe you are. Only a halfwitted moonling would have *you.*"

"Now, now. No need to be quite so insulting. It will undoubtedly astound you to know that Papa has had three offers for my hand to date. That's why I'm leaving home, you know. I do not wish to wed the gentleman he has picked out for me."

"Now that *does* astound me. To know that there are three fools loose somewhere in the countryside is shocking indeed, Miss Carteret."

"Do not be so stubborn. Call me *Georgie,* Sedgemoor. Hmm." Remembering the gold-edged calling card he had handed her the previous day, Georgie put her hand in the pocket of her now badly creased and dirty gown and pulled it out.

" 'Augustus Sebastian Stanhope St. Regis, Viscount Sedgemoor," she read. "That's quite a mouthful. Augustus. Such a grand name. So 'august.' Named after Octavian, the Roman emperor, were you?"

Sedge tried to ignore her provoking quip. He determined he would not give her the satisfaction of rising to her bait.

She tapped the card against her mouth for a moment. "I believe I shall call you . . . Gus!" she announced, her dimples very evident in her cheeks when she grinned so widely. "Yes. Gus. It suits you admirably," she informed him naughtily, her head tilted a little to one side as she regarded his severe frown. "And your addresses are very nice too, Gus. Number Thirty-Three, Brook Street, London, and The Oaks, Charfield, Near Chipping Sodbury, Gloucestershire. *Very* impressive."

"You seek to goad me, Miss Carteret. But I am determined you will not succeed with your hoydenish tricks. Why an incorrigible, shameless baggage like you is not still locked up in the schoolroom defies my understanding!"

"Why, Gus, I thought you would never ask! I'm sure you must be afire with curiosity to know why

I'm traveling all alone with only my groom and dog all the way to London." She gave him a saucy look, batting her lashes at him demurely.

"I have no wish to know anything about you. I am already better acquainted with you than I have any wish of being. You bore me," Sedge drawled.

She laughed. "Oh, no, no. That's not true, Gus. I'm sure I do many things to you, but 'bore' you isn't one of them. If you have no wish to learn my story, what shall we talk about?"

"I have no wish to talk to you at all," he insisted stubbornly.

"Indeed, I shall leave you to rest in a few moments, but Mrs. Thorpe will think me a poor sort of 'wife,' if I do not sit with 'my husband' for at least an hour to try to take his mind off the pain he must be suffering. She was only saying to me at luncheon, 'No need to help me in the kitchen, dearie. Ye're merry chatter's enough to cheer up the most dour soul. That poorly husband of yours must be pinin' away for a sight of ye.' "

She had captured Mrs. Thorpe's country accent perfectly. Sedge almost choked when he heard her, but it wasn't so much spleen that gagged him this time as an insane urge to laugh. The girl was a perfect mimic. And he had to admit, albeit grudgingly, her gaiety was beginning to infect him, despite the pain in his leg, and despite the fact that he did not trust her an inch.

"But before I go, won't you tell me about these women you mentioned who have tried to trap you into marriage. It sounds fascinating. Do they consider you uncommonly handsome?" she looked at him consideringly, with her head turned a little to one side. "I've always favored dark men, myself. I cannot imagine why any woman would want to tie herself to such an arrogant, bad-tempered man whose wits have gone begging into the bargain, but if such is the case, I am curious to know why."

"Want to learn some new tricks, do you?"

"Why, Gus, how can you think such a thing of me?" Georgie asked with a look of innocent outrage.

"I would be obliged if you would continue to address me by my title, Miss Carteret. I want no intimacy between us."

At those pompous words, Georgie went off into gales of laughter. "Oh, Gus, how you make me laugh. You *are* the most amusing man I've ever met. So cold and stiff and starchy, just like a sheet that's been hung out to dry on a frosty day." She busied herself wiping her streaming eyes on her handkerchief while he directed his most forbidding stare her way.

"You are enough to provoke a bloody saint!" he swore from between clenched teeth.

"Oh, but *you* are far from being a saint, aren't you, Gus? More in the nature of a sinner, I would say. And sinners deserve to have their patience tried, you know. It is part of the reparation they must make for their transgressions."

"Miss Carteret. Be so good as to leave off your moralizing. Your absurd reflections on the subject do not affect *me,*" he said coldly, exerting an almost superhuman control over his temper. He was unbearably frustrated that he could not rise from his bed and throw the provoking chit bodily from the room.

"Oh, come down from the boughs, Gus, do. I was

not moralizing, you know. No, no. I was only teasing you," she said outrageously, before she blew him a kiss and danced out of the room.

Sedge wished desperately he had something to throw at her rapidly retreating back, to vent a small part of his anger and frustration in some satisfyingly physical action. But he was left alone with nothing to do but lie still and brood in furious outrage.

He was as angry at himself for allowing himself to be goaded, despite his intention not to, as he was with Georgie for doing the goading—in the merriest, most lighthearted of ways, of course. And he was aggravated with himself for neglecting his first priority. He needed to get a message to Leftridge immediately. He had been expected two days ago. There was not a moment to lose now, yet he had wasted his time bantering words with the annoying red-haired menace, instead of insisting that she immediately send a message off to Leftridge at Grey Towers.

And he must send to the Oaks, his own home in Gloucestershire, too, so that they would know what had become of him and so that they could send his most luxurious, well-sprung coach to take him home where he would need to spend what promised to be a lengthy convalescence.

Thoughts of home and the comforts to be found there called up the image of his valet, Wilkins. Grey Towers could not be more than fifteen miles away. Wilkins would already have arrived there with his trunks, and so too would his groom with his horses. Ah, to have Wilkins with him, instead of relying on the Thorpes and that odd, little groom of Miss

Carteret's for his needs would be bliss. Well, not bliss exactly. Not with this broken leg, devil take it!

Never did he regret more his habit of driving himself everywhere alone. Henceforth, he would at least take his groom along with him in his curricle. Ah, his curricle. Made to his own exacting specifications. Smashed to bits now, without a doubt. And it was not even six months old. Well, that disaster would teach him not to take foolish chances. Never had he done a more ill-judged thing than try to overtake another vehicle on that slippery hill.

He closed his eyes and tried to put the incident from his mind.

Diana Carstairs was to be at Henderson's house party, he remembered suddenly. Beautiful Diana. Beautiful, sophisticated Diana. Who never put a foot wrong. So icily composed with her pale blond hair, long, slender legs and tall, willowy form. The young widow was just to his taste.

She had played hard to get the first few times he had met her. But just lately he thought that she had signaled her interest, that she would not be averse to his advances. He could just picture her cool green eyes looking into his, promising delights in store between the sheets. Sedge shifted in the bed. Devil take it, what did he want to torture himself by thinking of that? A man with a broken leg would have a hard time performing in bed.

He would just have to get used to the celibate life for the next few months, he thought, as an embarrassing picture formed in his mind of the awkward maneuvers he would have to perform were he to try to bed a woman in his present state.

Chapter 4

"Look what I've brought you, Gus," Georgie said brightly as she reentered Sedge's bedroom late that evening. She had left him to brood and sulk alone all day and she had heard from Mrs. Thorpe that he had looked "proper sour" when that good lady had taken him his evening meal. The only consolation for the poor woman was that he had eaten his dinner and praised her cooking.

"Brandy! Just what I need. Bring that bottle over here at once!"

Georgie skipped into the room, closing the door behind her. "Do high and mighty lords never say 'please'?"

"Please bring that brandy over here at once," he repeated belligerently.

"Please bring that brandy bottle over here at once, *Georgie,"* she coaxed him.

"Please bring that brandy bottle over here at once, *Georgie.* There. Does that satisfy you, you little tyrant."

"Yes, indeed ... for now," she answered with a

smug look, handing him the water glass and the brandy bottle. She was surprised to see that his hands shook slightly and the bottle clinked against the glass as he poured himself a large glass full of the rich, golden liquid.

He downed it in a long gulp, then poured himself another.

"Oh, Gus. Have you been in that much pain? I had no idea. Mr. Thorpe only returned a short while ago with the brandy. I was not hiding it from you, I assure you. You should have called for some laudanum."

"I will not take any more of that poison. And how am I to call for anything? There's no bell."

Georgie looked all around. "Oh, no, there isn't. But there wouldn't be, would there? This is only a simple farmhouse, after all. You could have used your lungs to shout for someone, you know."

He gave her a glacial stare, as though to say he wouldn't stoop to such common, vulgar behavior.

"Where's that groom of yours? Why didn't he go for the brandy?"

"As I mentioned earlier, Pip has gone to London to execute a commission for me."

"To London? What for?"

"Well, I've sent him with a message to my grandmother, letting her know when she can expect me."

"Yes, it's wise to warn people of your imminent arrival, so that they may prepare for the catastrophe. I feel for the poor woman."

"Oh, Gus, you can be so nasty when you put your mind to it, or I should say, your tongue to it." Georgie laughed at her own joke.

"Very funny, Miss Carteret," Sedge commented, relaxing back against the pillows once more with his third glass of brandy in his hand. He was only sipping at this one, for the first two glasses were already curling like warm fire down the back of his throat, up to his head and down through his stomach, spreading through his limbs and easing his pain.

When Georgie just stood there grinning at him, resting her elbow on the back of a large, wing chair, upholstered in a patterned fabric of yellow and red cabbage roses, Sedge cleared his throat and said with difficulty, "I would like your help in a matter of urgent importance, ma'am."

Georgie looked at him expectantly, her blue eyes wide open with interest.

"I need to get a message to a friend of mine who is expecting me. Has been expecting me for the past two days, in fact. His estate is not above fifteen miles from here, I believe. I was hoping to send your groom, but as he is unavailable and I do not think it would do to ask Thorpe, I would ask you to hire someone for me in the next village. I will provide you with the funds for the purpose, of course."

"Of course. And, yes, I can see that you had best inform someone of your whereabouts ... but surely you will not ask your friends to visit you *here*. What would the Thorpes think? You would not truly wish to see me compromised, would you, Gus?" Georgie asked, her brows lowered and a worried look on her face.

Sedge found that he didn't care for that fearful look. A wrenching feeling twisted in his gut to see her looking so unlike her usual insouciant self.

"I shall not ask them to visit me," he replied, though he had been thinking of sending for Wilkins, his valet. "I shall just send them an excuse. Say that urgent business arose to keep me away and tell them to send my valet and groom back home. Something of that sort." He waved his hand dismissively, trying not to think of how dearly he would miss Wilkins. It would cost him much to do without the services of his valet during the next few days. Of course, he would be forced to rely on the help of Mr. Thorpe and Pip, but they would suffice. Yes, he told himself with an inward sigh, it really would be best to continue to conceal his identity, and if Wilkins arrived word might well leak out about the incident.

"I shall not give away your game, Georgie, though why I should make such a concession to you, is beyond me," he admitted, running an impatient hand through his disordered locks before he raised his glass to his lips again.

"Thank you, Gus. That is indeed kind of you. You must wish for the services of your valet like the very devil!"

He smiled ironically at her. How could the chit read his mind like that? he wondered, beginning to feel pleasantly muzzy from the brandy.

Georgie smiled back at him. "That's *much* better. Do you know, you're not at all bad looking when you smile," she told him ingenuously. "That sneer you usually wear quite spoils the curve of your lips and puts lines in your face that, I daresay, make you look ten years older than you actually are."

Sedge looked incredulous. All his life he had been admired for his cold, classical features, had been told by a gratifyingly wide variety of women that he was uncommonly handsome. And he had never had reason to doubt them. He had been praised, admired, and courted, fawned upon and toad eaten all his life. Women of all ages had clawed their way over one another for a chance at him.

And now here was this impertinent red-haired witch standing up to him, taking all he could dish out and turning it back on him, laughing at his most chilling set-downs, *daring* to imply that his frown marred his countenance. The unmitigated nerve of the woman!

Georgie was looking at him brightly, questioningly.

Sedge had a hard time holding onto his temper. Only the languor invading his limbs and numbing his mind as he finished his third glass of brandy, kept him from taking exception to her remarks in his most cutting fashion. Famed for his masterly setdowns, one piercing glance from his cold gray eyes was usually enough to cause not only timid maidens to flinch and blanch and shy away from him, but had even been known to send brawny gentlemen scurrying away from his vicinity.

Georgiana Carteret should be lying crumpled up in a shaking heap at his feet by now.

"Well? How old are you, anyway?" she asked, unfazed.

"I shall be thirty at my next birthday. And you, Miss—ah, Georgie?"

"Thirty! Why, that's *old*, Gus! I will be one and twenty in six weeks time. That is one of the reasons why I decided to leave home and visit Grandmama in London at this time."

"Why don't you tell me about it," Sedge heard himself requesting sleepily.

"Well, you see, Papa wanted me to marry one of our neighbors. But, for various reasons, I could not agree to such a bloodless arrangement. So I decided to visit Grandmama. I never was presented at one of the Queen's Drawing Rooms, but I'm sure Grandmama will see to it, even though I am rather old now for such nonsense. But I understand you have to go through with all the rigamarole if you wish to go about in London society. Grandmama is nothing if not *tonnish*. She has lived in London forever. It's one of the reasons Papa never goes there."

"Afraid of his mother-in-law, is he? What does your mama have to say to that?"

"Grandmama Carteret is Papa's own mother. My mama died many years ago and Papa has recently remarried, you see."

"Ah, I see the hand of an evil stepmother in this. She drove you from home?"

"Roselyn!" Georgie exclaimed and made a comical face. "Oh, no, no. Roselyn is only seven years older than I am and the sweetest thing in nature. Papa dotes on her, you see. He follows her around like a lovesick calf all day long." Georgie assumed a soulful expression and pretended to be following someone around the room, to Sedge's secret amusement. He bit the inside of his mouth to keep from laughing aloud.

"Hmm. I've never seen a lovesick calf," he drawled, "but I will take your word for it one would look just as you do at this precise moment."

"Yes, well, we have already established what an

expert you are at issuing cutting setdowns, Gus. Do you wish to hear any more of my story, or do wish to find some other ways to insult me for your own amusement."

He waved a hand at her, amazed to hear that his barbed comments had penetrated her seemingly impregnable shield. It seemed to him she had managed to deflect them effortlessly ere now. "Pray, continue."

"Actually, that's really all there is. Papa had arranged to announce my betrothal to Tom—er, our neighbor later this week. I did everything I could to try to talk him out of it, but he wouldn't heed me. So I decided to take the old curricle and go to Grandmama. Actually, I think Papa will be relieved I've left. It's my belief he wants to be alone with Roselyn."

"I daresay you're in the right of it there, Georgie. A man does not like a grown daughter looking over his shoulder when he's on his honeymoon."

"Why, Gus, you speak as if you have daughters of your own." She looked at him inquisitively.

Sedge shifted himself to a more upright position, but the movement made his head spin. "No. I have no children at all, that I know of." He resisted the urge to lift his hand to clutch his dizzy head.

"Oh, you're a rake, are you? How fascinating. I have always wanted to meet one."

"I am *not* a rake, Miss Carteret," he said carefully. It was an effort not to slur his words, but the last thing in the world he wanted right now was to lose his dignity and make a damned fool of himself in front of this infuriating chit. "And I think it's high time for you to leave me and seek your own bed."

"But there is nowhere else for me to go. The Thorpes think we are married. They expect me to sleep in here. I can't suddenly ask them to make up a pallet for me in the kitchen."

"The kitchen? Surely there is somewhere else for you to sleep. You cannot stay in here," Sedge insisted.

"I stayed in here last night. What does a second night matter?"

It mattered because now he knew that she was to stay there. But he couldn't admit such a thing to her. Damn, but he had never in his life slept in the same room with a woman who hadn't been sharing his bed.

Except last night, he remembered. But he had been unconscious then. It would be just too tempting ... He caught himself up short. What in the name of all that was fiendish was he thinking of? He did not desire Miss Georgiana Carteret to sleep with him, did he? He must be all about in his head. That, or he'd drunk enough brandy to muddle his brains, turning them to mush. He stared down into his half-filled brandy glass and put it away from him on the bedside table.

"I suppose you will have to stay here," he muttered, grudgingly. "But if I should call out, don't come near me, do you understand?"

"Why? Are you afraid that you will want to kiss me?"

"No!" he shouted, but his bleary gaze strayed to her lips, soft and pink and inviting and he had a vague memory of having tasted their sweetness before. His blood stirred uncomfortably at the very thought.

Georgie walked over and stood next to his bed. "You seemed to enjoy it last night."

"What!" He glared at her. "I do not believe I did any such thing."

"What do you believe you did not do? Kiss me? Or enjoy it?" She smiled knowingly at him, the twin dimples peeping out in her cheeks and devilish lights dancing in her blue eyes as she teased him.

"Miss Carteret," he warned, "you are playing with fire. Take care, or you shall be burned."

Georgie laughed. "So you are a rake, after all. I thought as much. Well, I assure you, you do not appeal to me, Gus. I do not like cold, arrogant men. So you may put your fears to rest."

She walked over to the large chair where she sat down and began to remove her shoes in preparation for lying down on the truckle bed once again in her much creased and wrinkled gown.

"What are you doing?"

"Removing my shoes, so that I might entice you with my toes." She lifted one stockinged foot and wiggled it in his direction.

"Devil take it, Miss Carteret—"

"What? Shall you leap from the bed and attack me?" She laughed. "But I tease you too much. I shall blow out the candles and finish my preparations in the dark. That way you will not be tempted."

Her only answer was a grunt from the bed as she blew out the two tapers that lighted the room.

"Good night, Gus. I do hope you have a better night's rest tonight."

Georgie heard the chink of a bottle against glass as Sedge poured himself yet another glass of brandy.

Well, she should not have teased him so unmercifully. For a while there he was looking relaxed and pain free, but she had stirred him up again. She suppressed a small gurgle of laughter. She just couldn't seem to help provoking him. It was such fun to see the expression of haughty arrogance he assumed when he was vexed with her.

He really was a most handsome man, too, if one considered his looks dispassionately, Georgie decided. From the thatch of silky blond hair on his head and pale haughty brows that arched over his long-lashed smokey gray eyes to his aristocratic nose to his finely chiseled lips and firm, square chin, there was not an imperfection to be found.

And the way his various bodily parts were put together was nothing to sneeze at, either, she admitted, thinking of his trim, muscular frame with his fine pair of broad shoulders, slim waist and hips, and the well-muscled thighs and calves of his long legs.

Why, his physique could be favorably compared to the contours depicted in a statue of a Greek athlete, she thought on a giggle. She had had a good peek—more than a peek actually, quite a good long stare—when the doctor had removed his buckskin breeches in preparation for setting his leg. She had been too curious to feel any embarrassment at the sight of a near naked man.

But for all that, he was not to her taste. Her taste did not run to cold-eyed blonds, however attractive. Prince Charming, he was not. Princely, maybe—but definitely not charming! And he was so old, too.

With that thought she fell asleep.

Sedge tried to settle himself as comfortably as he

could against his bank of pillows without disturbing his leg, so that he could get to sleep. Shifting this way and that, trying to ease the pain in his neck, he lifted his hand to extract one plump feather pillow and toss it to the floor.

Why had the chit suddenly seemed so much more attractive—and desirable—to him tonight than when he had first met her yesterday? he wondered. Devil take it! He couldn't be *that* desperate for a female! She had the same provoking tongue, the same maddeningly cheerful laugh, the same wildly disarrayed copper red locks, the same short, slightly too rounded figure, the same freckled face . . . and yet, they weren't the same.

The copper-colored hair suited her sprightliness, the sparkling blue eyes, her vivacious nature, and the freckles, lightly dusting across her nose and cheeks, seemed downright attractive, in keeping with her effervescent personality. As for her laughter and teasingly provoking comments—well, if he were honest, he would admit her lively wit and manner cheered him more than they aggravated him, distracting him from his pain and from the uncomfortable situation he had landed himself in. Still, she was a mischievous madcap of a child, entirely too hot at hand. If he had the schooling of her . . . but such an untamed bundle of mischief was definitely *not* to his taste!

In the week that followed, Sedge's leg slowly mended. As it healed, it pained him a good deal less and he had to resort to the brandy bottle less and less often. He made himself more comfortable in the bed when he didn't have to lie flat on his back all day, and, after the first three days of bed rest, he was even allowed to sit up in a chair with his leg carefully resting on a padded stool.

Georgie had taken her own curricle and driven to the Cross and Keys in the hamlet of Little Bickton where she had learned that Baron Leftridge's estate, Grey Towers, was located at no great distance. She had been tempted to drive over and take the message herself, out of curiosity to see what Sedgemoor's friend was like, but discretion won out for once and she ended by paying a young lad to deliver the viscount's sealed message to his friend.

On the fourth day after Sedge's accident, Doctor Hamilton pronounced that he would be fit enough to travel at the end of the week. Sedge had grinned, actually grinned, quite boyishly, Georgie had seen with delight. She had clapped her hands and cheered, as much for the good news about his leg, as at seeing him smile happily for the first time since she'd met him.

Pip returned from his errand to old Lady Carteret in London where he had delivered Georgie's craftily worded message in which she advised her grandmother that she was about to pay her a visit, saying that her father was glad to see her embark for London at long last.

Georgie had added vaguely that she would arrive in a week or so. She had seen no reason at all to reveal to her grandmother that she had been delayed on her journey halfway to the metropolis and was at present masquerading as a Mrs. Moor, wife to the arrogant Viscount Sedgemoor, while she nursed that gentleman following a most unfortunate carriage accident.

Lady Carteret had sent a stern message to Georgie via Pip, advising her to travel with a large entourage and to take all the proper precautions to ensure her safety on the road. Knowing Georgie's overly friendly nature, her ladyship cautioned her granddaughter not to fall in with any strangers, and not to behave in her typical harum-scarum fashion.

In the rest of the brief, astringent note, Lady Carteret berated her son, for not sending his daughter to London sooner. She expressed her profound lack of confidence in her son's ability to make the proper travel arrangements.

Georgie had smiled as she read the sternly worded missive, disregarding the warnings. It's *much* too late for such chiding, Grandmama, she had thought humorously.

Pip was promptly sent on his way again to deliver Sedge's various messages, the funds to hire a good fast horse provided by the viscount. When he returned to the Thorpe's farmhouse from the viscount's estate in Gloucestershire, Pip reported that his lordship's coachman was preparing the luxurious traveling chaise and would slowly be making his way to Little Bickton.

Sedge greeted the news that his chaise and his servants should arrive within two or three days to carry him home with a fervent "Thank God!"

And Georgie was pleased too. "I'm anxious to be on my way to Grandmama's in London. I am so looking forward to the fun I shall have there. . . . Just

think, you need never see me again after this week,
Gus," she said, her eyes dancing.

"For which blessing I shall be eternally grateful,"
he drawled.

"Do you mean to say, you will not miss me just a
little bit?"

"Miss being hounded and nagged and contradicted
at every turn? Not one jot, ma'am."

"I think it's good for you. Takes some of the starch
from your spine," she said just before she whisked
herself out the room, closing the door loudly on his
outraged exclamation.

He refused to acknowledge the thought that he
would have gone mad if he hadn't had the distraction
of her entertaining—if often outrageously provoking—conversation and company.

When Georgie appeared in his room with a chess
set tucked under her arm later that day, Sedge was
ready not only to call a truce but to bless her. While
he did not believe for a minute that she would be a
match for him at his favorite game, he did realize that
she was the only person about who could provide
some relief from the inexorable boredom of lying flat
on his back in bed all day. He would try and teach
her something of the game so that she could give him
a good match, if she didn't plague the life out of him
first with her unrelenting cheerfulness and wide-
ranging series of chastening sallies and deflating
comments, designed to put him in his place.

He did not enjoy being an object for open pleas-
antry. However, he was soon able to let his little
imp's remarks pass without becoming unduly angry

or irritated, allowing himself, instead, to be diverted by her lighthearted chatter.

When Sedgemoor accepted her efforts to amuse him without a constant barrage of cutting comments and arrogant remarks directed her way, Georgie set herself to entertain her captive patient royally. Not only did they play chess, and various card games, but the viscount even so far forgot his dignity as to allow himself to be persuaded to indulge in the childish game of spillikins, spilling out the sticks on a tray placed over his lap and arguing lightly with her over who had the steadier hand in the game.

"I will just move my red knight here. Aha, got you! Checkmate!" Georgie exclaimed in delight. "Well, Gus, that's the first time I've taken your king. You will have to admit that I'm beginning to get the hang of chess."

"Hmm. Under my expert tutelage, perhaps you are beginning to grasp the rudiments of the game." He tossed his white king up and down in his hand for a moment, before clamping his fingers shut around it.

"The rudiments! I think I've learned more than the rudiments. But I must say, to take your king required all my guile," she admitted with a wide smile. "It took me twenty minutes to see how I was to accomplish the task, and then, of course, everything depended on your falling into my carefully laid trap. Which, I must say, you did most obligingly, Gus!"

Sedge's lips quirked up in a rueful half grin. Georgie's tactics had indeed fooled him. He did not believe someone so inexperienced at the game could be so cunning. After they had taken several of one another's rooks, knights, and bishops, he had been sent on a royal goosechase. She had enticed his remaining knight and bishop to leave his king unguarded and chase her queen across the board, trying to trap her between them. So intent was Sedge on teaching her a lesson by capturing her queen, he had not taken appropriate rearguard action and inadvertently left his king exposed.

"You were willing to sacrifice your queen to trap me, were you not?"

"Of course!" she admitted with a bright smile, her blue eyes crinkled up in amusement.

"Hmm. I did not expect such a ploy from a beginner. I congratulate you. If you continue to practice diligently in the months ahead, you should be able to give anyone a good game," he conceded magnanimously, reaching out to tweak one of the loose curls that fell over her ear, brushing his fingers across her soft cheek as he did so.

"Oh, you are a severe taskmaster," she complained, pulling a face at him. "As though I will not have anything to do in the next few months but practice chess! You know that as soon as I reach Grandmama's, I shall be so busy preparing to venture out into society, I will not have a moment to even *think* about chess!" Georgie went on to catalog all the things she expected to do and all the fun she expected to have when she reached London.

Sedge listened to all her enthusiastic plans about her coming presentation, one brow raised skeptically.

"I hope you will not be disappointed," he commented sardonically, thinking to issue a word or two of warning. Georgie was so full of gig and high spirits, he was sure she was doomed to disappointment. The London he knew was a cold, cruel place, ready to crush bright young things fresh from the country, no matter how sunny their outlook on life, or how much resilience they had.

"I fear you will find your enthusiasm for your surroundings is not the fashion in London," he sought to caution her. "To be *au courant,* one should complain of *ennui* and appear jaded with one's surroundings and the company."

Georgie pooh-poohed this joyless advice. It sounded decidedly flat to her. "What's the use of being presented, meeting new people, having new clothes, going to parties, and doing other exciting things, if not to have a good time? I certainly intend to, no matter what your silly fashion dictates," she stated, her blue eyes sparkling with eager determination.

Sedge sent her an exasperated glance from under hooded eyes. He had a grudging admiration for her attitude. It suited her personality, but it was not in vogue among his crowd to care about such things, to be so openly enthusiastic.

She was likely to be hurt, was little Miss Georgiana Carteret. And Sedge found he didn't care for the idea of her spirits being crushed. He ran a long finger over his bottom lip and sighed imperceptibly as she chattered on. Certainly his crowd evinced none of the interest or delight in the things she was looking forward to with such unalloyed glee.

He had grave misgivings about how Georgie would be received among the haughty *ton.* Blithe Georgie, so ready to make a friend of anyone and everyone, no matter how unsuitable, so ready to engage in all manner of fun and gig with her lively, unguarded tongue and madcap ways.

She would be like a lamb among a pack of wolves, Sedge thought. And he wasn't thinking so much of the gentlemen she would encounter in London, but of the high-born ladies of the *beau monde,* who ruled society with their iron fists encased in velvet gloves, their pointed tongues always ready with the latest lethal gossip to spread scandal and ruin reputations.

He frowned. The patrician female denizens of the metropolis would likely tear Georgie to shreds with their spiteful, denigrating comments about everything from her form, dowdy gowns, and untamed hairstyle, to her frequent merry laugh and exuberant manners. Those superior beings would be unlikely to condescend to welcome such a provincial.

However, he would be spared the sight for he would not be there to see how Georgie took to London, or how London took to Georgie. He was doomed to rusticate at his stately home in Gloucestershire until his leg was entirely better. The idea of showing his face in London while he still limped caused Sedge to cringe with mortification. And the doctor had told him that in all probability he would have such a limp for several months and need to rest his leg frequently. The invariable questions about the cause of his injury would have to be deflected with his famed chilling setdowns, or, if need be, outright obfuscation. He had no wish to undertake either.

He stifled a sigh. At least he could take comfort in the fact that his leg seemed to be healing satisfactorily and the pain in his limb had lessened considerably.

Chapter 5

An elegant black traveling chaise bearing a coat of arms emblazoned on its door rolled into the yard in front of the Thorpe's small farmhouse in Little Bickton eight days after the viscount had broken his leg. When the coachman came to the door asking for his master, Viscount Sedgemoor, Mrs. Thorpe's eyes almost started from her head. A viscount under her roof?

Georgie heard the commotion of the carriage's arrival from Sedgemoor's room. She flew to the bedroom window, overturning the chessboard in her haste, and watched the arrival of the impressive vehicle with the gold embossed crest of the St. Regis family coat of arms on the side panel gleaming in the sunlight.

"Your coach and servants are here, Gus. Don't worry. I'll deal with it," Georgie cried when the knock sounded on the farmhouse door.

Before Sedge could open his mouth to countermand her statement, Georgie had raced from the room.

She dashed down the stairs to intercept the coachman and a natty little gentleman she took to be the viscount's valet who were being greeted at the front door by Mrs. Thorpe.

"That's all right, Mrs. Thorpe. The viscount is our cousin," she called as her foot hit the last step of the staircase. "Lord Sedgemoor has kindly sent his coach to convey us to his home, so that Mr. Moor can recover there. These are his servants come to assist us on the journey."

The coachman looked flummoxed by this pronouncement. He lifted his hat and scratched his head, staring at Georgie in a puzzled way, then turned and shrugged his shoulders at his master's valet who stood stoneyfaced by his side.

Georgie took Mrs. Thorpe by the elbow and propelled her back toward the kitchen, explaining in a whisper, "I will take these good men up to see Mr. Moor, then we will send them along to the Cross and Keys for the night while we make ready to leave in the morning."

She returned quickly to escort the puzzled-looking coachman and the silent valet up to Sedgemoor's room. After she heard the viscount confirm the arrangements she had mentioned about the coachman taking the chaise on down the road to the Cross and Keys Inn for the night, Georgie turned to Sedgemoor and said, "Shall I send Pip to the inn with your coachman? Perhaps you will wish him to purchase something special for you. I think this evening calls for a celebration, do you not agree?"

Sedge gave her a warning look from under his brows as he sat in the large armchair with his leg

stretched out on a stool before him. He was glad he
had insisted on being dressed each day after the first.
He was also grateful to Mrs. Thorpe for providing
him with a pair of breeches. After she had laundered
them, the clever farmer's wife had been able to cut
and alter one leg of his garment in such a way that he
could get the breeches over his injured limb, and tie
the split side closed along the inside seam. With assistance from Thorpe or Pip each morning, he had
shaved and dressed and made himself perfectly presentable. Now he was decently clad in his jacket and
breeches.

Georgie almost chuckled at the stern look on his
face. She had taken care to phrase her suggestion so
that it was not the least bit indiscreet, even in front of
his servants, but the viscount still feared her tongue.
The poor man had never given up the belief that she
was out to compromise him.

Nevertheless, he did as she suggested and agreed
to send Pip to buy some champagne.

"But me'lord, shan't I stay and see to your needs?"
Wilkins pleaded, clearly outraged that his master had
been made to do without his services for more than a
sennight.

"Wilkins, I will gladly give myself over to your
care tomorrow. For tonight, you will leave my extra
clothing here and you will stay at the Cross and Keys
with Croyde here," Sedge decreed in a tone that
brooked no argument.

When the door had closed on his servants, Georgie
said, "Well, Gus, this will be our *last* night together."

"For which fact I shall never cease to give thanks,"

he replied sardonically, his eyes raised to the ceiling in exaggerated relief.

"I knew you would want to celebrate the event." Her freckles looked prominent on her cheekbones as she crinkled up her eyes and grinned at him.

He chuckled despite his best intentions to remain cool and unaffected by her provoking words. "Ah, how well you have come to know me, Miss Carteret. And in such a short time, too."

"Yes. Will you not miss me when we go our separate ways tomorrow?"

At seven that evening, Georgie bounced into the room without knocking on the door to find Pip helping the viscount change into the clean shirt, dinner jacket, and fresh white stock that had been provided by Wilkins. A bowl of dirty water and a razor resting on the small table at his elbow told her he had just been shaved.

"Oh!" she exclaimed. "Is dinner not ready yet? I quite thought Mrs. Thorpe said she would be serving us at seven o'clock sharp."

"As you can see, ma'am, you have arrived in advance of the dinner."

Unabashed by the sight of his dishabille, she gave him a bright smile. "I did not know you intended to be so formal tonight, Gus. What a signal honor you do me! I'm afraid I have nothing to change into," she said, spreading the skirts of her own much creased green Merino wool gown with her hands and holding them wide for his inspection. She made no move to leave the room so that he could finish his preparations.

Clearly discomfited to have Georgie walk in on him when he was in such a state of undress, Sedge said in his coldest voice, "Pray, Miss Carteret, grant me a moment of privacy to make myself presentable for this momentous occasion."

"What? You aren't embarrassed for me to see you in your shirtsleeves are you, Gus?" Georgie asked, looking her fill at his broad-shouldered form revealed by the thin muslin of his shirt. "There's no reason to be, I assure you. For a tall man, you are not at all fat."

"Thank you," he murmured in failing accents, closing his eyes at her typical lack of maidenly modesty.

"I daresay there's not an extra ounce of fat on you. You gave the impression of being a much larger man when I first saw you at the King's Head Inn."

"Georgiana!" he uttered in a strangled voice. "Is there no limit to your immodesty?"

"But, Gus, are you not proud of your body? I know I should be, were I a man."

"If you were a man, you would not be in my room at this moment ogling me and making such outrageously improper comments," he grated, then added in a sarcastic tone, "If you were a man, we would not be in this damned precious coil."

Pip assisted the viscount into his jacket. Sedge pushed his arms through the sleeves and said, "The show is over, Miss Carteret. If you have looked your fill, you may go now." He lifted his hands to adjust the jacket, before reaching for his neckcloth.

"Oh. I see I have shocked you, Gus." Georgie laughed, but made no move to leave.

"To the core of my soul, you brazen little hussy. I suppose I must be grateful you did not find me shirtless."

Over his lordship's head, Pip grinned and winked at his mistress, reminding her that he was a witness to their somewhat irregular carrying-on.

Catching her groom's eye, Georgie chuckled, then gave in. "Yes, well, since you are doing me so much honor, Sedgemoor, I shall take myself off and see if I cannot comb my hair into some semblance of order, at least."

She turned and left the room, much to Sedge's relief.

Georgie did not reappear again until the dinner had been laid out for her guests by the Mrs. Thorpe. There was no noticeable improvement to her mop of long, wildly waving red tresses, Sedge noted without surprise, before turning his eyes to the feast set out before them.

The farmer's wife had outdone herself in cooking up a dinner for them to remember. Barley broth followed by leg of lamb, roasted pheasant, trout en crout, stewed calves' kidneys, parsleyed potatoes, buttered carrots, beetroot and celery salad with vinegar were among the host of dishes she laid before her guests.

There was far more food than two persons could begin to do justice to, but Georgie and Sedge set to with a will.

Over an hour later, Mrs. Thorpe delivered a pot of fresh coffee and the dessert, a mixed fruit pie, folded in her best pastry and baked to a turn, topped with cream fresh from the cow. She watched her guests with a sentimental smile on her well-lined face as they sat on either side of a small table pushed up to the side of Sedge's chair. They both expressed unalloyed enjoyment of the feast she had prepared.

"Bless me, if'n I've ever seen a more devoted couple than the pair of ye lovebirds!" She lifted her work-roughened hands and lay them over her heart while she gazed at them with misty eyes. "Ye two hasn't been married long, has ye?"

At these words, Sedge choked on the piece of pie he had just bitten into, while Georgie smiled brightly and replied mischievously, "Why, no. I must admit, it seems like no time at all, Mrs. Thorpe. Sad to say, we had not had time to enjoy the married state with all its ups and downs for any length of time before Mr. Moor had his accident."

"Never ye mind, dearie. Soon's Mr. Moor's leg 'tis a bit better, he'll be a right proper 'usband to ye, and no mistake, from the looks of 'im." Mrs. Thorpe blushed violently at her own bold words, laughed to cover her embarrassment for daring to speak so broadly to the quality and quickly hustled from the room, carrying a stack of empty dishes in her arms.

Georgie laughed, looking over at the viscount to see that he was regarding her pensively, his complexion darkened.

"Oh, Gus, did you see the look on Mrs. Thorpe's face? What good actors we must be to have flummoxed her so thoroughly. Oh dear, what would she think, if she knew that we had never met but an hour before your accident?"

"You embarrassed the poor woman with your suggestive words. You must not be so indiscreet, or you shall quickly find yourself a social pariah in London, Miss Carteret."

"Oh, Gus, you're not going to lecture me again tonight, are you? I thought we would part friends. Here I've been enjoying our dinner so much. Don't spoil things now. Here, our glasses are empty. Let me pour us both another drink. I've never had champagne before, you know. I think I shall drink it every night when I'm in London. It tickles my nose most delightfully." She gave him a slightly muzzy smile as she lifted her refilled glass to her lips.

"If you should drink champagne every night while you're in London, you will soon find yourself with a reputation for loose behavior."

"Tell me, what is your definition of loose behavior, my lord? Is it something you engage in, I wonder? You must do, if you are a rake. And I think you are, though you poker up at me when I say so."

"Miss Carteret, guard your tongue! Your conversation is most improper."

"Well, I may as well ask an expert while I have the chance." Georgie rested her elbow on the table so that she could lean her cheek on her hand and watch his face closely for his reaction to her teasing—and so that she could admire his handsome visage. He really did have the most intriguing gray eyes, dark, dangerous lights flashing in their clear depths. He glanced away, guarding his eyes as his long, thick dark gold lashes came down to cover them and shield his thoughts. She continued, "Then I will know what not to do . . . or perhaps if what you do sounds fun, I may decide to try it." She hiccuped softly.

Sedge slammed his hand down hard on the table, making the dishes jump. "You most certainly will not do any such thing! Damnation, but I wish I had the schooling of you, Georgiana Carteret!"

"Do you, Gus? You have been so afraid I might try to compromise you, I thought you wanted nothing further to do with me." Still leaning on her hand, she regarded him mistily, her lips parted in a lopsided smile.

"Should your behavior go beyond the bounds of what is proper for a young lady, or if you ever so much as *think* about doing anything rakish, I should take great pleasure in turning you over my knee and administering suitable chastisement." While he issued this stern warning, Sedge tried to ignore that enticingly enigmatic smile, tried not to watch as she unthinkingly ran her little pink tongue across her full lower lip, catching the last taste of the champagne that lingered there.

"Would you, Gus?"

"By God, I would!"

"Well, I daresay you might try, but I would not stand for it, you know. You might find yourself upended and I would be the one to administer the punishment."

"Do not be absurd, Georgiana. Men do not live by the same rules, are not held to the same standards of behavior that govern young, unmarried females."

"Do I not know it?" she cried feelingly. "How unfair it is! Would that men and women were held to the same standards! 'Twould be much more just."

"'Tis not the way of the world, as I believe you know perfectly well."

"The world can be changed." She sat up in her chair and regarded him with a crusading light in her eyes. "Men should be just as virtuous as women. Then we all should be happier. I'm sure that's what the Church teaches."

"You are a dreamer, if you believe such a thing. Do not imagine that your trying to change the rules will ever make any difference. Break the rules, and you will find yourself ostracized by society before you can turn around."

"Well, look at us. We have spent several nights together and my virtue is still intact. Is it just because you've been tied by the leg? Or do you have some sense of virtue, too?"

"Georgie!" Sedgemoor closed his eyes in despair. How did one explain to her that her virtue was something she should not leave open to question, something that under no circumstances should she bandy about? He was at a loss to know how best to deal with such a madcap hoyden.

"Well? Would you have refused me, if *I* had attacked *you?*" she challenged, not quite relevantly.

"Good God, Georgie!" he exploded. "Do not be ridiculous!"

She giggled. "Oh, dear, Gus! I do admit that was a most improper question. I believe I have had too much of this delicious champagne."

"Yes, you have. And I will not be able to help you, if you become too foxed to walk. You must go to bed before you become quite disguised and I decide that you are open to improper suggestions and would be willing to accommodate me. Now let us go to sleep, before this outrageous conversation goes any further," he said before he realized that he had revealed his own lascivious thoughts, fueled by their highly irregular conversation, conducted behind the closed doors of a bedchamber, with a wide bed just behind them.

She opened her eyes wide and stared at him, then laughed merrily as she reached over and rested her hand on his arm. "Oh, you would never really do such a thing!"

"What?"

"Ask me to lie with you?"

"A man, finding himself alone with a woman, and with no other female company about, might well do such a thing." Sedge would never admit it, but he, too, was feeling the effects of all the champagne he had drunk. And Georgie *would* persist in putting lustful ideas into his head.

"But of course, *you* would not. With me."

"No. No, I wouldn't," Sedge lied through his teeth. All the thinly veiled talk of amorous dealings and sexual euphemisms had stirred his blood.

"You cannot abide me. And you are afraid I would try to compromise you."

"Georgie. Go to bed!" he ordered.

"Is that a request, an invitation, or an order, my lord viscount?" she asked provocatively, rising from her chair somewhat unsteadily and swaying toward him.

Sedge stared at Georgie for a long moment, opened

his mouth to speak, then closed it again with a snap, reaching for the champagne bottle instead.

"I shall find Pip and send him to you. When you're all tucked up in bed yourself, then I shall come back," she promised as she left the room, walking carefully.

Sedge lifted his hands to his face and rested his head against them. She was utterly, utterly impossible. Georgiana Carteret was the last female in the world he would actively pursue, but that did not alter the fact that she was a woman, and he was a man— and they were alone together in a bedchamber where the other inhabitants of the house thought them a married couple. The thought of singing bedsprings slipped unbidden into his mind. He uncovered his face and reached for his half-drained glass of champagne.

Next morning, Mr. and Mrs. Thorpe waved goodbye as "Mr. Moor" was helped downstairs by his "cousin's" coachman and valet and seated in the luxuriously appointed chaise. Georgie skipped along behind the entourage, calling out directions to one and all and giving cheerful, but not very helpful, advice about how to manage the incapacitated viscount.

Sedgemoor had instructed his valet to bring along adequate funds for the return journey to Gloucestershire and out of that he had left a very generous pourboire for the Thorpes.

The couple were suitably appreciative. "See Muthur," Farmer Thorpe remarked to his wife when he had received the handsome monetary gift, "Told 'ee we was dealin' with the quality."

"A viscount's cousin an' all. We's been honored," Mrs. Thorpe replied with awe. "Have you seen them a-lookin' at one another? 'Tis a love match, and no mistake, I'll be bound. . . . Wonder when their first babbie will come, I do," she said to her husband with a huge grin on her weathered face, nudging him in the side with her elbow.

Rufus, who had been shut up in the barn during Georgie's stay at the farm, was finally released from his confinement. He bounded across the yard to gambol joyfully at his mistress's heels.

The big dog leapt into the open door of the chaise after the viscount, who had been assisted inside and settled along one of the soft leather seats by Wilkins. Rufus put his paws on Sedgemoor's lap and would have licked his face, but he ceased immediately when his intended victim commanded "Down boy," in a steely voice.

"Oh, you are a naughty dog, Rufus. Where are your manners, sir?" Georgie asked in a shaking voice, holding back her laughter with difficulty as she saw her large dog drop to his belly and whine, cowed by the authority in the viscount's voice.

"Get down from there at once, Rufus," she instructed. "You are to ride with Pip. Come along."

The large hound scooted out with a frightened glance back at the viscount, then wagged his tail at his mistress, his tongue lolling out of his mouth happily as Georgie escorted him over to her curricle where Pip was sitting holding the reins of the restive team. He was to drive Georgie's curricle behind the viscount's chaise until his mistress joined him.

As earlier agreed upon, Georgie accompanied Sedge in his chaise a little way along the road in order to dupe the Thorpes. When they had once again traversed the dangerous hill where Sedge had overturned and had gone about a mile farther down the road, the viscount tapped on the roof of his vehicle, signaling his coachman to stop.

"I believe this is where we part company, Miss Carteret," he said formally. He reclined rather uncomfortably along one of the coach seats with his leg resting on a pile of pillows and blankets Wilkins had supplied to cushion his master's injured limb.

"Yes, indeed, Gus. I am anxious to be on my way to Grandmama's. I am glad we got such an early start and that it is turning out to be a gorgeous day for the first of March." She carelessly jammed her bonnet on her head, tied the strings in a lopsided bow under her chin, placed her reticule on her wrist and gave him a dazzling smile as she prepared to open the chaise door. "Goodbye, Gus. Godspeed."

"I wish you good luck in your season. Mind you conduct yourself with modesty—and some restraint. I trust you will not be too disappointed, if London and its, ah, amusements do not meet your expectations." He felt sure her high hopes and her high spirits would soon be dashed.

"Oh, how silly you are, Gus. I am sure I shall find great enjoyment in the season." She was brimming over with joy and excitement about her upcoming sojourn in London. "It is often what you look for, and where you look, you know, that determines if you

will enjoy yourself or not. Anyway, if there are one
or two things I do not like, I shall ignore them or
change them," she said airily.

"I just wish to—"

Georgie raised her hand to stop his speech. "No
need to thank me, Gus, for stopping to assist you
when you overturned and staying to see that you
were properly cared for. Anyone would have done
the same."

He shut his mouth, suppressing the urge to tell her
it had not been his intention to "thank" her for her
damned interference in his life and for the scandalous
charade she had propelled him into. *Thanking* the
maddening female was the very last thing he would
have wished to do. Wringing her neck would have
been nearer the mark.

"Hmm," was all he allowed himself to say, raising
one brow and looking at her broodingly.

"Well, goodbye, Gus," Georgie said, getting up
from her seat opposite him and impulsively flinging
an arm about his neck to give him a farewell hug.
Her soft lips warmly brushed his freshly shaven face
as she planted a light kiss upon his cheek. "I hope
your leg soon heals completely. But I'm sure it will.
Doctor Hamilton said it would. I have every confidence in his opinion."

She opened the door to see Wilkins standing there,
ready to assist her down. She smiled and gave him
her hand. The little valet had been riding on the driver's seat with the coachman, but now he stood ready
to take her place inside the vehicle with his master.

Wilkins was brimming over with curiosity about
the hurly-burly little female and her relationship to

his master, but he knew better than to question the viscount directly about his private affairs. He felt confident he could piece the story together bit by bit during the long, tedious journey back to Gloucestershire from any chance remarks his lordship happened to let fall. He had never seen the viscount with such a young lass before, and one, moreover, who certainly did not meet his exacting master's strict notions of attractiveness in the opposite sex.

Georgie turned and waved jauntily to Sedgemoor. "I shall take your king again the next time we play chess, see if I don't," she called with a laugh.

When he looked out, Sedge had to crane his neck to see her, for the top of her head was only just visible through the coach window. As he raised his hand in farewell, he saw that her bonnet was half off her head, her tumbled copper curls blowing wildly about her face.

Her headgear had been disarranged by her impulsive embrace of him, he realized with a sudden little jerk of his pulses. He had been caught offguard by that hug and kiss, but he didn't know why he should have been surprised by her impetuous—and most improper—action. The gesture had been so very like her, he should have expected it. What he did not expect was the sudden feeling of loss that had invaded his chest after the warmth of that brief embrace.

First she had provoked him, then she had rescued him, nursed him, and entertained him for more than a week, eight days to be precise, and now she was off to London to have her lively spirit broken, most like, he reflected moodily.

As she skipped away to where Pip was holding the

horses of her own curricle, Sedge told himself he was
well quit of her, interfering, provoking, incautious,
managing little baggage that she was. But he brooded
all the way back home to the Oaks, wondering what
would become of her when she entered the metropolis.

A mere six weeks after he had returned to Gloucestershire to recover from his broken leg in splendid
isolation at his stately home, vowing not to set foot
off his estate until he could walk without the aid of
a cane, Viscount Sedgemoor found himself once
more passing along the Marlborough Road on his
way to London. An elegant, but nonetheless sturdy,
ebony walking stick rested on the leather coachseat
beside him.

During the past month at the Oaks, he had been utterly unable to banish his memories of Georgiana
Carteret, despite every effort to do so. It was bad
enough that he thought about her during his waking
hours, but he also found himself dreaming of her at
night. Disturbing dreams they were, too. Dreams in
which all her physical imperfections that he had
disparaged so thoroughly suddenly became highly
desirable attributes.

Her impossible hair became the long, flowing copper tresses of a Venus, winding round her bare shoulders and falling provocatively over her creamy skin
to conceal and entice. Her sapphire eyes became the
sultry orbs of the most enchanting temptress; her soft
lips the sweetest he had ever tasted. Her flawed figure became impossibly alluring, feeling warm and

soft against him. Her never failing good spirits and gay laughter became infectious. He often woke finding himself grinning like a monkey at nothing at all.

Sedge began to suspect that his head had been broken as well as his leg when he had overturned in that curricle accident. He no longer seemed able to think clearly when he thought of Georgie.

He, who had had little use for women, other than as occasional bed partners, found himself obsessed by thoughts of a maddening little piece of mischief who had no business being in London on her own, with only an elderly grandmother to look after her. With her penchant for striking up conversations with any and all comers, she had undoubtedly already made a score of unsuitable acquaintances. She was likely deep into some sort of mischief by now, too. He only hoped she wasn't closeted in a bedroom with some other poor fool.

He brooded over the fact that they had spent seven nights alone in the same room together, and several people believed them married. She had let the farming couple who had looked after him and the doctor who had attended him believe that they were man and wife. She had given a false name and they had been in an isolated neighborhood, true, but people gossiped to their neighbors and the word spread.

He remembered, too, her quip about his having kissed her on that first night. Had he done such a thing? He had vague memories of tasting sweet lips and cupping a soft breast in his hand while he cradled a warm little body on top of himself in that bed. But he had been drugged and in much pain at the time.

Were his memories just the dreams he had been plagued with recently?

He feared they were not.

And she had assisted the doctor when his leg had been set. It was a completely unseemly thing for a young, unmarried female, who was in no way connected to him, to have done. Did the chit not have a modest bone in her whole incautious body? Did the proprieties mean nothing to her? His own conduct had always been governed by proper behavior, as far as women of his own class were concerned, at least.

And there was the nub of the matter. The family honor and the consideration he owed his distinguished name could be at stake.

The St. Regis had ever been a most upstanding family. No breath of scandal had ever attached to their exalted name. Every time he looked at one of the many mantelpieces in the house, the finely carved letters of the family motto set into each one fairly jumped out at him: *semper cum honore.* Always act with honor. His autocratic father had drilled the precept into him at an early age. Never do anything that would bring even a hint of disgrace to the irreproachable name of St. Regis.

And he always had acted with implacable honor where the family name was concerned. It was as precious to him as it had been to the generations who had guarded it so carefully before him.

Was the family honor at stake in this case? he asked himself. Had he compromised the girl through unfortunate circumstances, if not in deed? Being familiar with the way the censorious world viewed these things, he greatly feared so.

Argue with himself as he would that the scandalous situation been almost unavoidable under the circumstances, he came to the inevitable conclusion that he must offer Georgiana the protection of his name.

Good God! Must he offer marriage to that impossible little red-haired dowd? he asked himself in horror. He did not want to be saddled with a wife—was quite satisfied with his free and easy bachelorhood. But in a little over a week, the little wretch had thoroughly upset his ordered existence.

Was such a hoyden to become his viscountess? What would his sophisticated friends think to see him with such an unattractive child? He, who always had cool, statuesque beauties on his arm, would now be seen with this harum-scarum chit. The worldly gentlemen and elegant ladies of his circle would laugh themselves silly, thinking that he had lost his mind, most like.

But he was a gentleman. A *St. Regis* gentleman, he reminded himself, glancing again at one of the mantelpieces. His honor and duty compelled him to do the right thing. Therefore, much as he dreaded it, he must offer her marriage.

Once having decided upon his course, Sedge wanted to have the distasteful deed done as speedily as possible. He instructed his staff to prepare for an immediate journey to London. Once there, he planned to waste no time in visiting the girl's grandmother. He would persuade Lady Carteret that a quiet wedding was in order. Then he would spirit Georgie back to the Oaks where he could keep her safely under his eye while he recovered in peace and quiet, far from society's astonished, prying eyes.

So impatient was he to see Georgie again and fulfill the obligations of family honor, that he forgot his embarrassment at the fact that his limp was still quite pronounced and that he was still reliant on his cane to get about. He deliberately kept his mind a blank as to what their future life together would be like . . . what their married relations would be like. He thought that once he had the little wretch safely locked away, perhaps he would be able to get on with some semblence of a normal life once more.

Chapter 6

"My, you're a handsome lookin' fella, ain't you? Good thing wigs is out of fashion. Ain't seen so fine a head of yeller hair as yours in many a day. And your shoulders ain't half bad either," Lady Carteret said to Viscount Sedgemoor as he was shown into her best front parlor at Number Ten, Half Moon Street, one gloomy day in mid-April.

Affronted by Lady Carteret's outspoken words of greeting and her brusque manner, Sedge reached for his quizzing glass, but stopped himself in time. He was not used to being addressed in such blunt fashion, but she was an elderly woman, not worthy of a chilling setdown from him. Undoubtedly she had cut her teeth during the height of the raucous Georgian era, when manners among some of the upper crust had bordered on the crude, or so he had been given to understand.

Lady Carteret cackled with mirth at the look of indignation on the viscount's face. Leaning forward in her chair, she rested her slight weight on her walking stick and extended her bony hand, encased in a black

lace mitt, for his salute. "You'll excuse me not gettin'
up, young man. The rheumatics have settled into
these old bones of mine."

"Lady Carteret. So good of you to receive me,
ma'am," Sedge murmured smoothly, bowing over her
hand. "No need to disturb yourself on my behalf."

Reminding himself that his purpose was to ingrati-
ate himself with the older woman, he took care not to
adopt a superior tone, much as she provoked him. He
must not allow himself to be diverted from the task
at hand, but must concentrate his energies on explaining as succinctly as possible, the occasion, the
necessity of his visit. Also he must take care not to
reveal the full extent of her granddaughter's shocking, scandalous behavior. He would have to enlist
Lady Carteret's aid in seeing that his hasty marriage
to Georgie was made to seem quite above board.
Things must go smoothly so that no hint of the scandalous incident in Little Bickton ever came to light.
No whisper of scandal must attach itself to his
name—or to that of Georgiana, either before or after
she assumed that same exalted name.

"What happened to your leg?" Lady Carteret asked
forthrightly, seeing his cane and his limp. "Is it a permanent affliction?"

"I broke my leg recently, but it is on the mend.
Soon I will be able to do without this blasted stick
entirely."

He regarded his hostess appraisingly, noticing a
few streaks of copper red still visible in the iron gray
strands of hair that had escaped from her worked-lace
cap. So this was where his little imp had her hair
from. He wondered if Georgie had also inherited her

outspoken, madcap ways from her paternal grandmother. There were some similarities, but Lady
Carteret was a downy old bird, as haughty as her
granddaughter was friendly, as angular as Georgie
was softly rounded.

"Sit down. Sit down, young man. Come to see my
Georgie, have you?" She assessed him shrewdly,
more pleased than she would ever let him know by
what she saw. She liked the look of him. Her granddaughter's previous callers had been a pack of pup-
pies compared to this fashionable young buck who
had just limped into her room. He was lean and
powerful-looking, despite his injury, and as handsome as sin.

"Indeed, Lady Carteret, I had hoped to pay my re-
spects to your granddaughter today, but, as I was
given to understand by your butler that Miss Carteret
is out, I am glad to have this opportunity for a few
private words with you first."

"Private words?" She regarded him keenly. "What
has Georgie been up to now, heh?"

Her words alarmed him. There was no *telling* what
Georgie had been up to in his absence. The sooner
the thing was settled, the better for his immediate
peace of mind, if not for his future tranquility.

"Lady Carteret, may I speak plainly?" Sedge asked
with a straight look, deciding to get to the heart of
the matter without more ado.

"Wouldn't have it any other way. Been known as
a plainspoken woman all my life. I appreciate the
quality in others." She waved a beringed hand at him
nonchalantly, but her eyes on him sharpened, and her
mind was on the alert.

"Your granddaughter was delayed on the road to you here in London from her home in Wiltshire. Has she explained any part of the reason for that delay?"

"Delayed was she? No. I know of no delay. She sent that whippersnapper of a servant of hers, Pip, with a message to me that she planned to leave George's home—that's my son—and come to me here, if I would have her. Pish-tish. If I would have her, indeed! Been orderin' George to send her to me anytime these past three years. But would he part with the girl and do what's best for his own daughter? No. That selfish fool of a son of mine needed her at home. To see to his own comfort. My Georgie's had charge of the housekeeping—and of the stables, too—for years, you understand.

"Then George went and married that little flibbertigibbet, Roselyn Brascombe, a few months ago, and he's been makin' a cake of himself over his new ninnyhammer of a wife ever since. Makin' Georgie uncomfortable, not wanted in her own home, after she's had charge of it all this time. Well, men will be asses when they fancy themselves in love. Reminds me of my own youth. Some of the tales I could tell of the young mooncalves who followed me about!" She chortled, her faded blue eyes twinkling in her sunken cheeks as memories flooded her.

When she had regained her composure, she asked sharply. "Georgie was delayed on the road, you say? And you know something about it?"

"She was delayed by me, ma'am."

"Was she now? You begin to interest me greatly, young man. Scandalous goings-on were there?" she asked, looking at him acutely.

"Not precisely, Lady Carteret."

"Then what are you gettin' at? How did you delay her?"

"There was a curricle accident. I overturned and your granddaughter stopped to rescue me. She arranged for me to be carried to a farmhouse and stayed there with me for several days."

"Humph! Very heroic of her. Wonder why she hasn't mentioned any of this to me?"

Sedge ignored Lady Carteret's rhetorical question. "As we were forced to spend several nights under the same roof, I believe that Georg—your granddaughter was compromised. I feel it necessary to offer her the protection of my name."

"You want to marry Georgie?" she exclaimed in surprise. "Well, bless my soul! Make her a viscountess, heh? Never thought she'd do better than a knight, if that."

"Then we are agreed. The marriage will take place as soon as the arrangements can be made."

She put up a hand to stay his words. "You're in that much haste, are you? You go too fast, Sedgemoor. Have to see if Georgie'll have you first."

"She has been compromised."

"But not bedded, heh?"

"No," he answered emphatically, dampening down his annoyance, and his discomfort, at the question. "She has been compromised by *circumstances*. She has no choice but to marry me. Surely you will point that out to her."

"I can point it out to her as much as you like. Don't mean she'll take you, unless she fancies you. Georgie has a mind of her own. *I* can't compel her."

"I am highly eligible, I assure you," Sedge said, drawing himself up stiffly in his chair and looking down his aristocratic nose at the autocratic old lady. "Why wouldn't she have me?"

"High-in-the-instep, ain't you? Too high for my Georgie, mayhap," Lady Carteret replied sapiently, not at all intimidated by his haughty manner. "My Georgie's a warm-hearted little madcap. Needs a gentle hand on her reins. To my way of thinking, you wouldn't suit her. Used to getting your own way, ain't you? Too autocratic by half."

"*I* wouldn't suit *her!*" Sedge was deeply offended. Unknowingly, Lady Carteret had wounded him where he was most vulnerable, for his notion of his own importance was decidedly elevated.

" 'Struth, can't see why she wouldn't have you, though." Lady Carteret let her eyes run down her visitor's body appreciatively, taking note of his lean torso and broad chest and shoulders. Her eyes came to rest on his striking countenance. "You look virile enough. You'll keep her bed warm for her, I'll be bound . . . and she'll lead you a lively dance, too, sonny!" Lady Carteret laughed with bawdy delight.

Sedge felt himself flush at the audacious words.

"Aye, for my part, I'd like to see her hitched to you. You'll likely not be too long about gettin' an heir. I've a hankerin' to see some great-grandchildren before I stick my spoon in the wall."

As no appropriate retort came to mind, Sedge clamped his lips shut on an oath, silently damning all females by the name of Carteret, who seemed to have no qualms about riding roughshod over his carefully guarded dignity.

"But no use gettin' my hopes up. No tellin' what the gel will decide. She has an odd kick in her gallop, does my Georgie. Takes singular notions into her head and can be stubborn as a mule, if she takes against an idea. Mayhap she's taken against *you.*"

Sedge concealed his look of aversion. The thought of wedding a girl who bore any resemblance to a mule was decidedly unpalatable. He was reminded of all the reasons it would be imprudent in the extreme to tie himself for life to Georgiana Carteret. He would be well out of it if Georgie refused him, as her grandmother seemed to think quite possible.

There was a commotion in the hallway, signalling a new arrival. Georgie burst into the room, bringing a ray of sunshine into the gloomy chamber with her. "Grandmama, you will never guess where I have been invited!" She stopped abruptly, seeing Sedgemoor.

Sedgemoor put up his glass to survey Georgie, and to hide the light of gladness that had leapt into his eyes on seeing her again.

"Georgie, must you always come into a room in that harum-scarum fashion? We have a visitor, gel. Make your curtsy and say how-de-do," Lady Carteret instructed. But she may as well have spoken to thin air for all the heed her granddaughter paid her.

"Why, Gus! Whatever are you doing in town?" Georgie exclaimed. "Oh, this is of all things famous! How is your leg? Much better I trust, or you would not be here."

She rushed up to him as he rose to his feet with difficulty, using his left hand to brace himself on the ebony cane.

For half a second, Sedge thought she was going to

throw her arms about him and hug him as she had done in his chaise. His right arm began to rise of its own accord to receive her. However, she contented herself with giving him her hand and grasping his warmly, squeezing it tightly. She smiled brilliantly up at him, her eyes a brighter, clearer blue than he remembered as they twinkled up at him.

"Georgiana." He bowed unsmilingly, taking in her changed appearance. All her long, wild copper tresses were gone. And was her face thinner, too, or was it the new hairstyle that served to make it appear less round? Her hair had been cut and shaped around her head, leaving a mass of soft curls framing her face, and trailing down the back of her neck, just caressing the top of the ruched collar of her fashionable morning gown of sprigged primrose muslin. She looked like a red-haired cherub whose halo was slightly askew.

"I am fast recovering, as you see," he answered her.

Lady Carteret held her tongue and listened to the exchange between her granddaughter and her intriguing caller with a gleam of amusement in her eyes. So Georgie had captured the interest of this proud young lord, had she? What a dance she would lead him, Lady Carteret thought, shaking with silent mirth as she enjoyed the scene being played out before her sharp old eyes.

"Oh, this is lovely. I was wondering how you were getting on just the other day when your name came up in conversation," Georgie chattered on. "When did you get to town?"

"I arrived only last evening," Sedge replied stiffly. Georgie had not been thinking of him constantly since they parted, as he had her? Her words seemed to imply it. "You look well. How do you go on with your season?"

"Oh, Gus! I am having the most wonderful time. Grandmama has been a real Trojan to let me stay here with her and outfit me so extravagantly and arrange for me to be invited *everywhere!* I have just returned from the modiste's, and I have spent a fortune!"

"Can't have my own granddaughter runnin' about town in rags, even though I will likely be ruined before the season's out," Lady Carteret grumbled.

"Oh, I could never spend that much, Grandmama!" Georgie looked innocently at her elderly relative for a moment before turning to Sedgemoor. "How do you like my new gown, Gus?" she bubbled, twirling about in her new garment.

"I am lost in admiration, ma'am. It suits you admirably," he complimented her. And he meant it most sincerely. The gown was quite a stylish garment, all in the latest mode. She appeared slimmer, or did the new style just suit her short stature better? Belted softly under her full breasts with a satin ribbon, it flowed down her body in a smooth line, flattering her.

He looked closely into her happy, smiling face. Her freckles looked less prominent, too. He hoped she hadn't resorted to powdering her face and spoiling her freshness.

"Thank you for the compliment, my lord," she said, batting her eyelashes exaggeratedly. "I must say, you are looking extremely elegant, Gus." She exclaimed, openly admiring the way his fashionable coat of dark blue Bath cloth sat snugly over his wide shoulders.

"Quite an improvement from the last time I saw

you," Georgie teased, reminding him of the intimacy
they had shared during their sojourn with the Thorpes.

"Thank you," he murmured, hoping she would
quell the urge to reminisce about their time together
for her grandmother's edification.

Lady Carteret addressed a question to Sedgemoor,
asking him about the extent of his estate, and while
he politely answered her careful queries, Georgie
continued to smile up into his face, taking in his im-
proved appearance.

His blond hair looked freshly washed and gleamed
with golden lights. Just touching his collar in the
back, it was longer than it had been in Little Bickton,
giving him an appealingly romantic appearance, she
decided. Quite a contrast with the last time she had
seen him when his face had been pale and drawn
from his ordeal, and his hair had been all matted and
plastered to his head. Not a trace remained of the
dark shadows under his gray eyes either.

Her gaze wandered lower, to take in the form-
fitting buff inexpressibles that outlined his lower
torso to perfection, down to the gleaming leather of
the Hessian boots he wore on his feet, then skimming
over the ebony cane in his hand.

"Is that the Mathematical?" she asked when he had
finished speaking to her grandmother, indicating the
snowy-white cravat he wore carefully arranged
around his neck when her eyes had traveled up his
body once more. "I thought you would have favored
something more complicated, like the Oriental."

"You are quite right, ma'am. It is the Mathematical."

She laughed. "Are you not astonished by my
newly acquired vocabulary?" she quizzed him,

clearly pleased with herself. "I have grown quite fashionable. All the names and styles of modish attire are now at the tip of my tongue. I expect you to be suitably impressed, Gus."

He looked alive and vigorous now, despite the limp, she thought, smiling directly into his gray eyes. And quite impossibly virile. What a lucky girl one of her friends was going to be when she matched them up. Why, her own fingers itched to run through the silky golden mass of his hair. She could almost envy her unknown friend.

A smile played about his mouth. "You have learned fast, Georgie."

"Yes. Are you not proud of me acquiring all these useless fashionable terms? I am a good pupil, you know. Just remember how quickly I learned to best you at chess!"

"We shall have to have a rematch soon. I was not exactly at my best the last time we played."

"Oh, you seek to excuse your ignominious defeat because you were tied by the leg, do you, my lord? Well, we shall see what happens next time we play, when you are feeling quite at the top of your form! Next time, I shall take your king when you are wide awake, in possession of all your senses. It will be soon, I think, for you are looking quite, quite well now." Her eyes shone with mischief as she teased him, but a glint of admiration lurked there, as well.

He *did* look well, she thought. Exceedingly well. And formidable. He would make a challenging opponent in the game she intended they play, an opponent worthy of her mettle.

Lady Carteret sat back in her chair, hiding her in-

ner satisfaction as she keenly watched the interplay
between the two. Mayhap Georgie would have him
after all. The gel certainly seemed glad to see him,
glowing up at him like a firefly on the lookout for a
mate. And for all young Sedgemoor held himself so
stiffly, the look in the boy's eyes told her he admired
her granddaughter greatly. Ha! All his talk of offering
for Georgie as a matter of honor was only so much
balderdash. She laughed silently to herself.

"Well, it is wonderful to see you here in London.
Would you like to come with us tonight?" Georgie
asked impulsively. "Oh! Perhaps it is not proper for
the lady to ask the gentleman such a thing. Well, I am
sure it is not, and you already know my behavior is
not always prim and proper, do you not, Gus? But as
you have only just arrived, people would not think to
invite you yet, would they? Oh, the ins and outs of all
these genteel forms of social intercourse quite defeat
me. Now you are here, Gus, you will have to lecture
me on the correct way of going on as you were wont
to do at—Oh!" She came to a halt, casting a guilty
glance at Lady Carteret as she recollected that her
grandmother did not know of their previous meeting.
Realizing that she would somehow have to account
to Grandmama Carteret for her previous acquaintance
with the viscount, her inventive mind busily began to
spin a suitable tale.

"I would be honored to accompany you on your
evening excursion, Georgiana, if I can obtain an invitation on such short notice," Sedge replied formally.
"And if it is permitted?" He turned to look at Lady
Carteret, who nodded her approval gleefully.

"Of course, of course, sonny."

"Oh, good! It is a ball, you know. And I plan to dance until I wear holes in my slippers!" Georgie's hand flew to her cheek. She looked conscious. "Oh, dear. I have forgotten about your poor leg. You will not be able to dance. Perhaps you will not wish to come after all?"

"No, no. I wish to accompany you. There are some urgent matters we must discuss."

"But do not be standing here talking to me. Sit down again, Gus. I give you my permission to be seated in my presence."

Seeing that Sedgemoor was inclined to remain standing, Georgie took his arm and pressed him back until he was seated again. The feel of hard muscle under her hand sent a delicious tingle down her spine. She lifted her hand from his arm reluctantly.

"What are these urgent matters you speak of?" she asked curiously. "Can we not speak now?"

Sedge looked pointedly at her grandmother. "Not now, Georgie."

"Oh, you are cruel. You've piqued my curiosity and now you make me wait. I shall show you no mercy the next time we play chess, to pay you back, Gus," she warned him, wagging a minatory finger at him. "No need to look so arrogant and haughty and come all lordly with me. Your high and mighty airs will not work to quell me, as you know perfectly well, Gus."

"Have done, Georgie. Give the poor young man some rest from your waggin' tongue," Lady Carteret recommended with a cackling laugh. Seeing Georgie with the viscount had given her a new lease on life. She had the feeling she was in for some highly amusing entertainment in the coming weeks as her grand-daughter led the arrogant young man a lively dance.

Sedge took his leave after arranging to meet Georgie and her friends at Lady Carteret's at half past eight that evening.

Seeing Georgie again made him doubt the wisdom of his plan one minute, and fired him with impatience to get on with it the next. She had an ungoverned tongue. No telling what she would blurt out, or to whom, or under what circumstances. Just look at what she had said in front of her grandmother not two minutes previously.

Yes, the sooner she was under his control, the better—then the less chance of any indiscretion of hers causing the very scandal he sought to avoid. He would not have the good name of the St. Regis family, or his honor as a gentleman, impugned.

Sitting with his cane by his side and his leg propped on an embroidered satin stool in the ornate, gilded ballroom of the Duke and Duchess of Boscastle that evening, Sedge watched a vivacious Georgie dance by with yet another young admirer.

He was frustrated. He had as yet found no opportunity for private speech with her. Disgustedly, he saw that she had an army of gauche young men eating out of the palm of her hand, and some not so young and not so gauche, too. More than one gentleman of the first stare clamored for a chance to dance with her, right along with the youngest gentlemen freshly come to town.

While chatting to various friends and acquaintances,

his eyes kept straying to Georgie, wherever she might be in the ballroom. She went from one partner to another, a wide smile always lighting her face. Frequently, he could hear her merry, infectious laughter above the general chatter in the crowded, overheated room and whenever he looked at her, he could see that she was talking animatedly, enjoying herself to the hilt.

All his concerns about the disappointments she would face in town, about how she would face great difficulties in entering society with her outspokenness, disregard for proper behavior, and free and easy manners, had been for naught. After he had assured himself she would be on the fringes of society until he arrived on the scene to exert his considerable influence to ease the way for her, to assure her acceptance into society's highest circles, she had confounded him yet again.

She did not require his assistance. She seemed to be wildly popular not only with gentlemen of all ages, but with the young ladies making their comeouts, too. And, surprisingly, with the older set, as well. They treated her as a pet. He had even overheard her referred to as a "dear girl," by no less a personage than the haughty Countess Lieven, one of the lady patronesses of Almack's and a high stickler, if ever there were one.

Georgie seemed to have charmed the entire populace. He wouldn't be surprised to see Prinny himself go down on bended knee to her before her venture into society was over.

"Ah, Sedgemoor," the Duke of Boscastle greeted him. "Pleased to see you here tonight. Sorry about the leg. Healing well, is it?" his host asked him, disturbing Sedge's thoughts.

"As well as can be expected, Duke. I should be able to get on a horse's back before the summer's out." God, but he missed riding more than he ever would have believed possible! Sedge thought. Indeed, he would be more than glad when he had the full use of his legs again, for more reasons than being able to get himself over a horse's back.

"In time to hunt next autumn, eh? Glad to hear it. Margot tells me you escorted Georgie here tonight. Not surprised. You're never one to be behind the fashion. And the little minx is all the kick. Little Georgie's one of a kind, Sedgemoor, one of a kind," the duke declared, glancing appreciatively at Georgie as she danced by before he moved on to chat to other of his guests.

Sedge tried not to resent Georgie's universal popularity. With her open countenance, lively manners, and friendly, animated way of talking to anyone and everyone, all seemed to find her refreshingly different.

Deuce take it! he thought, if only they knew what a little imp with a decided penchant for devilment lurked beneath that surface charm, they would run for cover, as he should do before he was much older.

All his frustration stemmed from the fact that he had not been able to have two words alone with Georgie since he had collected her from her grandmother's residence earlier in the evening.

Lady Carteret did not often accompany her granddaughter out in the evenings, due to her "rheumatics," but she had arranged for Georgie to go about under the chaperonage of Lavinia Fraser, Lady

Widecombe, the daughter of a friend of hers. Lady Widecombe was presenting her own daughter, Miss Charlotte Fraser, and Charlotte and Georgie had become fast friends.

Lady Widecombe and her daughter had been waiting with Georgie when Sedge arrived in Half Moon Street to take them to the Boscastle ball.

Georgie had exclaimed over his appearance, never having seen him in full evening dress before. Each item of his apparel was praised as she noticed it, from his Prussian blue velvet evening jacket to his gray waistcoat woven with silver threads to his black pantaloons.

"Oh, Gus, your valet has taken special pains with this neckcloth, hasn't he?" she asked, touching his elaborately tied cravat lightly with the tips of her fingers. Even his black patent evening pumps did not escape her notice and came in for comment. "Even your cane is elegant, Gus!" She quizzed him, asking if she could expect to see a different cane with each different suit of clothes he wore.

At one point, to his chagrin, she had taken his hand in hers and lifted it, inspecting the lace that protruded from his jacket sleeve. "I do like the way this lace falls so gracefully down over your hand, almost covering your fingers," she remarked. "Our escort tonight is dressed in the height of elegance, is he not?" she asked her two companions, beaming at him proudly.

"Indeed, Georgie, Lord Sedgemoor is everything that is correct," Lady Widecombe had seconded, smiling approvingly at him.

Lady Widecombe was not behindhand in offering him every courtesy. Her daughter Charlotte was in looks tonight and she hoped that the bashful girl would benefit from being seen in the viscount's company.

Sedge had complimented all three ladies on their ensembles, his eyes roving over Georgie's evening gown and finding not a single fault in the modish peach silk with its modicum of trim. Anything too heavy or too elaborately decorated would not have done at all for Georgie. Someone had a good eye and had advised her well, he was grateful to see. With a plain satin ribbon wound through the new curls that suited her so well, she would not disgrace him in front of his friends in the *ton* tonight, he decided with relief.

The viscount had insisted on conveying the ladies to the Boscastle's mansion in his own elegant town carriage, explaining that they would be more comfortable in his modish, well-sprung vehicle, than in the ancient equipage Lady Carteret had offered for their transport.

When they had mounted into his carriage, the ladies had exclaimed and complimented him on the comfortable interior of the equipage that included luxurious velvet upholstery on the seat backs and cushions, as well as two glass-paned carriage lamps to light the interior. Even the quiet Miss Fraser had whispered a word of praise, though she had chosen a moment to speak when she was least likely to be heard over the chatter of her mother and Georgie.

When they arrived at the Boscastle's enormous Belgrave Square townhouse, they were swept along with a crowd of people, all of whom seemed to be calling out greetings to Georgie, to Sedgemoor's consternation. He had hoped his presence would lend her a certain cachet this evening. He had thought that, if her season had not been going well, his presence by her side would bring her to the notice of more people of consequence in the *ton*, and perhaps serve to add some excitement to her evening.

How wrong he had been! Sedge reflected from his seat at the edge of the crowded, festive ballroom.

Georgie twirled by him with yet another new partner, giving him a cheery wave and a bright smile. But he did not have time to brood over Georgie's defection for long moments. He found that his presence had created a stir of interest. Many friends and acquaintances who had not seen him for several months came up to speak to him, expressing pleasure at finding him in town and exclaiming over the accident to his leg, offering their commiserations.

Half a dozen married ladies had, at various times, seated themselves beside him during the dancing sets. Without fail, each had signaled her interest in his company . . . and her availability for his pleasure.

Sedge regarded them all with cynicism and a new-found distaste for such clandestine connections. He turned away their suggestive hints with arrogant ease. These sophisticated women, with their air of well-bred *ennui*, had formerly been to his taste, but he now found that they had become stale. Their sarcasm, their fatigue, their very boredom, bored him.

Margot, Duchess of Boscastle, came to sit beside him and tell him of her great happiness at seeing him in her ballroom. She not only forgave him for coming without an invitation, but blessed him for it. "You know you are always welcome here, my dear Sedgemoor. Your presence always adds that certain *je ne sais quoi* to an entertainment. I am only sorry you are unable to dance at present."

"My leg will soon be strong enough so that I may caper about with the best of them. And I insist on your partnering me when I am able to dance. If you would be so gracious as to grant me such a boon, dear duchess," he beseeched in a low, seductive voice.

She laughed and slapped him on the wrist with her fan. "Your blandishing tongue is still in perfect working order, I see. I was intrigued when I learned that I owe your presence here this evening to Miss Carteret. I shall be sure to thank her for bringing you to my little entertainment. . . . I am surprised you are acquainted with Georgie, though, Sedgemoor," the duchess continued, clearly fishing.

"I have that honor." He inclined his head slightly, an enigmatic half smile on his face. "Which I gather I share with the entire populace."

"Yes. She is wildly popular, of course, with that gamine charm and infectious gaiety of hers, and her nonstop chatter. She puts our shy young people at ease and flatters our elderly friends outrageously with her courtesy and care for their comfort. But you are neither a fresh young greenhead new come to town, nor one of our superannuated citizens." She looked at him expectantly, curiosity burning brightly in her large, pansylike brown eyes.

It was apparent the duchess wished to learn when and where they had first met, but Sedge refused to rise to the bait. "Is she? Popular, I mean. I would have thought with her rather average looks, she would not have taken."

Recognizing defeat, Margot corrected him. "Well,

you are out there, my dear Sedgemoor. Many gentlemen consider her a beauty. Oh, not a diamond or a
toast, of course. But, even with your stringent standards, you must admit, she is easy to look upon. It's
her most delightfully charming smile, I believe, and
her dancing eyes."

"Do you think so?"

"Yes, indeed, I do. And you will be amazed when
I tell you that almost single-handedly, Georgie has
brought several of our shy wallflowers into full
bloom, and helped some of the buffleheaded young
gentlemen get over their awkwardness. Her kindness
and friendliness eases their way. Why, I do believe
we can give her credit for the match between Baron
Greenlea's youngest daughter and the Earl of
Gunthorpe's heir. Their parents are in alt. And the
young people, both too shy to have more than two
words to say for themselves, seem to be very much in
love. But she's such a madcap romp, I expect her to
do something quite outrageous before the season is
much older to set us all on our ears!" the duchess
added with a laugh, then excused herself and went off
to speak to some of her other guests.

Sedge heard her parting words with well-concealed
alarm. He must speak to Georgie and convince her to
retire to the country with him as soon as they could
be married. If he did not remove her from London
with all haste, she would be sure to blurt out something quite indiscreet any day now, and then they
would be in a devilish precious fix indeed.

Chapter 7

"Sedge, you old devil, what's this I hear about an
accident to your leg?" Max Templeton, lately a captain in His Majesty's Fifth Dragoon Guards, arrived
at Sedgemoor's side, bringing the Honorable Henry
Edgeworth with him.

"Max, Henry! Where did you two reprobates
spring from?" Sedge, clearly delighted to see the two
newcomers, extended his hand to his friends and
started to get to his feet. Max put a hand to his shoulder, keeping him in place.

"No, no. Stay where you are, old chap. Henry and
I will join you." Max settled his large frame in the
chair the duchess had lately occupied. Edgeworth,
the smaller of the viscount's two friends, quietly took
the chair to the other side and greeted Sedge in his
usual reserved way.

"What are you doing in London, Sedge?" Max
asked. "Thought you was fixed at Leftridge's, enjoying the company of the divine Diana."

"Had this blasted accident and had to cancel all
those plans."

"Is the delectable Diana coming up to town to join you here, then?" Max continued. The last he had heard Sedgemoor was determined to bed the chilling, formidable, but extraordinarily beautiful, Diana Carstairs, before another season had passed.

"Don't know what the lady's plans are," Sedge answered with a bored look. "Haven't seen her for an age."

"By Jove, you're mighty cool about it. She didn't send you away with a flea in your ear, did she, old chap? There's a stack of wagers riding on the outcome of your chances at melting My Lady Iceberg at White's, Watier's, and, I daresay, a dozen other places, you know. Wouldn't be surprised if even Prinny has a packet laid on it. Don't tell me you're going to disappoint him now by spoiling all bets. Our spendthrift future monarch needs the blunt, you know."

The viscount frowned. "No, I didn't know there was betting on the outcome of my acquaintance with the lady. If a pack of fools will wager on which raindrop will fall down a window faster, I can't say I'm surprised they are laying down their blunt on who takes whom between the bedsheets.... As I said, I didn't go to Leftridge's and I have no idea where Di—Lady Carstairs is now, nor do I much care."

Max gave a low whistle between his teeth. "Have bigger game in mind now, do you? Who can it be?" Max grinned at his friend, creasing the white scar that ran from his ear across his cheek to his jaw.

At Sedge's noncommittal shrug, Max glanced all around the ballroom, looking for a woman of outstanding beauty who would be worth his friend's mettle. "Can't be that yeller-haired Armitage chit, can it? Grant you, she's a diamond of the first water, but hardly out of leading strings yet, and a brainless peagoose into the bargain. Not your type, really. Besides, her father would have you tied up in parson's mousetrap fast enough to make your head spin, if you tried such a thing."

"Pray, Max, rid yourself of the deuced bloody notion that I am out to seduce any willing female at the moment," Sedge responded irritably. "I have other things on my mind."

"No need to take that damned stiff-rumped tone with me, Sedge, my boy. We were at school together. Remember?"

Sedge lifted his hand and pressed his thumb and forefinger to his eyes, rubbing them for a moment. "Sorry, Max. I would not admit it to anyone but you, but I've been up too long today."

"Leg's paining you, isn't it, Sedge?" Henry asked from the viscount's other side. He had been quiet, not participating in the general conversation, but listening avidly to his companions' words. He realized that, as much as Sedge tried to hide it, his friend was still suffering from the effects of his injury. Henry himself was in the habit of keeping his own counsel, so he was particularly sensitive at knowing when others were doing likewise.

"Like the very devil," Sedge admitted with an apologetic grin for his friends.

"Why didn't you say so, man?" Max asked gruffly. "Why don't you take yourself off home, then?"

"Can't. Brought a young lady and her chaperone.

Two young ladies actually, as I recall. Must wait on their pleasure before I take my leave."

Max's eyebrows shot skyward when he learned that his friend had escorted some young chits and their chaperone to the ball. It was unheard of for Sedgemoor to involve himself with the infantry. He was immediately on the alert. What exactly was going on here? He watched the viscount carefully, noting the direction of his friend's eyes.

Finally, he realized just who it was Sedge was watching so keenly. Max was stunned. No! It couldn't be, he thought.

"You know Georgie, Sedge?" he asked, his warm hazel eyes full of incredulity.

The viscount recollected himself. His face closed as he admitted, "I am acquainted with Miss Carteret."

"Miss Carteret!" Max hooted with laughter. "Everyone calls her Georgie. She's the friendliest, liveliest, most easy-going girl around this season. There must be a dozen bucks ready to pay her their addresses."

"Oh? And does she favor any one of these young, er, bucks?" Sedge asked carefully, trying not to betray too much interest.

"Not that I've heard. Seems impartially friendly to everyone. Doesn't seem to favor anyone special, but it's early days yet. Perhaps she already had her eye on some poor bast—er, lucky devil. Henry, here, would like a look in, wouldn't you, my lad?" Max reached behind the viscount and cuffed Henry on the shoulder.

The taciturn Henry blushed and admitted somewhat haltingly, "I'm lucky if she has space left on her dance card by the time I get up enough nerve to ask her. But she usually manages to fit me in. She's so kind, I don't think she ever turns *anyone* down."

"You're too modest, my boy," Max said bluntly.

Sedge's eyebrows snapped together at this news. Even his friend Henry was interested in Georgie. Bashful Henry, whose modest looks were not his most outstanding attribute. As enthusiastic and accomplished a sportsman as they came, Henry pursued all the manly sports—riding, driving, fencing and boxing, hunting and shooting and fishing. But he had never been involved in any petticoat dealings before that the viscount was aware of.

Georgie skipped up to Sedge and his friends just then, sparkling with high spirits and smiling brilliantly. "Oh, Gus, Charlotte does not have a partner for supper. I have volunteered your services."

"Gus!" Max sputtered under his breath, turning almost purple with the heroic effort to smother his shout of laughter when he heard Georgie address his toplofty friend by this playful diminutive.

Sedge saw the laughter dancing in Max's eyes and shot his friend a quelling glance. No one, *no one,* ever dared call him Augustus and here was Georgie embarrassing him by addressing him as "Gus" in front of his friends. Devil take the little wretch!

"Oh, hello, Max. And dear Henry, too." Georgie greeted them with delight. "I didn't know the pair of you were acquainted with Sedgemoor."

"Indeed, Georgie, we've known this devilish stiff-rumped character since our school days," Max told her with a wide grin. So, the little Carteret even dared to tease the mighty Sedgemoor. Here was food for amusement, indeed. "We were all at Winchester together, you know."

"Well, you two can join forces with Gus to take Charlotte in to supper. The three of you will make a most impressive triumvirate."

"Sorry, Georgie. I'm already engaged, but Henry here would be pleased to do the honors, wouldn't you, old boy?" Max said to his diffident friend.

Henry bashfully agreed, but the viscount was not to be ordered about so easily.

Sedgemoor looked sharply at Georgie. "You seem to have forgotten that you are engaged to *me* for supper, Miss Carteret," he reminded her with a hardening of his jaw and a lift of his arrogant blond brow.

"Oh, Gus, I know we have so much to talk about since I saw you in—oh, ah, well, I'm sorry if there was a misunderstanding, but I promised to go in with Tiny Bigelow, and the poor boy had such a time even getting the invitation out, that I simply *cannot* disappoint him now. Why do we not all go together?" she exclaimed brightly as this brilliant solution to the dilemma occurred to her.

It was agreed that they would all make a large party at supper. Max and his partner were to join them, too.

"Come along, Henry. Let us find Charlotte and Tiny. Do not get up just yet, Gus. Rest your leg a moment until we come back to join you," she ordered, sailing off on the arm of Henry Edgeworth.

"Tiny Bigelow!" Max exclaimed in an aside to Sedge. "The fellow's as big as an ox, and as tongue-tied as all bedamned. Trust Georgie to make a friend of such an ungainly chap." He chuckled even as he eyed her with approval.

"Trust her to make a friend of *anyone,*" Sedge cut in, an edge to his voice. "She seems to be on first-name terms with every man in the room."

"Why, Sedge, you sound as if you don't approve. Surely such a charming, friendly girl deserves admiration. No airs. She's certainly not puffed up in her own esteem, nor a giggling, empty-headed peagoose, like most of the widgeons who come to town to display their wares on the marriage market. Many men appreciate that—it's refreshing after all the cloying misses and their matchmaking mamas closing in on a fellow."

"Perhaps, but she is not discriminating in her choice of friends. She gives herself no airs, I grant you, but she has no graces either."

"You are too severe, Sedge," Max commented, coming to Georgie's defense. "She's graceful enough for such a little squab. I think she is a positive delight." He looked carefully at his friend to gauge his reaction.

"She will have to learn to show more moderation in her behavior, or she will soon find herself the object of censure and unpleasant gossip. It would not do for her to make herself a by-word in the *ton.*"

"Hmm. You sound as though you would like to have the schooling of her. You have more than a passing interest, do you? What's between the two of you?"

"She's an acquaintance, that's all," the viscount prevaricated, waving his hand dismissively.

"So much heat about a mere acquaintance, Sedge? Well, I can see you are determined to reveal nothing. I had best go and seek out Miss Adams, before some-one else runs off with her for supper. She's a comely girl. Hope she'll prove conversant." Max wandered off, leaving Sedge to his thoughts.

As it fell out, Henry was the one who took Char-lotte on his arm with Georgie and Bigelow following behind. Sedge limped along beside them, feeling con-spicuous as he leaned heavily on his cane, while they made their way to the supper room.

Their party was very merry indeed, and many eyes were turned their way during supper, Sedge saw un-comfortably. Max was flirting with Miss Adams, bringing a flush to her pleasant, youthful face, and the taciturn Henry was speaking quietly with Miss Fraser, who was responding to him shyly. The pair seemed to be getting along famously. To his exasper-ation, Georgie was seated diagonally opposite him, chatting animatedly with Bigelow, trying to bring him out and make him laugh.

Sedge's frustration increased. Not once did she ad-dress a remark to him.

He caught Georgie's arm as she prepared to leave the supper table. "I must speak to you, Georgiana," he commanded in a low voice. "Can you not sit out this next dance with me?"

"Oh, yes, Gus, let us do so. I am dying of curiosity to know what you wish to discuss with me." She smiled up at him brilliantly and slipped her hand through his elbow, resting it warmly on his sleeve. "Let us go into the Duchess's anteroom immedi-ately," she whispered conspiratorially.

"Miss Carteret. Our dance, I believe," Lord Robert Lyndhurst, youngest son of the impoverished Duke of Miramont, was bowing formally before Georgie and extending his white satin-clad arm for her hand.

"Oh, heavens, I forgot!" she cried, giving Sedgemoor an apologetic look.

"You wound me, Miss Carteret, assuredly you do," Lord Robert was saying, assuming a hurt look, the twinkle in his spell-binding emerald eyes belying his words. "Do you mean to stand me up? That would be a novel experience."

"Oh, no, no. It is to be a waltz and I love to waltz. I have waltzed with you once before, and I must say, you do it divinely."

He looked deeply and seductively into her eyes as he drawled, "Hmm. I assume that if it were a country dance, I would find myself forsaken?"

Georgie laughed, releasing the viscount and taking Lord Robert's arm. "La, but you do seek for compliments, do you not, Robin? As if you have any need of them," she teased.

The virile young gentleman who stood before her with a lock of his longish sable brown hair falling negligently across his forehead, was quite impossibly attractive. With his seductive good looks, trim physique, and devastating smile, Lord Robert was accounted one of the most handsome, fascinating men in London—and one of the most dangerous. One glance from his thickly lashed, mesmerizing green eyes was enough to slay any female's heart.

Looking from one to the other, Georgie compared the two gentlemen she stood between. Molded in a coldly classical form, Sedgemoor's handsome features looked as though they had been chiseled from marble by a master sculptor.

As strikingly dark as the viscount was light, Lord Robert had a more earthy appeal. As devilishly charming as Sedgemoor was coldly formidable, there was a seductive warmth burning brightly in Lord Robert's bewitching eyes that easily drew women to him. A member of the Carlton House set, Lyndhurst was an intimate of Prinny's—*and,* it was rumored, a rake of the worst kind. One who loved women and left them with broken hearts without a second thought.

"Do you know Sedgemoor, Robin?" Georgie asked, seeking to introduce the two gentlemen, who were eyeing one another with covert hostility.

"'Evening, Sedgemoor. Haven't seen you in town this age," Lord Robert drawled. "Thought you would be in Berkshire. Heard your latest interest was situated there. How is Lady Diana Carstairs?"

"I wouldn't know, Lyndhurst. As you see, I am in London. How is Miss Ann Forester?" Sedge countered, referring to the girl whose heart it was rumored Lyndhurst had captured, then callously broken, during a house party over the past Christmas season.

Lyndhurst shot him an annoyed look from under his brows, his complexion somewhat flushed.

Sedge's eyes gleamed when he saw he had scored a hit off his rival.

"The music begins, Miss Carteret," Lord Robert said to Georgie.

"I shall see you after the dance, Gus," she called gaily to Sedgemoor as she went off on the arm of the most notorious rake in London.

Sedge watched her go with impotent fury, a ferocious frown marring his features. The devil! he swore. If Georgie were to fall under Lyndhurst's spell she would be ruined before the night was over. Remembering that she had once said she favored dark men, he cursed the injury to his leg more vehemently than ever.

If only he could dance, he would have snatched her from Lyndhurst's clutches and taken her onto the floor himself, even if it had resulted in a meeting in the park at dawn.

The viscount ignored the fact that he and Lyndhurst had competed for the same woman once before. Indeed, he himself could have matched Lord Robert in the number of females who had succumbed to his charms, but Sedge was more discreet in his affairs, and did not have the habit of publicly breaking the hearts of the young, unmarried ladies.

The Boscastle ball finally wound down to a conclusion in the wee hours of the morning. Sedgemoor saw to it that a pleased Lady Widecombe and a very sleepy Charlotte were conveyed home before he continued on alone with Georgie to Lady Carteret's Half Moon Street residence. Georgie had been the belle of the ball, and, of course, had not wanted to leave until the last set was danced. Her energy seemed to be boundless.

"Here we are alone at last, Gus!" Georgie exclaimed in a teasing tone after they had bid farewell to Lady Widecombe and Charlotte in front of their

Russell Square townhouse. "Now we can have a comfortable coze."

"I don't know how comfortable it's like to prove," Sedge answered sardonically.

"Oh, Gus, you sound weary and cross. Is your leg paining you?"

He denied it, but Georgie didn't believe him. "Of course, it must be. How selfish of me to have kept you out all night! You should have said something, and I could have gotten someone else to take us home—Robin would gladly have done so."

"Indeed, ma'am, you have a strange notion of my honor if you think I would have abandoned you to the tender mercies of that rake," Sedge ground out.

"Oh, well, perhaps I would have asked Max or Tiny, or, well, anyone would have been glad to do so."

"Indeed, I'm sure you are correct, ma'am," he agreed sarcastically.

"You *are* in a bad skin! Well, it is late and you are in pain, so I will forgive you, this time. . . . I was so surprised to see you in Grandmama's parlor this afternoon, Gus. I quite thought you wanted no more of my company after we parted in Little Bickton."

"Yes, at the time I had assumed that would be the case. But while I have been recuperating, I have had time to think about the ramifications of our sojourn together with the Thorpes. There were certain improprieties that cannot be overlooked. As little as the idea might appeal to either of us, I have reluctantly come to the conclusion that in order to preserve the honor of my family name I am compelled to offer you my hand."

"Wha—at! You are offering me m—*marriage?* You must be roasting me, Gus!" She laughed gaily.

"It is no laughing matter, Georgiana."

"Augustus Sebastian Stanhope St. Regis, have you lost your wits? The idea is completely ridiculous!" She stared at him with her mouth open. He looked steadily back at her.

Seeing that he was in earnest, Georgie lifted her hand and rested it for a moment against his brow. "You must have contracted a fever that has turned your brain, Gus."

He grabbed her hand and held it tightly. "Now listen to me, Georgiana. You were compromised."

"Was I? I must have been asleep at the time, for I don't remember a thing about it."

"Georgiana, you make light of it, but the fact remains that we spent seven nights alone together behind the closed door of a bedchamber. No one would believe that the episode was entirely innocent, should word get out. Your reputation could suffer irreparable damage, were it ever discovered."

"But who would discover it? Do you think the Thorpes will come to town and expose us as Mr. and Mrs. Moor?" she asked jokingly.

"There is no alternative."

"But you could hardly move, and were in dreadful pain much of the time. Surely, that one little kiss didn't compromise me, even if we were lying in your bed at the time."

"*What!* What 'one little kiss?' "

"Oh! You see, you don't even remember. That goes to show how insignificant it was."

He turned on his seat and took her by the shoulders. "Tell me!"

"It was nothing. It was the first night, after you had had the laudanum. You were in the throes of some dream about someone called Polly."

"Polly? Oh God!"

"Yes. You seemed to think I was Polly."

"What did I do, Georgie?" he asked in a low, menacing voice, demanding an answer. His hazy recollections had got mixed in with his sensuous dreams, so that now he could not be sure what had actually occurred and what was only imagined.

"You just kissed me. It seemed to ease your pain."

"By God, I would wager it did!" He muttered an oath under his breath, releasing her shoulders and sitting back. He closed his eyes briefly. "It is far worse than I thought. We must be married immediately."

"No, no, Gus. We would never suit. You are too high a stickler for me and I would drive you mad within a fortnight. . . . Besides, I have already picked out a girl for you."

Sedge choked. "You have picked out a girl for me?" he ejaculated. He had forgotten how managing Georgie could be. Why, in God's name, had he decided that honor compelled him to offer for the meddling female?

"Yes. She is sweet and shy and good-natured. And I'm sure you will be able to bend her to your will. She likes to observe all the formalities. And, oh, I should mention that she is *very* beautiful. I am sure you will be able to love her."

Dare to defy him, would she? He would not allow her to do so. The chit would *not* be the cause of any scandal attaching to the St. Regis name, of any stain on his honor. On that point he was determined.

"Now see here, Georgie. That is a preposterous idea! *You* must marry me. You have been compromised, even more seriously than I had thought. My honor demands that I make amends."

Hearing the implacable note in his voice, Georgie sobered. "Oh, Gus, you could never love me. I would drive you mad. I like to have fun. I like to laugh. You are formal and stiff. You insist on observing all the proprieties in public, even though I think you pursue your rakish activities on the quiet. . . . And that is another reason I could never marry you. I will not have *my* husband bedding other women!"

She rested her hand on his arm, her fingers pressing into his flesh. "I could never conform to your notions of what a proper wife should be. Can you imagine *me* a viscountess? No, no . . . I would always be doing something to draw your censure. I cannot help what you call my impetuous behavior. It is just *me,* you see."

In the glimmering light cast by the swaying coach lanterns, she looked straight into his eyes. He looked back at her determinedly.

"You would be lecturing me from morning to night, day in and day out, Gus. You know you would. I do not want to be like a daughter or ward to my husband. I want to marry someone who will treat me as an equal—someone whom I can love with all my heart. A marriage to you would not be like that, I fear. . . . So, I think you should be profoundly thankful that you are off the hook." She smiled at him, thinking he would be sincerely relieved.

Sedge heard her words and clenched his hands at his side. He was inexplicably hurt. He didn't know why that should be so. Yes, what he proposed was a rather bloodless alliance, a marriage of convenience, but they must marry. His family honor was at stake. Her own reputation was at stake. Neither of them had the luxury of waiting for a love match. It was far too late for such mawkishness. Not that he believed in that particular philosophical abstraction, anyway. He had always scoffed at the idea of everlasting, true love. He saw it as just so much poetical nonsense.

"I am not 'off the hook,' as you so inelegantly phrase it."

"Oh, stuff!" Georgie exclaimed.

"You have been compromised," he repeated inflexibly, a harsh note in his voice as he looked at her. "You will be made to see that you must marry me to save your good name, as well as mine. You would not want your grandmother hurt, would you?"

"Heavens, no. But how can she be hurt, if you and I say nothing of the matter?"

"I shall obtain the license tomorrow," he insisted, ignoring her arguments.

"What shall you do if I refuse? Capture me and ride away with me like a daring knight of old?" she asked humorously.

"Do not underestimate me, Georgiana. If I am forced to, I shall resort to whatever means necessary to see that you agree," he said roughly, looking at her with an intense expression in his gray eyes.

Georgie refrained from further protest. Good lord!

she thought, he was entirely serious. Well, she would just have to maneuver him into a match with Charlotte before he did indeed resort to kidnapping her and carrying her off over his saddle bow.

What a famous notion! If Gus were to behave in such an impetuous, romantic way, perhaps she would have him after all, Georgie thought on an inner chuckle. A marriage between them begun in such a way would be more exciting than she would ever have imagined.

Chapter 8

"Hello, Gus!" Georgie called, waving her hand gaily to Sedgemoor the following afternoon as she walked along a pathway in Hyde Park with Charlotte Fraser. "Here we are." She was holding Rufus on a long lead and one of Lady Carteret's footmen trailed discreetly behind the trio.

Sedgemoor directed his coachman to drive along the carriage track to where Georgie waited so that he could take her up in his open barouche for a drive through the park.

He clamped his lips shut on a curse. Devil take it, he thought, why did she have that insipid Fraser chit with her today? He wanted to discuss their wedding plans, convince her that the thing should be done as quickly and in as quiet a manner as possible. A third person would spoil their opportunity for private conversation.

He had been miffed when he called in Half Moon Street to collect her for their previously arranged drive only to find that she had set out on foot for the park. Lady Carteret had looked at him with a laugh in her rheumy old eyes, putting him forcibly in mind of her granddaughter, and told him that Georgie had gone to walk her dog and left instructions that he should follow along after her.

Did these women have no compunction about offending his dignity? He had been tempted to tell his coachman to drive back home, but had swallowed his anger and gone on to the park.

"Here, Sykes, you take Rufus, please. You may as well walk him home now." Georgie said to her grandmother's footman, to Sedge's great relief. Accommodating Georgie's large, unruly hound in his elegant barouche would have presented something of a problem.

"Well, is it not a beautiful spring day, Gus?" Georgie asked as she reached up a hand so that he could assist her into the barouche. Under other circumstances he would have climbed out to help the ladies in, but his stiff leg prevented him from performing that gentlemanly office.

"Indeed it is," he agreed.

"And does not Charlotte look beautiful today?"

"Indeed." He murmured his assent to Georgie's question as he handed Miss Fraser to a seat opposite him, beside Georgie.

"Look at how well this primrose sprigged muslin with its green lace trimming becomes her. Does she not look like the very embodiment of spring?" Georgie asked happily, pointing out the beauties of Charlotte's ensemble. "How I wish I had her soft blond hair instead of my unruly red mop," she continued cheerfully, with no real hint of envy in her voice. "The two of you look perfect together. With your almost matching coloring and gray eyes and straight, aristocratic profiles, you are a perfect pair. . . . What beautiful children you would have!"

"Georgie!" Charlotte whispered in an agonized voice, red flags flaming in her cheeks.

Sedge had been lounging back, his arms spread to either side of him along the seat back, but now he straightened, and his brows drew together in a frown. So that's what Georgie was up to—trying to pair him off with the little Fraser chit. He should have realized sooner.

"Indeed, ma'am," he said.

"Oh please, my lord, disregard Georgie's foolish chatter. She is only roasting us, you know," Charlotte whispered in a strangled voice, looking down at the gloved hands clenched in her lap.

"Ah, Miss Fraser, you are indeed a beautiful young lady, and will make some fortunate man a lovely bride," he drawled at his most urbane, "but I believe Georgiana is aware that plans for my future have quite definitely been made. You see, Miss Fraser, I find myself promised to someone else." He fixed Georgie with a gimlet stare.

"Do you, Gus? And who is the fortunate lady?" Georgie asked innocently. "Are you quite certain her plans match with yours?"

"Georgiana, I have been to Doctors' Commons and obtained the license. We may be married in two weeks time," Sedge informed Georgie.

They stood on one side of the enormous drawing room of Emily and Marcus Whaleon, the Marquess

and Marchioness of Benningham. There the cream
of the *ton* had gathered to attend an anniversary
dinner with dancing afterward to commemorate the
Benninghams' engagement some ten years previously.

For the past several days Sedge had been trying
without success, and with mounting frustration, to pin
Georgie down about a wedding date. She had evaded
his attempts with teasing comments, skirting the issue, saying she did not think it wise that they marry.

"I do wish you would give up this mad scheme,
Gus," she said in a low voice. "Hello, Teddy. Yes, I
shall dance with you later," she promised a young
sprig of the nobility who greeted her shyly, requesting a dance. "And I do not know why you will not
consider Charlotte instead, if you are in such haste to
wed. She is lovely and so perfectly well behaved, she
would be a credit to you," she continued speaking to
Sedgemoor in a quiet voice, while she smiled broadly
and greeted various friends and acquaintances who
happened to catch her attention.

"You know very well why I cannot consider any
other woman. I do not wish to be married at all. But
it is necessary."

"Aha!" Georgie exclaimed triumphantly. "I knew
you had no great inclination for the wedded state. I
release you from any misguided obligation you feel,
Gus. I will not wed you."

"We must wed. And soon. Your grandmother
agrees with me."

"Yes, she does. I give you my permission to pay
your addresses to her." Georgie laughed merrily at
the look on Sedgemoor's face. He was not amused.

"Then *she* would be the one who had to live with you for the rest of her life. You can be a bear at times, you know, Gus, with that temper of yours."

"I am *not* a bear," Sedge muttered between his teeth, while he tried to maintain a look of polite nonchalance for the many people who were drifting by offering their greetings to him and Georgie. "It would no doubt astound you to know that I have always been known for the particular evenness of my temper and correctness of my behavior—until I met you, *Miss* Carteret."

"Well, all the more reason for us to keep our distance in the future. You would soon lose that reputation if you were wed to me."

"I will not take no for an answer, do you understand?" he insisted, his polite social half smile strangely at odds with the steely determination in his voice.

"Georgie. You are looking particularly lovely tonight." Lord Robert Lyndhurst interrupted them, paying his compliments to Georgie, whose gown of pale blue silk lent a deeper hue to her sparkling turquoise eyes. Her simple necklace and earrings of gold filigree and the trimming of gold passementerie along the edges of her bodice, hem, sleeves, and in the twisted cord around the high waist of the gown brought out the burnished copper lights in her soft red curls.

"Dare I hope you have a space left on your card for a dance with me?"

"Oh, this is not a formal ball, so Lady Benningham has not issued cards to the ladies, but I believe I *might* be persuaded to favor you with one set,

Robin." Her blue eyes sparkled flirtatiously. "But you must be *very* good, and promise to dance with Charlotte and Ann before I will consent to dance with you."

"You exact a high price for your favors, Georgie," Lord Robert replied with a glinting smile, his green eyes quizzing her.

She tilted her small chin and looked adamant. He sighed and lifted his hand to promise.

"Very well, I shall obey you, oh Demanding Mistress."

"You are a good boy, Robin," she said, reaching out to tap him playfully on the cheek.

A cold look came into Sedge's eyes at the sight. To hear Georgie treat the notorious Lyndhurst so familiarly sent a nerve of temper jumping in his right cheek. And to find that she allowed herself to become a subject for gossip by flirting and dancing with the man irritated him almost past bearing.

Sedgemoor regretted more than ever that his leg was still not strong enough to attempt to dance. He would have made sure there were no opportunity for rogues of Lyndhurst's stripe to claim Georgie's hand for so much as a single set.

Lord Robert lifted Georgie's hand, turned it over and pressed his lips to the skin on the inside of her wrist where the button of her glove left her skin exposed. With a sideways glance at the glowering Sedgemoor, he promised to collect her for their dance when the pianist struck up the first waltz.

Sedge opened his mouth to scold Georgie for her continued friendship with Lyndhurst, but before he could speak, she let out a shriek and flew across the room to embrace a pair of newcomers.

She actually threw her arms around the neck of a very tall, dark young man and hugged him right there in the middle of the ballroom. A strong desire to do murder surged through the viscount's breast as he viewed the scene. Whether he most wanted to strangle Georgie or run the young man through the heart with a sword, he didn't know.

He closed his eyes, trying to control the urge to stalk across the room and break his cane over the boy's head. Imposing calm on his mind, he told himself it was Georgie's impetuosity that was at fault. He feared she would never learn to behave in a proper, sedate manner, would never learn to show proper decorum. He flinched at the thought of making such a harum-scarum female his viscountess . . . making her a St. Regis.

No, they would not suit in the least. He should take her at her word and give up on the plan to offer her the protection of his exalted name. Perhaps he could take an extended trip abroad, now that Napoleon was safely ensconced on St. Helena and the continent safe for travel once more. Italy's warm climate was said to be beneficial to invalids—not that his almost-healed leg put him in such a distasteful category. Aside from a slight stiffness and ache in the injured limb, he was feeling quite as strong and vigorous as he ever had.

If her cohabitation with him in Little Bickton should ever come to light, Georgie seemed confident enough to weather the storm alone. She wasn't concerned much about what the *ton* thought of her behavior, and was quite capable of laughing off any scandal that broke about her head.

Yes, he should leave her alone. Return to the Oaks tomorrow. Return to his peaceful, quite satisfactory existence, perhaps get up a house party and invite Diana Carstairs and forget all about Georgiana Carteret.

When he opened his eyes again, he saw that the broad-shouldered young gentleman had a satisfied smirk on his face, looking highly gratified by Georgie's very public, very enthusiastic greeting of him.

Sedge wanted to wipe that smirk from the boy's face with his fist. Who the devil was the young cub, anyway? he wondered, his blood beginning to boil once more.

Georgie had turned to the girl who stood beside the young man and embraced her in equally enthusiastic fashion. The young lady, whose midnight dark hair was looped round her head in a crown of braids, was quite striking. Under winged black brows, the girl's dark eyes glowed when she smiled, and she carried her tall, elegant figure gracefully. Perhaps she was the boy's sister, Sedge thought, for the dark good looks of the pair were of a similar nature. He had never seen either one of them before.

He limped over to where Georgie stood speaking animatedly to the pair and overheard the barrage of questions she fired at them.

"Oh, Tom and Susan! It is so lovely to see you here in town. And *together.*"

Catching her friend's eye, Georgie nodded almost imperceptively and immediately changed tack. "When did you arrive? Where are you staying? Is your mother come with you, Susan? You are never putting up in an hotel, Tom? How come you to be here tonight?"

"Lady Benningham is a cousin of mama's," Susan explained.

On discovering Sedgemoor at her side, Georgie immediately turned and presented her friends to him. "Gus, here are Miss Susan Tennyson and Mr. Thomas Cunningham, my very dearest friends from home in Chitterne St. Mary's. Susan and Tom, this is Augustus Sebastian Stanhope St. Regis, Viscount Sedgemoor."

Susan was awed by the tall, austere good looks of the viscount who regarded her out of coolly assessing gray eyes. She curtsied to him and stammered a bit as she acknowledged the introduction.

"Charmed, Miss Tennyson," Sedge drawled, touching her outstretched hand briefly.

Tom withstood the introduction to so much cool, aristocratic consequence standing before him with more equanimity. He narrowed his eyes when he saw the viscount move beside Georgie and rest a hand on her waist possessively. What was the relationship between Georgie and this arrogant-looking lord? he wondered jealously.

Tom had come to town to persuade Georgie to marry him. He was satisfied that he had done the right thing in following her to London after she had run off from home so unexpectedly just before their engagement was to have been announced. He had been in a towering fury with her for pulling such a trick and had brooded at home for the past two and a half months, nursing his offended dignity. But her ardent greeting of him reassured Tom that Georgie was now ready to receive his addresses, and that the letter she had left for him telling him otherwise had been just so much feminine coyness. His youthful confidence in his own attractions was high. He would not stand for another man in his way.

"Gus, take care of Tom for me, would you?" Georgie asked. "Introduce him around to your friends. I must have a few words with Susan before the first set begins."

Each gentleman was seething with fury at Georgie's casual words. They eyed one another warily while the girls walked off, arm in arm, Georgie prattling non-stop as she and Susan disappeared out the drawing room door.

"Viscount Sedgemoor looked at me as though I were an insect pinned to a board," Susan whispered to Georgie as the two girls exchanged confidences and news from home. "However did you come to be acquainted with him, Georgie?"

Georgie laughed and made a light answer. "Yes, he can be rather intimidating, can't he? But I have never allowed him to quell *me!*"

"Is he smitten with you, Georgie?" Susan asked in surprise at her friend's smug answer.

"Viscount Sedgemoor? Heavens, no! He considers me a pestilential nuisance. But tell me how things go with Tom. I thought when I left I had made it clear to him that I would not fall in with my father's plans for me to marry him. I was sure that as soon as I was out of the vicinity, Tom would turn to you, my dear

Sukey. And now he has escorted you to town. Are things well in train for your engagement?"

Susan sighed eloquently. "No, I'm afraid not. Your father encouraged Tom to come here in search of you so that he could press his suit. Although he was very angry with you for running away as you did and making him look foolish, from what he let fall on the journey here, Tom is determined to marry you anyway."

"Oh, botheration! Has he not given up on that ridiculous idea?" Georgie exclaimed. "I thought I had made it clear to him that I would never have him."

"You did not tell him the reasons why?" Susan asked worriedly, pressing one of her hands to Georgie's arm.

"No, you goose. I did not say, 'Dear Tom, you are wonderfully handsome, but I will not have you because my best friend is in love with you and I am not.' "

Susan gave a little moan, knowing that it was not impossible for her outspoken friend to incautiously blurt out just such a thing. "Oh, Georgie, pray have a care what you say to him. I will just die, if he ever finds out I am breaking my heart over him."

"No need to worry, my dear." Georgie patted her friend's hand. "If he has not yet realized that you are a pearl without compare and that he is fortunate beyond his just deserts to have won your heart, he is a fool and does not deserve you. Now that you are here, perhaps we can find you someone else," she said optimistically.

"Oh, no, Georgie. I could never love another. Please do not even think of it."

"Hmm. No, I guess you could not—it has been an ingrained habit for too long, has it not? Well, this complicates matters considerably. But if Tom has not yet come to realize your charms, why is he here with you, then?"

"When Tom learned that Mama had received an invitation from her cousin, the Marchioness of Benningham, inviting her to bring me up for a few weeks, he volunteered to ride along beside our traveling chaise as escort, as he was coming to town to seek you out anyway," Susan explained. "Mama, of course, was in alt at the prospect of having a gentleman escort, someone besides the servants to protect us from danger or any unforeseen problems on the long journey. Tom did nothing on the journey but talk of how his father's land and your portion of the estate, that is not entailed on your papa's successor, will be joined one day."

"Oh, stuff. Can he not see that your beauty and sweet nature are worth ten times what I would bring him in terms of a few hundred acres of land? He cannot remain indifferent to your sweet charm and your devoted love forever, my dear Susan."

"He has known me forever and sees me as a little sister, I believe."

"Dear, dear, dear. Something must be done to change the way he regards you, to open his eyes," Georgie said, tapping one finger against her lips. "Aha! I have it!"

"Oh, no, Georgie, not another of your schemes! The last time I fell in with your plans everything went badly awry. I did not live down the embarrassment for a six-month!"

"Now Susan, don't be a goose. Think of Tom's warm brown eyes—you have always said you could drown in their dark depths. And that tall, muscular physique of his, with his broad shoulders and lean hips and long legs—you have always sighed over how wonderful it was to dance with him, being held close. Think of that thick black hair of his that falls down over his collar most romantically. Do your fingers not itch to twine themselves in his silky curls as he holds you in his arms? Think of him riding hell for leather in the hunt last year, when you swore the sight of him in a red coat was enough to make your heart do somersaults in your breast."

"Oh, Georgie, please stop. You are torturing me." Susan sighed, twisting the handkerchief she held in her hands into knots.

"You do love Tom, don't you?"

"Of course I do. I always have. I could never love any other man."

"Good! then you must do exactly as I say and we will have him at your feet in a fortnight."

Susan looked alarmed, but knew that it was next to useless to try to resist her determined, energetic friend. If there was a chance that Tom could be made to return her affection, then she supposed it was worth taking the risk of allowing herself to become involved in one of Georgie's madcap schemes.

"You will suddenly become popular with a lot of gentlemen, perhaps even including his almightiness, Viscount Sedgemoor. And perhaps if Robin paid you some attention, too, it would do you no harm."

"Who is Robin?"

"Robin? Oh, you have heard of Lord Robert Lyndhurst, haven't you?"

Susan gave a low shriek. "Not the rake they write all those scurrilous, satiric verses about?"

"The very same. He's a friend of mine. He is pretending to be smitten with me, just for the joke of it, I think, and to make G—er, someone jealous. But he is a blood of the first water, as I'm fond of saying, and quite handsome enough to turn any lady's head."

"Oh, no, no. Those two gentlemen sound much too high flying for me. And how could you get them to pay attention to me anyway? Surely you could not just ask them to take some notice of me and they would immediately fall in with your request, Georgie? Viscount Sedgemoor seemed quite a cold, proud man to me."

"Oh, yes. He is the highest of high sticklers. But you see, he will do it, if I do something for him in return. He wants a particular favor of me."

"N—nothing scandalous, Georgie?" Susan asked in alarm.

Georgie laughed. "No, no. Quite the reverse. Gus is forever lecturing me about my lamentable tendency to ignore the proprieties. He can be all prim and proper when it suits his purpose, though I suspect he has indulged in his own share of rakish activities in the past. He is just more careful to avoid detection than poor Robin. Speaking of Robin, have you ever met Miss Ann Forester?" Georgie asked, then went on to confide her plans for that couple into her friend's ear.

Susan listened with deep foreboding, fascinated despite herself.

Eventually the strains of music recalled Georgie's attention and she hurried back to the company, pulling Susan with her. Georgie was afraid the young man to whom she had promised the first set would think she had deserted him and she did not wish to hurt his feelings.

Sedge stood fingering his quizzing glass, eyeing Cunningham coldly, while he considered what best to do with him.

"Hello, Sedge," Max Templeton said, putting a hand on the viscount's shoulder.

Sedge damped down his irritation at Georgie for putting him in such an uncomfortable situation and introduced Cunningham.

"Well, Cunningham, I suppose you have a whole slew of things planned for your stay in London?" Max asked, doing the polite.

"Well, I'm not at all sure as yet how long I shall be here," Tom replied. "It all depends on Georgie and when she will be ready to return home to Chitterne St. Mary. She will have a lot to see to before the wedding."

"Georgie's getting married?" Max exclaimed. "Who's the lucky chap?"

"*She* is to marry me," Tom replied, his tone strongly implying that Georgie was the lucky one. "The arrangement between our families was made long ago. Our land marches together, you see."

Max glanced at Sedge to see that his friend was looking astounded by the news. He looked ready to do murder, Max thought on a chuckle. "Well, I'll be damned," he said, slapping Cunningham on the back. "She's said nothing about getting married to us, has she, Sedge?"

The viscount did not reply. He was stunned—and furious.

It seemed the match she was running from when he had first encountered her at that inn on the Marlborough Road was with young Cunningham! Sedge could not have been more confounded. He had assumed Georgie's father was trying her to force her to marry some old codger, some elderly farmer she couldn't stomach.

He had pictured a grossly overweight, ill-featured, ill-mannered, lecherous old bore with a red face and a receding hair line. To see that she had run from a handsome young buck like Cunningham defied understanding. Was Georgie a confirmed manhater? or had she conceived some harebrained scheme to force Cunningham into a romantic declaration, or to induce him to perform some highly melodramatic deed of daring-do before she bestowed her hand? Knowing Georgie, the latter seemed likely.

Determination hardened within him. Georgiana would marry her childhood friend over his dead body, Sedge decided, concern for family honor having nothing to do with his emotions at the moment. Even if he did *indeed* have to carry he away over his saddle bow, as she had once facetiously suggested, he would do it to prevent her from marrying such a conceited, swaggering young stripling as Cunningham.

Chapter 9

"Now, Gus, there is no need to shout. I assure you, I do not plan to marry Tommy Cunningham."

Georgie was closeted with Sedgemoor in her grandmother's small first-floor library the morning after the Benninghams' party.

He stepped forward and gripped her shoulders hard, his gray eyes stormy as he looked down at her. "By God, Georgiana, you had better not. I will not have any taint of scandal attached to the St. Regis name!"

"I do not see what your name has to do with anything, Gus. As I said, I am not going to marry Tom, nor am I going to marry *you* right now." She looked steadily up at him, quelling the urge to lift her hands to smooth away the frown on his face. To stop herself, she broke from his clasp and paced about the room.

"Indeed, ma'am," Sedge drawled. "I believe you will find that you are mistaken. You are my responsibility."

"Oh, I can not think about that now. Since Tom and Susan have come, I have more important things to see to." He was in a bad skin. She wondered how she could best tease him out of this fit of temper and persuade him to help her. She turned to him and said brightly, "I want you to help me make Tom jealous."

"I see." Sedge drew himself up stiffly. Her words hit him like a blow, low and hard.

"Now, Gus, what I want you to do is to take Susan about so that—"

"So that you will be left free to gad about with Cunningham," he supplied sardonically.

"Yes! I mean, no! Gus, you must help me—"

"I will *never* help you wring some sort of romantic declaration of everlasting love from Cunningham, if that is what you are asking."

"No! . . . Oh! How can you be such a muttonhead?"

This was too much for a man of Sedgemoor's pride. It was far better to extricate himself from the whole sorry tangled mess now, before he made even more of a fool of himself, he decided with cold fury.

He gave her an ironic smile as he grasped his cane and prepared to quit the room. "Yes. I have been a 'muttonhead,' as you so inelegantly phrase it. As you have pointed out on numerous occasions, we would not suit. I fear I shall have to deprive myself of your delightful company for the foreseeable future, ma'am, as I find that my engagement calendar is quite full. Goodbye, Georgiana."

Somewhat alarmed by his cold manner and the finality of his tone, Georgie took hold of his arm and coaxed, "Gus! Do not desert me now. I had hoped you would help me with Susan. Escort her about a little, while I try to make Tom see that—"

He wavered for a moment as he looked down into her pleading blue eyes, then shook off her hand.

"Good day, Miss Carteret. Accept my best wishes for your health and happiness."

Georgie bit her lip as she watched him go. Sedgemoor was proving more difficult to manage than she had anticipated. Well, he was in a snit, but he would come about, she thought, deciding that she would persuade Lord Robert to help her make Tom jealous of Susan instead.

" 'Morning, Georgie." Max Templeton hailed Georgie as he came upon her in the park before the fashionable world was stirring. "You're up and about early, considering that you danced until dawn last night, I make no doubt."

Rufus was pulling Georgie behind him on the end of his long lead and she was skipping along, holding onto her bonnet trying to keep up. When she stopped to greet Max, she handed the dog's leash to Sykes, her grandmother's sturdy footman, who accompanied her.

"Max! How lovely to see you." Slightly out of breath from exercising her dog, Georgie returned his greeting with a sunny smile. "I have not seen you for ages! And I must say, you are certainly in no position to know how late I danced last night, sir, as you were not at the party. Indeed, you have been quite the stranger of late. Have you been out of town this past fortnight?"

"No, no, I assure you, I have never put a foot outside of London in all that time."

"Aha! so you have just been eluding *me,* then!"

"Yes, indeed so. You're in the right of it there, ma'am," he quipped.

"Now why would that be, Captain Templeton?" she asked, looking up at him with twinkling eyes.

"Well, you see, the thing of it is . . . I'm afraid of you, Georgie."

"Afraid of me? Oh, Max, you're gammoning me!" Georgie laughed merrily, looking up at the very tall, strong man who towered over her.

"Not at all."

"What in the world would you find to fear in *me?*"

"If I remain overmuch in your company, I will find myself looking at a leg shackle before I know what's hit me."

"I'm sure I don't know what you mean," she replied innocently, taking hold of his arm so that they could stroll along the pleasant park lane. "Surely you do not think I am a danger to a large, strong fellow like you. Why, I am nothing but a small, tottyheaded female who tends to chatter too much."

"Hmm, so you say, but I see Edgeworth and Lyndhurst and young Cunningham and even Sedge dancing to your tune, Georgie. I'm afraid I balk at being one of your puppets, my dear."

"Oh, Max. Am I so fearsome?"

"Indeed, ma'am, we poor males don't stand a chance when you decide that it's time for us to become tenants for life. I would rather face a cavalry charge than become the object of one of your matchmaking schemes." He grinned down at her. "Ain't ready to be caught in Parson's mousetrap for a few more years yet."

Georgie smiled secretly. She had indeed been full of lively schemes and plans in the past fortnight. She had been playing matchmaker for her friends, Susan and Tom, while trying to mend matters between Lord Robert and Ann Forester. And, though Sedgemoor had maintained a cool distance, he came in for his fair share of her busy thoughts.

"Oh, dear," Georgie had confided jokingly to Susan. "I feel as though I'm playing three games of chess at once, maneuvering my pieces about here and there, trying to set clever traps for my opponents, catching them offguard without getting caught myself. . . . I must confess, it is all I can do to keep track of the ins and outs of each game!"

Susan, whose knowledge of chess was severely limited, had just looked bewildered.

"Sometimes, dear Sukey, I fear I have mixed my ploys. Who knows which gentleman will end up with which lady? Though I hope that some of you at least will be mated at the end of the game." Georgie had laughed.

"Tell me, my dear, while we're sharing this most delightful little coze, what do you have planned for Sedge?" Max asked, recalling Georgie's wandering attention. "I confess, I am burning with curiosity."

"Well, I know you are a trustworthy gentleman and will not broadcast my secrets, so I will tell you that I had my heart set on matching Gus and Charlotte. However, I'm afraid that scheme has come to naught. They are both so unaccountably recalcitrant. It is a mystery to me why each cannot see the sterling qualities of the other, both so fair and noble looking. But I must confess, Max, I was a little worried that Charlotte would not have been able to manage him," Georgie continued. "You know, Gus tends to be a trifle touchy. . . .

He needs the starch taken out of him from time to time, someone to stand up to him. I would have been more than happy to give her the benefit of my advice, if she got into difficulties."

Georgie gazed straight ahead, not seeing the broad grin of amusement that lit her companion's war-scarred face.

"Well, that's so much water under the bridge," she chattered on. "And, I must say, just lately I have noticed that Henry, of all people, has begun to pay attention to Charlotte. Now there's a pair I had not thought of."

"Cupid works in mysterious ways, shooting off those naughty arrows of his, pairing off the most unlikely candidates."

"Yes, you are perfectly right, Max. But Henry and Charlotte are both so quiet, I can not imagine how they manage to communicate."

"Well," interposed Max, "I suppose that's why they are so comfortable in one another's company. Birds of a feather, you know."

"Oh, I daresay, you have the right of it, Max. Well, that's two of my friends I don't have to worry about anymore."

"And what about you, Georgie? You are to marry Cunningham, are you?"

"No, no. Whatever gave you that idea, Max?" She looked at him in surprise.

"Er, Cunningham did."

"Well, Tom is all about in his head. No, I have other plans for him, if only he will not be so pigheaded . . . and it is proving most difficult to reconcile Robin and Ann, too." Georgie put one gloved finger up to her lips as she contemplated a new strategy in that particular game.

"Perhaps you should abandon the attempt, my dear. Er, what will you do with Sedge now that he has failed to succumb to Miss Fraser? Pair him off with your friend, Miss Tennyson?" Max was finding it difficult not to laugh aloud as they carried on the hilarious conversation. He restrained himself with a superhuman effort, determined to learn the extent of Georgie's devious plans for his proud friend.

"Sukey and Gus? No, Susan is already taken, or she soon will be, if all goes well. And Gus is still in a miff with me, and not likely to fall in with any of my suggestions at the moment. But he will come about. . . . You are perfectly right, though. I must do *something* about him. He does present quite a problem, but problems always have solutions."

Max looked at her inquiringly, but she just gave him a mischievous grin. It was obvious she was not yet ready to reveal her scheme for the viscount.

"Oh, I quite agree. He needs to have *something* done about him."

"You are laughing at me, Max, but it is for his own good, you know."

"Umm. If you say so."

"If he continues with his profligate ways, he will come to a bad end. Be unhappy, I mean."

"I'm not at all sure you should view Sedge as a dissipated rake, you know. Nothing sinister about him in the least. Fairly upstanding gent. Actually rather full of moral rectitude and all that."

"Exactly!" Georgie beamed at him, like a proud teacher at a very bright student.

162 *Meg-Lynn Roberts*

"But even if he does succumb to temptation now and again, perhaps he finds it pleasurable, rather than wicked, to behave in such a way," Max suggested mildly.

Georgie gave him an exasperated look. "Another man might, but Gus is too straightlaced underneath. He cannot reconcile all that rakish behavior and sneaking around on the quiet with his inherent prudery, you know. I can't bear to see any of my friends unhappy."

Max stifled his hoot of laughter. "Er, what do you know of his rakish ways, Georgie?"

"Well, I have heard all about how he was on his way to seduce Lady Diana Carstairs before I met him. . . . I long to meet her."

"You do? I would have thought she was the last person you would wish to know."

"Not at all. I would like to see what her attractions are."

"Georgie, you make my head spin. You have more irons in the fire than a blacksmith."

"Oh, Max," she tugged his arm, giving him a mock fierce look, "you seem to think I am the worst kind of managing female."

"No, no, my dear. I think you are the *best* kind of managing female. Indeed, I am enjoying seeing everyone dance to your tune."

"And what about you, Max? Should you not like to dance, too?"

"Well, you see, the thing is, my dear, I don't find myself ready to join the dance just yet. And I have the distressing wish to pick my own partner . . . I am quite content to watch from the sidelines."

"Your turn will come, Max," she said, slanting him a provocative glance.

"Deuce take it, that's just what I'm afraid of, you little minx! But I hope not too soon."

Indeed, Georgie reflected with an amused smile, Max was all too knowing. She must beware, or he would discover *all* her secrets.

How she wished she had met someone who would do for him! He was a lively, witty gentleman, one of the most entertaining of her acquaintance. Attractive, too, despite his somewhat harsh features and the scar that ran down his cheek from his ear. He often joked about the sabre cut he had sustained honorably in action during the Peninsula War at the Battle of Salamanca. She was afraid he felt that the long thin white line of his scar marred his looks. She thought it made him almost unspeakably attractive.

With his very tall, muscular build, square, firm jaw, and military bearing, he personified strong, dependable manhood. He fairly radiated dependability. Warm lights danced in his golden hazel eyes and lit his face with a rare intelligence and understanding, too. How lucky the woman would be who won him! she thought enviously.

"Shall I see you tonight at Sarah McIntyre's engagement party?" she asked, preparing to turn about and return home.

At the exaggerated look of fear on his face, she laughed and held up her hand. "I promise, no matchmaking, Max. I have yet to see the woman who would do for you."

He grinned and said that he had had a card from Colonel "Mac" and thought he would look in for a brief time if Georgie would save him a dance and give him her solemn promise that she would not to try to pair him off with anyone.

"Sarah McIntyre has not disappointed her parents in her choice of husband, I see. The young man stands heir to his uncle, Earl Bicester," Stella Withers, widow of Sir Randolph Withers, remarked to Sedgemoor when she joined him at the edge of the McIntyres' ballroom.

The viscount leaned against one of the decorative Ionic columns bordering the overly ornate room, taking the weight off his leg and looking on as brightly gowned ladies and equally well-dressed gentlemen waltzed past him.

"They both seem fortunate in their choices," he answered shortly as he watched Susan Tennyson twirl by in the arms of Lord Robert Lyndhurst.

Since Sedgemoor had returned to London that spring, Lady Withers had been trying to reignite the very satisfactory flirtation she had enjoyed with him at a house party during the hunting season the previous autumn. Earlier this year, she had heard rumors that he was pursuing Diana Carstairs, and had cadged an invitation to Grey Towers when she learned both he and Diana were to be among the houseguests, wanting to see how the land lay for herself. But when she reached Baron Leftridge's estate, she found that Sedgemoor had begged off and that Diana Carstairs had abruptly left Grey Towers after the news arrived.

So the much whispered about liaison had come to an early end, she had thought in satisfaction. With the beautiful Diana no longer a potential rival, Stella hoped to take her previous byplay with the fascinating, elusive viscount to its inevitable conclusion. But thus far he had proved unresponsive to her blatant lures.

"It was quite a coup for the McIntyres to have captured Bicester's nephew," she continued in a low, sultry voice. "I believe Colonel and Mrs. McIntyre spared no expense in presenting their daughter to the *ton* this spring, so perhaps their investment has been rewarded. . . . I wonder how the young couple will fare when it is borne in on them that her dowry is virtually nonexistent and her young man is a fool," Stella continued maliciously, fanning herself languidly with a silver-rimmed fan.

"I gathered it was a love match," Sedge responded with an edge to his voice. He was in a foul mood. Georgie had arrived on Lyndhurst's arm that evening.

"Oh, *love*. What would two young innocents know about that? Does such a thing exist anyway, do you think, Sedgemoor?" Stella looked at him enticingly, making play with her fine dark eyes.

"You are asking the wrong person, Stella," he responded curtly. "I know nothing of such sentimental claptrap. Momentary physical attraction exists, from which much pleasure may be derived. Such things are transitory, however. In my experience, the overdramatized emotion poets and other sentimental fools rant and rave about does not exist."

She moistened her lips and looked up at him. "Yes, I agree. So-called love among the young and inexperienced is a dull, lifeless thing, not to be compared with the full-bodied passion a mature man and a woman of experience may share. Two persons who are attracted to one another may enjoy much pleasure in, ah, certain exciting intimate situations."

She pressed up against his arm, brushing her breasts back and forth against his jacket sleeve, feeling the heat of him through the thin material of her gown.

He did not move away, neither did he look at all interested in her invitation. "Indeed, Stella. Two persons who are *attracted* to one another certainly may."

His clipped answer was a chilling setdown to her thinly veiled invitation. Snapping her fan shut, Stella looked daggers at him.

Georgie danced past just then in the arms of Tom Cunningham, drawing a frown from Sedgemoor.

"The little Carteret is becoming a byword in the *ton*, the way she flirts with any and every male who comes within her orbit," Stella commented slyly when she saw the direction of his gaze.

She had been annoyed to learn that Sedgemoor was acquainted with the wildly popular Georgiana Carteret, and had even lowered himself to squire her about on a few occasions. Now, unable to help herself, Stella was determined to make sure the elegant, exacting nobleman saw the little hoyden in as unfavorable a light as possible.

"It's being said that even Max Templeton has come under the little witch's spell. They were seen walking arm-in-arm in the park before nine o'clock this morning. Obviously a planned assignation at that early hour."

Sedgemoor made no comment to his companion's malicious remark. He was feeling angry with Georgie himself, but he would not give Lady Withers the satisfaction of agreeing with her catty criticism.

"Looks as though the little ninny is Lyndhurst's latest victim, too. Though why he should bother with such a blowsy infant, I have no idea, when any number of rich, ripe plums are his for the picking."

"Perhaps he is *her* victim," Sedge cut her off with a haughty lift of his golden brows. He was excessively annoyed. He had known Stella Withers for the past two years, and he had derived much amusement from her sharp, wicked tongue. However, he was not at all amused by her present comments, though he was very much afraid they bore some grain of truth.

Stella was furious. How dare Sedgemoor defend the vulgar Carteret chit. She gave a tinkling laugh. "You know, I believe I saw Georgie Carteret in Little Bickton this past February when I was staying with Leftridge at Grey Towers. If 'twas not her, 'twas someone very like, only the dowdy child I saw was even wilder looking. She wore no hat and her long, unkempt red hair was blowing about in the breeze. What was she doing there, I wonder? Keeping some assignation or other?" she asked slyly. "What man of any discrimination, of any taste, would want to be linked with such a freckled-faced child? She chatters incessantly and her constant merriment and enthusiasm over every new thing becomes tedious in the extreme. Such schoolgirlish high spirits and countrified manners are a bore."

"Do you think so, Stella? You must be alone in that opinion, to judge by Miss Carteret's popularity among not only the young gentlemen present here tonight, but with the other young ladies, and their chaperones and parents as well."

With that sharp setdown, Sedgemoor limped away

from the voluptuous widow. He could find fault with Georgie himself, but it annoyed him extremely to hear anyone else doing so.

Stella stared open-mouthed after the viscount. Sedgemoor defending such a vulgar creature? Surely such a discriminating high stickler wasn't caught in the little red-haired nobody's net?

Good God, Sedge thought in alarm as he walked away, Georgie had been seen in Little Bickton! Damnation, it must have been the time when she had gone to arrange for his note of regret to be sent to Leftridge.

It only remained for someone to learn that he had been in Little Bickton at the same time for the scandal to break about their heads. He would have to speak with her tonight, he decided grimly. So much for his determination to stay away from her.

Sedge took a glass of champagne from the tray of a passing footman and stood sipping it while he mulled over how he should handle Stella's revelation. He had not spoken with Georgiana in over two weeks, leaving her to run about with Cunningham or Lyndhurst, sometimes in tandem with both of them, her friend, Miss Tennyson, making a fourth member of their party. He had stayed away from her, but often saw her from a distance when he went out, and he heard of her doings from everyone.

He had even seen Lady Carteret being driven out in her ancient landau in the park one sunny day. She had quizzed him, commenting on what a slowtop he was to allow himself to be outmaneuvered by her madcap granddaughter, and wondering querulously why a virile young man like him couldn't seem to bring Georgie up to scratch, hinting that he should pursue more amorous techniques to persuade her.

His eyes were drawn to Georgie. She was waltzing with Cunningham.

His hand tightened around his glass. Her gown was entirely too low cut. What had Lady Carteret been about to approve such a daring style for a young girl like Georgie? he wondered disapprovingly. And neither did he approve of the way she was clinging to Cunningham, looking up at him with stars in her eyes.

Why had she run away from the boy in the first place, if she favored him now? Had the blasted young gudgeon not shown enough ardor to suit her? He certainly seemed to be making up for it tonight, Sedge thought angrily.

No matter what Georgie wished now, it was far too late for her to choose her own husband. She could not marry Cunningham.

Nothing had changed. She had been thoroughly compromised with him in Little Bickton.

"Well, Georgie, I suppose you are determined to complete the season before we go home to wed," Tom declared resignedly, as he and Georgie walked to the side of the room at the end of the set.

He had been arguing the point for days, but he could not get a satisfactory answer from Georgie about when their wedding was to take place. She held him in check, changing the subject every time the matter came up.

"Tom, do not be such a numbskull. I have never

promised to marry you. The marriage was all plotted between my father and your family. My wishes were never consulted."

Taken by surprise at her direct answer, Tom halted in the middle of the floor. "But, my dear girl, what objections could you possibly have? We've been friends forever. I thought you liked me well enough for marriage. You've never given me any reason to think I was not to your taste."

"Oh, Tom, of course we are friends. I like you very well—but not in the way that a woman wishes to feel toward her husband."

Georgie had decided the time had come to set him straight. He would not be seriously hurt by her rejection, she was certain. There was not a loverlike aspect in the whole of their long relationship. No, Tom's life would not be blighted when she made him see that her refusal was final.

"Been lookin' forward to havin' you as my bride, Georgie," he insisted, not easily letting go of his single-minded purpose to wed her.

"I am sorry, Tom. It would never do. I do not think your heart is in a marriage between us. Not really. And besides, I'm afraid I've gone and fallen in love with someone else." She had hoped not to have to resort to telling him this, but it seemed he would not accept her refusal otherwise.

"Georgie, you ninnyhammer! Why did you do something goosish like that for? You will just have to fall out of love. Our families expect us to wed. And so do I!"

"I told you in my letter when I left home that I

would not marry you, Tom. You will just have to re-
sign yourself to the fact that I meant it."

Tom was so thick-skulled, Georgie felt like braining
him over the head with a large club. She had contrived
to throw him and Susan together frequently in the past
fortnight, often leaving them alone together. But her
ploy had not worked. Tom had taken Susan just as
much for granted as he was wont to do at home.

The time had come for more drastic action. She
would just have to try her gambit sooner than she had
intended.

"It's that Lyndhurst chap, isn't it?" Tom growled
pugnaciously, his jaw hardening. "Well, you'll catch
nothing but trouble there, my girl. Haven't been in
town long, but have heard of his wild reputation. He's
the worst kind of rogue. They call him—well, never
mind," he mumbled. "Ain't fit for female ears. Sure to
make you miserable, Georgie."

"Robin's reputation only makes him more attractive to us females, you know, Tom," Georgie answered blithely, deliberately playing up Robin's wild
reputation, which she had good reason to believe was
much exaggerated. "But I'm sure he is not interested
in *me*. His taste runs to beauties, and I have certainly
never had any claim to beauty—and never will have.
But I have deliberately befriended him and been
much in his company of late because I believe he
may have an eye to *Susan*. Now she is to his taste,
being so very beautiful, you know."

"Susan, beautiful?" Tom asked, turning in surprise
to look at his childhood friend. She stood across the
room from them in conversation with Lord Robert.

"Of course, you idiot! Why do you think she has

attracted the attention of such discriminating, sophisticated men as Lord Robert? She is tall and elegant and graceful. And with her gorgeous black hair and creamy white complexion and those lovely wide dark eyes of hers, men are flocking to her side. She is being hailed as an Incomparable in some quarters. Haven't you been paying any attention to the success of our childhood playmate, Tom?"

"No, guess I haven't," he answered vaguely, his gaze still fixed on Susan, seeing her suddenly through new eyes.

Finally, Georgie thought. She plunged ahead while she had his attention. "For all Robin is not as bad as he has been painted, I think we must have a care for Sukey. I do not think they are at all suited to one another. I saw them dancing the last set together, and look! See them over there! Why, he is whispering in her ear and pointing to the open doors that lead to the balcony. I think we should join them before he persuades her to take the air outside *alone* with him."

"By Jupiter, you're right, Georgie!"

Georgie was pleased to see that Tom's eyes narrowed with concern as he turned to look at the couple.

"Susan should not be allowed to associate with that damned bast—dashed philanderer! Where is Mrs. Tennyson? I don't see her. Come, Georgie, we must rescue Sukey."

Georgie almost laughed aloud as Tom immediately grabbed her hand and set off at a fast pace in Susan's direction. One of her bold moves seemed to be working, at long last!

Chapter 10

Sedge moved purposefully to where he had last seen Georgie and Cunningham standing together with Miss Tennyson and Lyndhurst after the previous set had finished.

There was Cunningham rather solicitously handing a glass of lemonade to Miss Tennyson. The boy looked as though he had just been hit on the head with a poleax. He couldn't take his eyes off his companion. Now here was a new come-out. Had Georgie lost her faithful suitor?

"Evenin', Sedge."

"Max."

"Seen Georgie about anywhere? I believe she promised to partner me in the set just getting up."

"No, I have not seen her since the last set ended," Sedge answered curtly. So Max, too, had joined Georgie's cadre of admirers, he thought angrily, remembering Stella's earlier comment.

"Guess I'm stood up then. Ah, well, we ancient bachelors should not be surprised to find ourselves cast off for these younger bucks. Think I'll console myself with some of the champagne punch. Care to join me, Sedge?"

"Not at the moment, Max." Sedge scanned the room, looking for Georgie, keeping his ears open for the sound of her distinctive laughter. "Perhaps later."

Max quirked a brow at his friend's preoccupation and sauntered off in the direction of the refreshment room.

There was not a sight or sound of Georgie anywhere. Or of Lyndhurst, Sedge saw with an ominous tightening in his gut.

His eyes glittered dangerously. With a grim set to his mouth, he gripped his cane tightly in his hand, forgetting to use it as he limped purposefully toward the curtained door that led to the balcony.

"Georgie, I know I have promised you to try to make it up with Ann. But, as hard as I've tried, she rebuffs me. I have made every effort to reignite the friendship we shared at Christmas, but I'm afraid it is no longer possible," Lord Robert was saying. "She no longer has any wish to see me—and the feelings I once had for *her* have changed."

"But Ann is so sweet and kind. And intelligent, too. With quite a lively wit. Surely you could not fall out of love with her so quickly. Your heart is good, I've learned for myself, and you have been falsely maligned by detestable gossip for some time. Most of the women with whom you have been linked threw themselves at your head, I know. You are just too handsome for your own good, Robin."

"I am gratified to hear that *you* find me attractive,

Georgie." Lord Robert rested his elbows against the balcony railing, one leg, elegantly clad in black velvet knee breeches, was bent at the knee and his foot cocked back so that it rested against one of the stone balustrades. His eyes glittered at Georgie in the moonlight.

"Hmm. Did I say that? Yes, I suppose I did. However, I appreciate you only as an object to be admired. I do not desire to *have* you for my very own, Robin."

"Do you not, Georgie? I would not object, if you did."

"Fie, sir. You speak like a coxcomb. 'Tis your relationship to Ann I wish to speak about, as you well know. You promised me that you would make it up with the poor girl."

"Yes, I know I did, and I have tried. Just as I have tried to flirt with your friend, Susan, to make Cunningham jealous, but my heart is not in it. Susan is an attractive girl, and Ann is . . . Ann. But I'm afraid my heart is no longer my own. I am no longer free to offer it to Ann, even if she would have me."

"Oh do not say that, Robin!" Georgie exclaimed, wishing there was some way to reconcile the pair.

"You see, Georgie, I'm afraid I have fallen in love with someone else. My heart has been captured by the most vivacious little bundle of energy, the veriest little sweetheart it has ever been my privilege to know. I am deeply and completely in love with her." He moved from his negligent position against the balcony and captured her gesturing hands in his.

Georgie pulled free of his hold and paced about the stone floor in front of him. "Oh stuff and fiddle! You are being utterly nonsensical, Robin. I have kept you so busy with my errands and commissions, I know you haven't had time to fall in love with anyone else—unless it's Susan. Oh, Robin, you haven't gone and fallen in love with *Susan,* have you?"

Lord Robert moved closer to capture Georgie's shoulders between his hands. He held her tightly captive, pinning her against one of the stone columns that bordered the balcony, his hard thigh pressing against hers. "I know you find it next to impossible, but just keep still for a minute, my dearest girl. I wish to say something serious and I can't do so with you moving about all the time."

He tilted up her chin with one long finger so that he could gaze deeply into her eyes, while his other arm snaked about her waist, pulling her fully against him.

"It's you, Georgie," he whispered ardently. "I find I love you quite madly, darling. Will you marry me, my dearest girl?"

"Robin!" Georgie breathed in amazement just before he lowered his mouth and took hers in a passionate kiss.

Sedge came out through the curtained door to the darkened balcony, glanced one way, then the other. A flicker of movement caught his eye in the farthest, darkest corner of the balustraded balcony that ran along the entire length of the rear of the house. He could just make out a couple locked in an intimate embrace.

It could have been anyone. But in a flicker of light,

as the moon broke through the thick overcast of cloud, a glint of gold from some ornament the lady wore in her hair caught his eye.

The moonlight pooled over the couple and glinted off the woman's copper-red hair.

He limped toward the couple to see his worst nightmare coming true. Georgie was caught up in a fierce embrace with Lyndhurst. Embracing her? Hell, he was ravishing her mouth ruthlessly.

Thought retreated and pure instinct took over, as he lurched toward his rival.

Roughly, he pulled Lyndhurst away from Georgie. His balled fist crashed into Lord Robert's face, sending him sprawling on the hard stone floor of the balcony.

"Gus!" Georgie cried. "What in the world have you done? Oh, good Lord, I believe you have knocked him out! Help me," she commanded, as she knelt beside the inert form of Lord Robert Lyndhurst.

"The blackguard can rot in hell, for all I care," Sedge snarled, refusing to lend a hand as he stood two feet away, legs spread wide and hands clenched, ready to strike again.

His blinding anger was not even close to being assuaged by that one satisfying punch. The term red-hot rage had always struck him as fanciful, but there was a definite red glow blurring his vision now as he looked down at his fallen rival.

"Oh, Gus, you are jealous!" Georgie smiled radiantly up at him from her position beside his fallen rival. "How lovely!"

"I am *not* jealous," he denied savagely, his teeth clenched. "I know how to protect my own, however."

Lord Robert moaned.

"Robin, Robin, can you hear me?" Georgie asked, slapping his cheeks lightly.

He sat up, clutching his head.

"Was that really necessary, Sedgemoor?" Lyndhurst asked. "What are you to Georgie, anyway? You hadn't been appointed her guardian, the last I'd heard."

"Listen to me, Lyndhurst," Sedge ground out. "In the future, you are to stay as far away as possible from Miss Carteret, or you will be answerable to me in the same kind of punishment as I have doled out here tonight. That, or you will find a glove slapped in your face, before you are much older. And be well advised—I can handle a small sword as well as a pistol. Makes no matter to me how I put a hole through you, for kill you I certainly will."

"What the devil—" Lord Robert began, getting up and clenching his own fists.

Georgie had to bite the inside of her cheeks to conceal her delighted grin at this bit of unlooked for drama. My, Gus was positively bloodthirsty, he was so jealous. "Now, now, gentlemen, calm yourselves," she counselled sensibly. "It was all a misunderstanding. You are both too impetuous by half." She clucked her tongue. "We must get you inside, Robin, and see to your face. There's blood coming from your nose and I believe your lip is split."

Georgie reached for his elbow to assist him, but he brushed her aside.

"I think it would be better for me to leave quietly this way, Georgie." He pointed to the steps the led down from the balcony to the garden below. "I would not want to shock the ladies by my disheveled appearance," he said lightly, but with a steely gleam in his eyes as he glared at Sedgemoor. "I shall see you tomorrow, Georgie, to continue our discussion."

"Over my dead body!" Sedgemoor took a step toward him, but Georgie put her hands on the viscount's chest and held him in place as Lord Robert left.

"Come, Georgiana. I will take you home," he said, putting an arm about her shoulders.

"Oh, that's not necessary, Gus. I am not at all overset, you know."

"If you are not, you should be. Any woman of sensibility would be shocked witless by having the attentions of a debauched rake forced upon her like that."

"A woman of sensibility? *Me?* I thought it was widely understood that I am sadly lacking in that insipid trait," Georgie said, laughing. "What in the world made you hit him, Gus?"

"He was treating you dishonorably," he replied belligerently. The insanity of his fury was abating somewhat, leaving Sedge wondering uncomfortably what had prompted him to feel such murderous rage.

"'Oh, no, Gus. Robin was not treating me dishonorably."

"He was kissing you, ravishing you!"

"I was enjoying it."

"By God, Georgie," he thundered, raising his hands and seizing her shoulders in an iron grip, "you had better not enjoy any such thing in future!"

"Oh, Gus, Robin was kissing me because he was proposing to me."

A shock like a bolt of lightning shot through him. *"What!* Proposing to you? You can't mean marriage!"

"Oh, yes, indeed. You do not think Lord Robert would propose something improper, do you?"

"Certainly I can believe that of him. He is London's most notorious heartbreaker."

"But he is no worse than you, is he, Gus?"

"I am not a debauched lecher!"

"Neither is Robin."

He cursed violently under his breath. "Surely you were not planning to accept that—that *philanderer* . . . were you?"

"Well . . ." Georgie put her finger on her chin and pretended to consider the matter. "It would be quite a feather in my cap to be able to claim that I tamed a 'notorious' rake. And he *is* awfully handsome."

"Marriage to that lecherous devil!" Sedge's head was spinning. Georgie married to Lyndhurst? Sharing his bed? *"No.* I absolutely forbid it!"

"If I did not know better, I would think that your jealousy was prompting this outburst of temper. You want to save me for yourself."

"It is not jealousy—" he insisted, then recollecting himself, continued in more measured tones, "I know how to protect my own. I consider you my affianced bride, Georgiana."

"Do you? I thought you had washed your hands of me. . . . I have seen nothing of you for a fortnight, Gus. Is that how a fashionable gentleman behaves toward his fiancée in London? Leaving her alone to fend for herself for weeks at a time?"

He waved away her quip. "You know you must marry me and I will not have any scandal attached to the name of my future viscountess. I want you to have nothing further to do with Lyndhurst. He is exceedingly bad *ton.* Your name linked with his can bring nothing but censure down upon your head."

"Do you know, I have been thinking. Perhaps I might be persuaded to marry you after all, Gus." She looked up at him, a provocative smile curving her lips. She stepped closer, resting one hand against his chest.

Sedge raised his brows and looked down at her incredulously.

It took him a moment to recover from the suddenness of her surrender. "You *will* marry me. Without delay."

"Perhaps we could announce our engagement and cancel it, after it has served its purpose."

"Served its purpose? What on earth can you mean, Georgiana?"

Georgie almost blurted out that its purpose was to permit Tom to fall in love with Susan, and to give Robin time to admit that he still cared deeply for Ann. But she gathered her wits quickly enough to realize that such matters would not weigh with Sedgemoor.

"Why, Gus? Why do you insist on marrying *me?* And in such haste, too."

"The purpose is clear. I have told you. My honor demands it. I must protect you from scandal and prevent any dishonor from being attached to the St. Regis name," Sedge declared forcefully.

"Is that the only reason?"

"You would not want to wed a man who was without honor, Georgiana."

"No, indeed. But I would not want to wed a cold fish either."

"I assure you, madam, I am not a cold fish," he replied heatedly. "If such a thing is worrying you, let me assure you that you would not suffer from an inexperienced husband. I have some little experience in amatory matters. I trust you would find my attentions in that regard quite satisfactory."

"Hmm." She considered this for a long moment, then said suddenly. "Kiss me, Gus."

"Do you think to test me? Do not be ridiculous, Georgie."

She closed the space between them, winding her hand in the folds of his pristine neckcloth, pressing it against the hard wall of his chest. "If you kiss me, perhaps I will marry you," she coaxed shamelessly. "Sometimes a woman likes to be persuaded with more than mere words, you know." She smiled up at him saucily.

He glared at her, his nostrils flaring with temper at her audacious request. "Very well."

If she sought to put him through some kind of trial, perhaps compare him with Lyndhurst, he would show her just how much skill he had.

He bent to touch her lips with his, hoping he would not find it too repulsive to kiss the outrageous, hurly-burly female whom he found far from physically attractive, but whom it was his unpleasant, and equally undoubted, duty to wed.

Georgie stood on tiptoe, letting her hands run up his chest until they reached his broad shoulders. Rock hard muscle met her touch through the smooth material of his modish evening jacket. She wound her arms round his neck and tangled her fingers in the silky hair at the nape of his neck.

Coming fully against him, she met his light touch on her mouth, firmly pressing her lips to his, wanting to feel his mouth on hers with surprising urgency.

Sedge found himself kissing her back. His hard lips softened over hers, melding their mouths together.

His breathing coming faster, he angled his head, sliding his lips from one side of her eager mouth to the other. He ran his tongue softly over the edge of her full lips. Pushing between her lips insistently, he sought entrance to the sweetness within.

Her lips sought the warmth of his, then softened further and opened slightly at his insistent probing.

He plunged within, seeking the warm moistness behind her lips.

Georgie lost the ability to breathe properly, her breath suspended in her throat. Suppressing the urge to moan aloud, she sagged against him, her arms tightly wound about his neck the only anchor that kept her upright.

The cool evening suddenly became as hot as high noon on a summer's day.

Sensation sizzled through him at the feel of her warm, curvaceous body against his. His pulses leapt. Immediate arousal, followed by shock, rocked him.

One hand sought and found the fullness of her breast. His hand covered it, sliding back and forth, caressing it through the soft muslin of her gown.

Moving his arm down from her back to her hips where they flared beneath her softly draped muslin gown, he pressed her intimately closer.

He wanted to lie down with her right there on the hard balcony floor and take her body with his, burying himself in her soft, warm feminine flesh.

"Oh!" Georgie exclaimed breathlessly, breaking contact for a moment. "I didn't know about that part—with the tongues, you know. How strange it makes me feel! And how wonderfully well you do it too, Gus!" she congratulated him.

"Georgie, you—," he protested huskily. Whatever he had been about to say was lost as she pulled his head down to hers once again to experience more of the stomach-churning excitement.

After an eternity, Sedge lifted his head, fighting for air, his breath coming hot and fast. His eyes were unfocused as he gazed down at the seductive little bundle of sensuality he still held so tightly in his arms her feet hardly touched the ground.

He found her irresistibly desirable.

"Umm. Yes. I believe I *will* marry you after all, Gus," Georgie breathed dreamily when he set her on her feet. "If you promise to kiss me like that at least once a day."

Her teasing remark brought him up abruptly out of the fog of his passion, all desire quickly doused. Why should Georgie arouse him so? he wondered, confused. She had none of the attributes he admired in a woman. He must not let her know how much she affected him. To let her gain the upper hand in their physical dealings would be disastrous for their future relationship, for an orderly marriage, for his *sanity*.

"Georgiana, you should not make such an improper suggestion!"

"Improper? To kiss your own wife. Oh, Gus, surely not!"

"You *will* behave with decorum as my viscountess. I will insist upon it. If necessary I shall take measures to assure that you do."

That kiss had been quite out of bounds for an innocent girl like Georgie. He had never before experienced such immediate arousal, such utter loss of sense of time and place, such utter loss of *self,* even when he had been with women of experience, women whose favors he had purchased, and whose profession it was to minister to his physical pleasure.

He must not lose control and kiss Georgiana so in the future. It was too dangerous.

"Oh well, if you will not promise, Gus, perhaps I will marry Robin, after all. He kisses *almost* as well as you."

She knew just how to arouse a different sort of passion in him too—rage.

"No! I absolutely forbid it!"

Georgie laughed, pleased at his show of temper, and agreed to marry him whenever he liked.

Thinking of the license that had been resting in his bureau drawer for more than a fortnight, Sedge told her he saw no reason for delay. He instructed her to be ready when he called for her at eleven the following morning.

"Oh, Gus, so soon? Can we not wait a day?"

"No. If you are not ready, I will carry you off willy-nilly."

"That sounds a bit impetuous and romantic for you, my dear Gus, if typically high-handed. . . . Whatever shall I wear for my wedding?"

"Anything that covers you up to your neck and down to your ankles, will do."

Georgie chuckled, thinking that that definition would cover anything from her nightrail to a horse blanket!

"And, Georgie, don't forget to wear a hat!"

Well, Georgie thought optimistically on the way home in the coach with Tom and Susan, she had taken an irrevocable step tonight. She had agreed to wed Viscount Sedgemoor. For better or for worse.

Never one to shy away from bold action, she had moved quickly when the opportunity presented itself. It was a necessary tactic in her game to secure the happiness of several persons. She was confident she could manage her new husband in such a way as to secure her own future happiness, too. And his.

She did not share her news with her two friends who were talking quietly together on the seat opposite her, not liking to spring such a thing on Tom. She conceded that he would be upset when he learned of it. With some reason.

It would be best to quietly wed the viscount tomorrow and let the news come as a surprise to everyone after the deed was done.

Her change of tune was sudden, but did not come about on the spur of the moment. Her affairs were becoming more complicated by the day. She could not be entirely sure Tom had given up his plans to marry her, though tonight's most satisfactory display of jealousy over Susan's relationship with Lord Robert gave her considerable hope that all would be well for her two old friends.

She hoped her marriage to the viscount would be just that extra nudge Tom needed to send him into Susan's waiting arms.

Not only had Tom proved difficult to manage, but now, astonishingly, here was Lord Robert issuing a marriage proposal in form! She would have to send him a note first thing tomorrow, declining his most flattering proposal as kindly and gently as she could.

Even though Robin professed that his *tendre* for Ann Forester had been shortlived, Georgie was certain he still cared deeply for her. He was very hurt that his attentions to Ann had become common gossip.

The rumor had circulated that Lord Robert had not embarked on one of his famous seductions, but that his attentions had been serious for once. After all, it was said slyly, *she* was a considerable heiress, and *he* was the scapegrace younger son of an already impoverished family. So it was no surprise that he had been seriously courting her. But, as the gossipmongers reported it, when Miss Forester caught him with another woman, her eyes had been opened to his real character and she had jilted him. His philandering had broken her heart, or so rumor had it.

At an evening party during the past week, Georgie had caught Robin in a rare confiding mood after Ann had rebuffed his request for a dance. She had wormed the whole story out of him about his first meeting Ann, their falling in love, and their subsequent disastrous falling out through a misunderstanding concerning Robin's attentions to another woman.

Georgie liked Ann enormously, finding her to be one of the most intelligent women she had ever met, though she had been surprised that Lord Robert, so devastatingly attractive himself, had been drawn to Ann with her at her rather ordinary looks and her reputation as something of a bluestocking.

Reminded of a French saying she was fond of, "A man has never loved, until he's loved a plain woman," Georgie was pleased to think that Lord Robert hadn't fallen in love with Ann for reasons of physical beauty. Yes, Ann was just the woman to hold Robin in line.

Georgie judged that Ann was still breaking her heart over Lord Robert and was proud of the self-possessed young woman for holding up her head and showing herself in London, not burying herself in the country while the scandal was still fresh news in everyone's mind.

Robin had been most obliging when Georgie had asked him to help make Tom Cunningham jealous by flirting with her friend, Susan. Using Robin for her own purposes, she never dreamed he felt anything more than friendship for her.

She still did not believe it. He was just suffering still from Ann's rejection and had turned to her on the rebound.

Well, Robin was a gorgeous specimen of virile, young manhood, and Georgie enjoyed his friendship. She had been quite willing to indulge in a playful flirtation with him, but she could not take him for her husband when she knew Ann still cared deeply for him.

Besides, there was Gus.

As she had said that morning to Max, *something* had to be done about him.

Her head full of what it meant to love truly, her thoughts turned to the man she was to marry on the morrow. After tonight's quite spectacular display of jealousy, she had some hopes that Sedgemoor was not completely indifferent to her. Even if she could never win his fastidious heart, she certainly did not want to spend the rest of her life with a cold husband.

Tonight's kiss and heated embrace gave her some hope of turning Sedgemoor into a satisfactorily passionate lover. She had learned that it would be easy enough to make him respond to her physically at least.

She had moved boldly, sooner than she had planned to. But perhaps if she could cut through the heart of his defenses ranged against her, his affections, as well as his sense of honor, would ignite toward her.

She grinned suddenly, restraining her gleeful laughter at the way the pieces of the game were falling into place.

Chapter 11

"Oh, no, Georgie, you haven't married Viscount Sedgemoor on my account!" Susan exclaimed to her friend, the day following Georgie's quiet marriage.

"Now, Sukey, don't be a goose. I had reasons of my own for marrying Gus. And if it accomplishes the purpose of finally convincing Tom that I am *not* available, perhaps his eyes will turn in your direction, where they should have been any time these past four years!"

Georgie sat with Susan in a bright and airy little nook off the breakfast room in her new home, Sedgemoor's quietly tasteful Brook Street townhouse, fashionably situated just off Grosvenor Square. Sharing a lively coze over a mid-morning pot of tea and fresh scones, they were discussing Georgie's sudden marriage.

Susan had been happy to comply when she received Georgie's request to visit her that morning, but her eyes had almost popped from her head when she had read the address and seen that Georgie had subscribed herself as Georgiana St. Regis, Viscountess Sedgemoor.

"But to sacrifice your whole future and marry such a man!" Susan exclaimed, concerned for her friend's future happiness.

"You forget, Susan, Sedgemoor is wealthy and titled. How can I be sacrificing myself?" Georgie twinkled at her friend.

"Yes, but he is such a cold, austere man, for all he's so handsome. I'm sure you must be frightened to death of him," Susan remarked with a shudder. "I should be shaking in my shoes in your place."

"Frightened of Gus!" A ripple of laughter issued from Georgie's throat. "No, never, my dear. He is a tiny bit arrogant, I grant you. But I will take the starch out of him before he's much older, see if I don't," Georgie replied with a martial light in her eyes.

"Why, just this morning Gus informed me that we would leave for Gloucestershire tomorrow. That's where the Oaks is located—his estate, you know. Imagine, leaving town before the season is over! You have been acquainted with me long enough to know that I soon put paid to that idea!"

There were several more weeks left before the season began to wind down. Georgie planned to enjoy every minute of that time before she allowed the viscount to spirit her away to the country. She wanted to make sure that Tom engaged himself to Susan before she left London, and she hoped something could be done about Ann and Robin.

"Oh, Georgie, no!" Susan cried, putting her hand up over her mouth to hide her shock. "How can you oppose him like that? He is your husband now. You owe him obedience in everything."

"Susan Louisa Tennyson! Don't be a ninnyhammer! I hope you do not plan to behave like the downtrodden little woman when you are wed to Tom, and allow him to ride roughshod over your wishes."

Susan sighed eloquently. "I doubt that event will ever come to pass."

"Umm. I think things may have begun to change for the better at Sarah's engagement party." She teased her friend lightly.

Susan blushed, then an unwelcome thought struck her. "Oh heavens, Georgie!" she exclaimed, raising her hand to cover her mouth. "Whatever will you tell Tom?"

"You, my dear Sukey, will tell him for me."

"Oh, no, I could never do that. He will be furious!"

Georgie's eyes gleamed. "Exactly! When you leave here, send a note directly round to his rooms and bid him come to see you. You can give him the shocking news and when he flies into the boughs, you will be there to comfort him."

"Georgie! Another of your mad schemes. I will not do it!" Susan shook her head.

"Well, if you don't tell him, he will just have to read about it in one of the newspapers. Gus has gone this morning to puff it off in the *Morning Post*, the *Gazette*, and *The Times*. I teased him about such wretched excess, but he only told me that he wished to be sure that everyone knew."

"Everyone will be so shocked by the news," Susan ventured.

"Probably . . . they will recover shortly, however. I intend to have a party of my own here next week and invite all my friends, and Gus's friends too, of course, to celebrate our wedding after the fact. I want you to help me plan it, Sukey, dearest." Georgie bubbled with excitement, thinking how she could put all her newfound resources as a viscountess behind her matchmaking plans.

"Tom will be invited, of course. But I will ask Robin to escort you and your mother. We want Tom to feel the green-eyed monster biting into him when he sees you on Robin's arm. Wear that white confection you bought at Madame Celeste's last week. You will look even more beautiful with the pale gown setting off your dark hair and eyes!"

"Georgie, I don't think—" Susan tried to remonstrate with her friend, but Georgie would not hear any protests.

Georgie's enthusiasm was infectious. Though she was still shaking her head over her friend's sudden extraordinary, and perhaps unwise, marriage, Susan soon entered into the plans for the new viscountess's first entertainment. The two girls talked and schemed and planned for the next hour.

During the carriage ride to White's, Sedge was experiencing very mixed feelings about the wisdom of his hasty marriage.

He cursed himself for a fool. A whole lifetime stretched before him where he could repent the rashness of his recent actions at his leisure. He had no one to blame but himself. It was he who had insisted on the match.

By all odds Georgiana Carteret—with her lively ways, penchant for mischief, merry laughter, her too brightly colored hair, and imperfect figure—was the very *last* woman he would have chosen for his viscountess. Red-haired women were nothing but trouble, as he had learned long ago.

Certainly, if he had ever decided to wed for the sake of the succession, he would have chosen someone quite unexceptional, a dignified, *serene* woman who knew how to behave with decorum and propriety, someone who always acted according to the dictates of her station in life.

And of course, she would have been a beauty. Yes, if he had ever *freely* chosen to wed, it would have been to a well-born lady whose beauty and taste and good manners would have won the admiration of his friends. Someone who would fade into the background, a beautiful ornament, who did not interfere in his day-to-day life.

Definitely *not* someone like Georgie!

It was just unfortunate—damned unfortunate—that circumstances had forced him to wed her in order to preserve his honor.

Semper cum honore. He would not be the St. Regis to bring dishonor to the family. Nor would he ever allow a chit of a girl to bring scandal to that name.

And, he admitted reluctantly, he had been angered by her stubborn refusal to bend to his will when he had first informed her of his decision. She should have been abjectly grateful that he had so lowered himself as to offer her his hand. She should have been thanking him on bended knee, instead of laughing in his face and arguing the matter with him, refusing to consider his proposal for weeks, then abruptly giving in.

He buried deep inside the knowledge that he had been beside himself with rage when he had seen another man holding her and kissing her, and refused to acknowledge it as one of the reasons he had pushed the wedding forward with such haste.

His jaw hardened as he remembered how Georgie had mocked the very idea of becoming his wife. Well, he had won that battle. She was indeed his wife. His viscountess.

What on earth was he to do with her now?

He ran a hand over his face in weariness. The little wretch had addled his wits. He couldn't seem to think straight. Hadn't been able to think straight since he had met her.

The fruit of his precipitate action yesterday was already bitter in his mouth. That morning she had stubbornly refused to leave for the Oaks on the following day as he had planned, telling him it was no part of their bargain to rusticate. She fully intended to enjoy a few more weeks of the season, she had informed him with a bright gleam in her eyes.

"Anyway, Gus dear, tongues would be wagging if we were to run off with our tails between our legs, as though we had something to hide," she had argued, never losing her cheerful smile or the lively twinkle in her eyes. "Why do you want to leave town so soon, anyway, my dear?"

"I believe that it is generally the custom for a

newly wedded pair to go on a honeymoon," he had replied coolly.

At her laughing comment that they could enjoy their honeymoon in London as well as in Gloucestershire, he had retired behind his newspaper.

"No, we cannot leave town now," Georgie had insisted, "with everything so unsettled."

He glared at her over the top of his paper. "Unsettled? Things were settled yesterday. What else is there left to settle?"

A mischievous look crossed her face and she had dodged the question, reminding him instead that this was her first season, and that she was having a marvelous time.

She had several engagements planned in the next few weeks that she could not possibly miss, she had told him, a devilish light dancing in her blue eyes as she sat across from him at the breakfast table. "And we must give our own evening party before we leave town, too. Next week, I think."

Not bothering to ask his permission or consult his wishes, she had announced the fact to him as coolly as all bedamned, saying that as the Viscountess Sedgemoor she was now in a position to return some of the gracious hospitality she had received over the past few weeks.

He had tried to take a fierce line with her. He threw down his newspaper beside his plate and fixed her with a stern look. "Georgiana, could you not have the goodness to consult me first? This is my house and—"

"Our house," she had corrected with a smile.

"What?"

"It is *our* house now, Gus," she said, speaking slowly and kindly, as though he were an imbecile. She had reached out to lay her hand on top of his that was clenched over the tablecloth and patted it. "I believe I became mistress of this establishment when I married you yesterday."

"I wish to leave for the country. Perhaps next year you can come to town and give an entertainment for your friends, after you have had a chance to become accustomed to your new role as Viscountess Sedgemoor."

"Oh, Gus, you will enjoy yourself *this* year. I will see to it. I will invite all your special friends—except that Stella person. She is not very nice, I believe. I hope you do not count her one of your bosom bows."

"Lady Withers is nothing to me," he had answered negligently, mildly amused that Georgie should show a bit of jealousy. There was no need. He had never felt the least desire to bed Stella. "Next year will be time enough to be planning entertainments."

"Who knows, next year I may be otherwise occupied," she had said archly, looking up at him from under her lashes.

One blond brow had risen in query. "Otherwise occupied? How so?"

"Yes. Married people often produce children early on in their marriage, or so I believe. Perhaps it is not universally the case."

Feeling a flush mounting in his face, Sedge had clamped his lips shut, unable to utter another word. He had not gone in to Georgie the previous evening to consummate the marriage. Worry over how he would manage the business with his customary expertise with his stiff leg to hinder him had stopped him cold. Now she was teasing him about the delicate matter. The little imp!

When his barouche pulled up in front of Thirty-Seven St. James Street, Sedge made no move to descend and enter his club. Instead, he sat in the elegant equipage, preoccupied with his memories of that morning's unsatisfactory conversation still weighing on his mind.

How could he tolerate a wife who refused to obey him, who refused to acknowledge that he was now her lord and master, her superior in understanding? How could he make her understand that as his wife, she owed him total obedience?

He had remonstrated with Georgie again, but she had paid absolutely no attention to his wishes. She had jumped up from her chair, come around to where he sat, put her arms around his neck, hugged tightly, and given him a smacking kiss on the cheek, saying sweetly, "Oh, dear, Gus, your leg must be bothering you this morning. Your temper is always so uncertain when you are in pain."

To his annoyed chagrin, she had continued, "I quite understood why you did not come to me last night. I do wish you would rest today, rather than going out to your club." She had set her soft cheek against his rough one and rubbed gently. "And I do not think a journey to Gloucestershire would be at all beneficial to your poor leg at this time. Just think of all the jostling it would receive on a long, tedious

carriage ride. No, no. We are best fixed here for the
next few weeks."

How on earth was he ever to regain his sangfroid
with a wife like Georgie to contend with?

Bracing himself for the unpleasant task ahead,
Sedge stepped down from his barouche, waving away
the attentions of a hovering footman. He used his
cane to support himself as he left the vehicle, limped
up the steps, and entered the large double doors that
led into the inner sanctum of White's.

As he set foot in the room, he was greeted by a
chorus of excited, curious voices, all exclaiming
about his recent marriage.

He had intended to announce the thing himself, as
casually as possible to a few special friends and let
the news filter down to others before the announce-
ment that would set the *ton* on its ear appeared in following day's newspapers. But the tidings were before
him.

Through the mysterious means by which these
things became known, undoubtedly from servant's
gossip, word had already spread like wildfire. News
of his marriage to Georgie was greeted as though it
were the eighth wonder of the world.

Not quite in command of the situation, as he would
have preferred, Sedge felt somewhat ill-at-ease and
nettled by the volley of congratulations and ribald
comments that poured forth on his appearance.

"You here today, Sedgemoor? Should have thought
you would be too exhausted to show your face for a
week or more," one wag commented brazenly. "A
new bridegroom, after all! And such a lively bride,

too!" Desmond Stiles gave an unpleasant neigh of a laugh after he delivered his salacious sally.

Sedge fixed the unfortunate speaker with a cool stare through his quizzing glass and replied languidly, "As you can see, Stiles, the rigors of the married state are not too onerous. I have survived quite nicely, I thank you."

He steeled himself to counter similar sallies with cutting setdowns, should the taunting continue. He was surprised when several men heartily congratulated him instead of offering bawdy jests, telling him he was a lucky man and expressing envy that he had been the one chosen by the incomparable, much beloved Georgie.

"She's a rare handful, Sedgemoor, you lucky dog!" Lord Smythefield, the Duke of Hightower's heir, said to him. "She can charm the birds out of the trees. Even the guv loves your Georgie. Never seen the old man so taken with a chit before. She discovered his bark's much worse than his bite one evening at the opera and he has been after me to join the hordes that dangle after her ever since. The duke said he wouldn't mind having such a lively chit for a daughter-in-law. Damn your eyes, Sedge, for beating me to her!"

"Sedge, you dark horse!" another friend exclaimed. "Imagine stealing a march on the rest of us like that. I can't imagine a more charming companion than Georgie Carteret. You will not know a moment's rest—or a moment's boredom with Georgie. What a happy life you will have with her." The man shook him vigorously by the hand.

"Yes, I'll go bail Georgie will never treat you to

the vapors, or ruin your best new jacket from Weston's with floods of tears," another crony assured him. "You will not have to put up with sulks, fidgets, or hysterics like poor St. Clair yonder. Look at him slouched in his chair. Already been at the brandy bottle this early in the day. Comes to the club first thing in the morning and don't go home till after midnight. Only way to escape Serena's caterwauling."

Sedge smiled until his face ached, saying yes, he knew what a lucky man he was. However he wished he had not ventured there that morning and was looking for a way to take his leave gracefully when he was accosted by Norman Mayhew.

"Heard you'd gone and married the little Carteret. Not in your usual style, Sedgemoor," Mayhew drawled in a bored voice, offering a snide comment rather than congratulations.

"Oh? You presume to know my tastes do you, Mayhew?" Sedge retorted cuttingly, not liking the sneer on the man's face when he spoke of Georgie. "Do you think to offer a comment on my viscountess?"

Not mistaking the lethal threat underlying the viscount's smooth words, Mayhew backed off. "Sure you know your own mind, Sedgemoor." He turned and sauntered from the room, leaving Sedge seething.

Max came up and clapped him on the shoulder. "Is it true what I've just heard, you close-mouthed old devil?" he asked. "You've taken on a leg shackle at last and married Georgie?"

"Quite true, Max," Sedge assured him.

"Knew a match between her and Cunningham wouldn't fadge." Max offered his most sincere congratulations. "Georgie would make any man a bang-up wife. But for you, I can't imagine a better choice. She will make you a superb viscountess." Max grinned at him.

"Is that observation supposed to convey some deep meaning, Max?"

"No, no, my friend. I envy you. Truly. But you had best keep an eye on Mayhew," he added quietly. "I fear your Georgie's made an enemy there. He could cause trouble."

"Why so?"

At the inquisitive lift of Sedge's brows, Max continued. "The man's at point-non-plus. Hasn't a feather to fly with. Fixed his interest with the little Waverly heiress—you know the one, small, dark girl with no looks or style. Well, Mayhew had been planning to elope with her a few weeks ago, but somehow Georgie got wind of his plans and spiked his guns. The Waverly girl came off safely. But he bears no good will toward Georgie for putting a spoke in his wheel and ruining the match."

Max did not add that he had overheard some mendacious gossip Mayhew had spread about Georgie. He did not want his newly wed friend to go off and challenge the blackguard to a duel.

"I'm grateful for the warning, Max. Sounds like Georgie. Always busy about other people's affairs, where she has no bus—ah, I mean, you know how she takes an interest in the affairs of others." Sedgemoor cursed his loose tongue. It was hardly discreet, or gentlemanly, of him to be criticizing his new wife, even to his friend Max.

He had married her partly to shield her from the

consequences of her own indiscretion. He should not be giving others cause to question her common sense. If only he could get her away to the country, by this time next year she would be model of propriety and good manners. He would see to it.

Max laughed. "Never mind, Sedge. We all know how warmhearted Georgie is. She isn't afraid to step in, if she sees an injustice being done. Can't help but get into trouble sometimes because of it. Good thing she will have you to bail her out of any scrapes now. But, know what I think, my lad—she's a real heroine. Georgie loves everyone and everyone loves her. You're just the lucky devil who will get more of her 'loving' than any other." Max winked at his friend and was amused to see a faint flush touch the viscount's cheeks.

Sedgemoor took his friend's comments in good part, but he resolved to be on his guard. His new wife bore close watching. He should make it a policy to know what she was up to at all times. He would be damned if he would let her embarrass him or bring any disgrace to the St. Regis name.

Chapter 12

After Susan left, Georgie called Mrs. Finch, Sedgemoor's competent housekeeper, pointed to the muddle of papers—guest list, menu consisting of her favorite foods, ideas for decorations and so forth— spread out over the breakfast room table and explained her desire to hold an entertainment in a week's time.

Saying she had every confidence in Mrs. Finch's ability to take care of all the details, Georgie gave her such an ingenuous smile, that the housekeeper was thoroughly charmed by her new mistress and promised to see to all the arrangements.

Full of restless energy on the bright, sunny day and not knowing when she could expect Sedgemoor to return, Georgie decided to take her hound out for a walk in the park. She did not yet have a lady's maid, so she decided she had best request the company of one of the viscount's servants to accompany her to help with Rufus.

"What is your name?" she asked the young footman who was standing to attention outside the ornate, unused drawing room. The boy's ginger hair stuck out oddly at all angles from his head. Georgie thought him quite endearing.

"Eugene, my lady."

"Oh! Yes, I suppose I am 'my lady' now. How funny it sounds! However, I shall soon grow accustomed to it. Eugene, do you like dogs?"

"Yes, my lady. Me mum always had a dog about the house when I were a lad."

"I am pleased to hear it. I would like for you to help me with Rufus, Eugene. The viscount has provided housing for my dog in the mews, but Rufus cannot remain confined there all day. He must have lots of exercise. If I am unable to take him for a walk in the park, I would like for you to do so for me. He must go out every day, preferably twice, morning and afternoon. And he likes to play. I must warn you, Eugene, he never gets tired."

"Beggin' your pardon, your ladyship, but Mr. Stillman, the butler, says I'm to be on duty in the hall at all times, unless he wants me to polish the silver or do other jobs for him in the butler's pantry. He don't like changes to his orders, your ladyship."

"Stuff and fiddle! I shall deal with Mr. Stillman. I am the mistress here now." Georgie drew herself up to her full five feet, two inches and tried to look autocratic. She failed miserably. "You will be in charge of Rufus, Eugene. *And* you shall accompany me when I wish to pay morning calls or go shopping, or any time I wish to go out otherwise unaccompanied."

"Yes, your ladyship. It will be a pleasure, your ladyship." Eugene hid his grin as best as he was able to hear the little lady say she would deal with Mr.

Stillman. That would be a confrontation he would not want to miss.

As Georgie walked along in the park, smiling and greeting many passersby, she thought back over her hectic wedding day . . . and her disappointing, *lonely* wedding night.

The brief ceremony had gone swimmingly. The viscount had collected her and her grandmother promptly at eleven o'clock for the short drive to St. Margaret's Church, Westminster, where the wedding took place. Sedgemoor had exerted his considerable influence to have the nuptials conducted in the famous old building on such short notice, telling Georgie that they might as well follow in the footsteps of Samuel Pepys and John Milton, both of whom had said their marriage vows in the church.

Dressed in a claret jacket and biscuit-colored pantaloons that set off his manly figure to perfection, and with his hair brushed until it had shone like spun gold, Georgie thought her groom had looked quite devastatingly handsome, despite the fact that there was a grimly determined rather than an ecstatically happy look on his face when he had arrived at her grandmother's.

Georgie had thought she looked quite up to snuff herself, considering she had had so little time to prepare. She wore a new dress of soft creamy silk edged with pale blue piping. Instead of the hat Sedgemoor had commanded her to wear, her grandmother's maid had fashioned a fragrant wreath of roses and delicate white camellias for her hair.

She had thought to wear a veil, but her grandmother said that a long piece of lace over her head

would drag her down and make her look even
shorter. Lady Carteret had given her as a wedding
gift a simple gold necklace with a sapphire pendant
and sapphire earrings and bracelet to match. She
had beamed happily at Georgie, taking all the credit
for the match herself. She had been sorry not to have
a large society "do" so that she could puff off
Georgie's new status to all her acquaintances, but had
decided it was best to get the pair buckled before one
or the other of them changed their mind. She was in
haste to see her granddaughter a viscountess, she had
told Georgie, wagging a finger at her.

When Sedgemoor had complimented Georgie on
her appearance, she had smiled radiantly up at him.
He had rarely done so before.

She had been as merry as a grig after that, sure that
she was doing the right thing in agreeing to this wedding.

Henry Edgeworth had stood up with him. She had
been surprised. She had thought he would have asked
Max. But Henry was all but engaged to Charlotte, so
perhaps Gus felt more comfortable with another man
who was contemplating matrimony, rather than with
one of his staunch bachelor friends. And then, too,
Henry was very discreet.

Sedge's pale golden hair gleamed in the light from
the candles flickering on the altar and there was a
warm light at the back of his gray eyes as they held
hers when they said their marriage vows to one another.

Georgie had felt quite breathless just *looking* at
him. What would she feel when he kissed her? she
had wondered with tingling excitement.

They had gone back to Half Moon Street where Lady Carteret had had an elaborate wedding breakfast set out for just the four of them. Afterward, the viscount had whisked Georgie off to his townhouse in Brook Street.

After meeting the servants and viewing the house, Sedgemoor had escorted Georgie to her set of rooms on the second floor that was located next to his own bedroom and dressing room suite.

He had bid her rest before dinner, saying she must be tired. Georgie had not been at all tired, but she had seen that he was looking somewhat worn and drawn. She remembered that he had been standing for a good deal of the day, and he had dispensed with his cane for the first time since he'd been in London. No doubt *he* needed a rest.

She had risen on tiptoe and kissed his cheek, saying that she would be glad of a lie-down and that she would see him at dinner. She had been too excited and restless to lie down, however, so she had explored her own room, then wandered downstairs again where she met the housekeeper who seemed somewhat startled when her new mistress expressed a wish to explore the kitchens.

Mrs. Finch had been all politeness, guiding Georgie belowstairs where she had spent an hour getting in the way and making the servants laugh when she would insist on tasting everything that was being prepared, taking an interest in the daily lives of the staff and learning all about them before she rushed away to dress for dinner, realizing that she would be late, if she didn't hurry.

Georgie had tripped downstairs for dinner in an

ebullient mood. This was her wedding day—with the night to come. She had sparkled during dinner, not noticing at first that her new husband seemed to have something on his mind that took his thoughts far away from her.

She had retired rather early, surprised to find herself somewhat nervous about what was to come. She had not had time to have a new nightgown made, but she owned a fine lace and silk confection that she thought was suitable.

There had been no time to procure a lady's maid as yet, so she undressed herself, drawing the nightgown down over her head in excited anticipation.

Clasping her hands together, she had paced about trying to calm herself, then slipped into bed and lay there . . . waiting . . . for what had seemed like hours.

Gus had not come to her.

Obviously he did not intend to consummate the marriage that night, she had realized in disappointment. Did he intend to do so at all? Did he want a marriage of convenience only?

Perhaps he had not come because his leg had been paining him.

Well, whatever the case, Georgie would not have it. There was no lack of desire on his part, she knew. There was that shattering kiss they had shared the previous night after all.

If he did not come to her soon, she would take matters into her own hands, she thought on a slightly embarrassed chuckle. She did not know exactly what people did in bed, but she had shared a passionate kiss with Gus and she wanted more. . . .

Jerked suddenly out of her reverie, Georgie realized that Eugene had let Rufus off his lead. The big red dog was cavorting through the park, chasing a squirrel, running in the path of a foppish dandy and tripping him up, then creating havoc as he got in the way of horse and carriage traffic.

"Oh, Eugene, catch him," Georgie called after the running footman, trying to restrain her laughter at the comical sight. "Oh dear, we have come at the wrong time. I have never seen it so crowded at this hour. The sunshine has brought everyone out early," she said aloud to herself. "We will have to come back at a time when the park is more deserted tomorrow."

When the viscount still had not returned home by mid-afternoon, Georgie gave up waiting for him. Casting about for something to do, other than exploring her new house, she remembered guiltily that she owed Lord Robert an answer to his proposal of marriage.

She really should have found the time on the previous day to write to him, explaining that she could not marry him and that she was going to marry Sedgemoor instead.

But yesterday—her wedding day—had been so busy, she had not had time. Events had unfolded quickly and overtaken her good intentions.

She sat at Sedgemoor's large gleaming mahogany desk in his rather dark, book-lined study, took up pen and paper and prepared to write a long, explanatory letter to Lord Robert.

Sheet after sheet of paper was balled up and thrown into the empty grate.

"Oh botheration!" she exclaimed after she had been at her task for over half an hour, her fingers ink-stained and cramped from her efforts.

She could not seem to strike the right tone. She wanted to express her thanks for his thinking of her in such a way. She wished to tell him that she had enjoyed their kiss. No, she must not do that!

She wished to let him down gently, telling him how much she enjoyed his company even though she did not think it wise that they marry. But she reached a sticking point when she attempted to explain how she came to marry Viscount Sedgemoor the very next day.

"Fiddle! I can never explain by letter. There is nothing else for it. I must go and see Robin."

Heedless of the impropriety of such a visit, Georgie marched purposefully up to her room and prepared to go out. She put her hand on the bellrope to summon a carriage, then hesitated. Lord Robert lived in Chandler Street, only a stone's throw from her new home in Brook Street. She decided to walk.

She reached Lord Robert's rooms in a matter of minutes and was shown into a small receiving room by his astonished man of all work. She had not long to wait before Robin entered the room.

Clad in a splendiferous mauve silk dressing gown over his open-necked white shirt and black panta-loons, and sporting a motley collection of discolored bruises marring his heartstoppingly handsome face, Robin rushed into the room and greeted her with a glad light in his green eyes, though one of them was still half closed.

"Georgie, my dearest girl!" he exclaimed, taking

her hands in his. "You have come to console me for the undeserved punishment I took at the hands of that madman Sedgemoor, and to set our wedding date, I hope."

"Oh dear me, no, Robin. That's not why I have come at all. I am so sorry, but I can't marry you, my dear."

"But whyever not? I thought after our kiss—you don't find me distasteful, surely?"

"No. Oh, no. It's never that, Robin. I, too, enjoyed—but I must not say so."

"Georgie!" Laughing, he lowered his head and rested his forehead against hers. "You are not making perfect sense, my girl."

She drew away. "Well, you see, Robin, the thing is . . . I'm afraid I have gone and married someone else instead!"

"What! You're married!"

"Yes. I am so sorry, my dear. I feel that I *might* have been able to love you, but it's my firm belief that you are still in love with Ann."

"No, no. That's all over. She would not have me back if I were served up to her on a platter. Oh, Georgie, we would have been good together."

"Yes, I mean, no. We would not have suited."

Robin moved closer to her. He took up her hand and pulled her to him, gazing at her seductively, smoldering lights flashing in his emerald eyes.

Georgie reached up to touch his bruised cheek, wishing to offer some consolation. "I am sorry, dear Robin."

His head slowly descended toward hers, his eyes on her lips.

Recollecting herself suddenly, Georgie pulled away. "No, no. You must not kiss me, Robin. I am married now."

"I can't believe it!" Releasing her, he turned to pace about the room. He ran his long fingers through his dark hair distractedly, leaving tufts of it standing up on end.

"Oh, but I'm afraid it's true. I was married yesterday."

Robin struggled to control his emotions. He was overcome with the overwhelming and equal desires to moan with despair, howl with fury, and hoot with laughter. His face worked convulsively as he demanded, "Who the devil is the lucky man, Georgie?"

"Gus—I mean, Sedgemoor."

"*What!* You've married *Sedgemoor!*" Lord Robert goggled at her. "Leave. Now. At once!"

"Robin! Do not be so nonsensical!"

"Nonsensical? I am being wise beyond my years. Go, Georgie. If you hold me in any kind of affection, or even simple friendship, please leave! Now!"

He put his hand on her shoulder and propelled her to the door of the small room, picking up her hat, gloves, and reticule where she had carelessly tossed them on a chair and stuffed them into her hands.

"You are actually serious, Robin!"

"Of course I am serious, my dear child. As I value my life, I am serious. This could be a killing matter, should Sedgemoor learn of this extremely unwise and indiscreet meeting. Only think of how he reacted when he saw us together two nights ago, when, I presume, you were not even engaged!"

"Oh! Oh dear, I suppose he might kill you."

"Thank you for that vote of confidence. Has it occurred to you that I might perhaps kill *him*, instead? I can see by that horrified look on your face that it has not. He had the advantage of me the other night, you know, taking me by surprise as he did. Yet, I assure you, my girl, I am no weak shot or slow-wristed swordsman. I believe I could hold my own against, or even best, your new husband. Then you would be a widow. How would you like that, eh?"

"Not at all," Georgie said, jamming her hat on top of her head with more haste than care and heading for the door to the street as she rushed along the hallway. "Oh heavens, Robin, I never thought—"

The door closed on whatever else Georgie had been saying.

Lord Robert propped his shoulders against the closed door and shut his eyes in disbelief. How could such a vivacious, knowing little female be so innocent and ignorant of propriety? So lacking in *sense?* He could only hope that Georgie's indiscretion would go undetected by her fiercely jealous husband.

Georgie hurried away down the street, never glancing around to see if she had been observed coming out of the residence of London's most notorious rake unaccompanied by so much as a maid or a footman. She had no notion that Norman Mayhew stood across the street, watching her with a malevolent look on his face while she left Lord Robert's rooms.

* * *

Sedge had taken luncheon with Max after he had spent a lengthy session with Livermore, his man of business, directing him to draw up an extremely generous marriage settlement for Georgie. Livermore had tried to dissuade the viscount from transferring such a large sum from his own account, but Sedge did not believe he was being soft. It was only right and proper that a man in his position do the honorable, generous thing by his wife.

He had come home, wanting, wishing to see Georgie and make it up with her over their earlier disagreement. He grimaced at the news that she was out—and at the renewed pain in his leg.

He had put too much strain on it in the past week and now it ached. He went up to his room, shrugged out of his jacket, carelessly kicked off the Hessian boot on his good leg and carefully removed the other. Then he pulled off his neckcloth, drew his shirt over his head, and lay down with a sigh of the large bed that dominated the master chamber.

His thoughts were all of his new wife and how he should proceed in his relations with her. He had not gone to her last night. Georgie was just a child, a naive young girl, not yet ready for the intimacies of marriage. She would not have known what was expected.

Well, he rationalized, she was young and innocent . . . not so very young though, he remembered. She had recently turned one and twenty.

Tossing and turning, he was unable to sleep or to find a comfortable position. He folded his arms under his head and stared up at the canopy of the bed. Despite the pain it would cause his leg, he would have to bed her soon, and damn the embarrassment his stiff limb might cause while he made love to her.

God! The very thought of making love to Georgie was enough to send the blood pounding through his veins. He swallowed and shifted his position.

He must convince her to leave for the Oaks.

If only she would agree to go with him, they would not be facing this dilemma. Surely it would be easier to consummate the marriage there in the privacy of his country estate, without feeling that every neighbor on the street would learn through servant's gossip how the marriage bedding was going.

He smiled slightly, recollecting that at least he would have no excuse to avoid sleeping in the same bed with her, once they were at the Oaks, for there was only the one chamber for them to use, not a set of connecting rooms as here in London.

Chapter 13

Georgie returned home, more than a little agitated. She had realized during her unaccompanied walk back to Brook Street that perhaps her visit to Robin had not been *quite* the thing.

Learning that her husband had returned and was above stairs in his dressing room, she rushed up, needing to glimpse his face and reassure herself yet again that she had done the right thing in marrying him so precipitously.

She burst into Sedge's dressing room where he was bending over a china bowl at the wash stand splashing water onto his face. He was shirtless. In fact, he wore nothing at all, except a pair of form-fitting buff-colored pantaloons.

"Oh!" Georgie exclaimed loudly at the sight of his bare back turned toward her.

Sedge looked sideways when he heard Georgie enter his room. He straightened and drew a towel over his wet face and chest.

"To what do I owe this unexpected pleasure, ma'am?" he drawled.

"Oh, Gus, I wish you would not talk in that affected way. I am your wife, after all. I can seek conversation with you without an ulterior motive, can't I?"

"Conversation, my dear?" His gray eyes gleamed at her as he continued to run the towel slowly over the glistening golden hairs on his chest and shoulders and upper arms.

"You can at least listen to what I have to say without glowering at me, can't you? As your wife, I think—"

"Indeed you are, madam. And as such, owe me obedience. Or have you already forgot your vows of yesterday?"

"Do not be so odiously sarcastic, Gus. I take it you are still miffed that I will not agree to go to Gloucestershire before the season is over."

"Do you?" he asked, giving her an ironic smile. "How perceptive of you, madam wife. But my wishes as a mere husband have no influence with you, do they?"

"Oh, Gus, of course your wishes count for a great deal with me. You are my husband. And I *do* wish to please you. But, my dear, I am greatly looking forward to this party we are to give next week. I think you will enjoy it too!" she said coaxing him with her brightest smile. "Perhaps after that, if all goes well, we can leave for Gloucestershire."

He flung down the towel he had been using and leaned against the washstand, resting his hands on the stand behind him for support.

For perhaps the first time since she had met him, Georgie felt unsure of herself, and the tiniest bit intimidated. Sensing that they had reached a turning point in their relationship, she walked up to him, determined to show no fear.

Water droplets still clung to his face and hair. And there was a hint of moisture gleaming on the curling golden hairs that ran from the base of his throat down his broad chest to disappear in the waistband of his skin-tight pantaloons. Georgie's mouth went suddenly dry as her eyes fixed on those softly curling hairs.

He was magnificent.

He was her husband.

A sudden memory of helping the doctor unclothe him in Little Bickton assailed her, flooding her cheeks with color.

She could not seem to raise her eyes to his face. Mesmerized, she moved even closer, until she could smell the musky masculine scent emanating from him. Her hand rose of its own accord and just touched his chest, resting against the soft hair gleaming there. She resisted the urge to twist her fingers in that soft mat.

She could feel his heart beating strongly under her hand.

She looked up at him and swallowed awkwardly. Finding her voice at last, she said, "Gus, please allow me to give this party. Call it my bride gift, if you will. It is very important to the future happiness of several people."

"What about *my* future happiness?" he demanded, one brow lifted cynically.

Still holding his penetrating gaze, she faltered. The hot gleam in his smoky gray eyes was something she had never seen there before. It was not anger. She was quite familiar with *that* emotion leveled at her. This was something entirely different.

She looked down again, only to find herself staring at his naked chest, her eyes on a level with one flat male nipple. She stared fascinated at the whirl of golden hair surrounding the flat brown areola.

She took a deep breath, and the damp masculine scent of him assailed her nostrils once more, sending her senses reeling.

Feeling the tension crackling in the air, Sedge looked down at Georgie. Her turquoise eyes transformed themselves before his astonished gaze. One moment they were wide open, sparkling with high spirits, the next, they were great limpid pools, seducing him, drawing him down into their deep blue depths.

He reached out his hand and tipped up her chin. "Georgie, let us be friends. We will work out our differences," he whispered, bending his head to cover her mouth with his. His arms came fully round her and he pulled her up against himself, crushing her mouth beneath his.

Georgie's response was gratifying in the extreme to his masculine pride. She moaned and sagged against him, opening her mouth to his probing tongue and grasping his face between her hands as though it were a lifeline.

His hands held her, moving over her back to her waist to her hips, touching, caressing, arousing her through the thin muslin of her gown.

His hand moved to the back of her gown where he began to undo the buttons with impatient fingers. He stroked down over her neck, her back, pushing the material aside as he went, until he cupped her large, soft breast in his hand. His fingers played there, stroking back and forth across the sensitive flesh.

She moaned. Her hands fell to his shoulders and she caressed the skin of his back and arms and chest, reveling in the feel of smooth, hard muscle under her fingertips. One hand dropped to his chest where she ran her fingers through the soft mat of golden hair that so enticed her.

Her fingers entwined in the damp, softly curling tendrils, tugging the fleecy mat gently.

"Georgie!" he murmured thickly, his warm, moist mouth following his hand down her soft skin that was bared to his touch.

They touched and kissed and explored one another's bare flesh with mounting urgency, mounting desire. Bringing his mouth back to hers, Sedge kissed her deeply, deciding she was ready and eager for him. He bent his arm lower under her hips to pick her up, intending to carry her to his bed, but pain shot through his weakened limb when he lifted her.

He lowered her again, never taking his mouth from hers, and instead of carrying her, he propelled her backward to the bed. He lifted his mouth from hers to say huskily, "Now, will you do as I say and pack your things for our journey to the Oaks?"

Somehow his arrogant words penetrated the fog of Georgie's passion. "Oh, you, you . . . rake! You think to seduce me into doing your bidding!" she cried, bristling with indignation, knowing she must get away before he discovered he could easily do exactly that.

She ducked beneath his arms and pushed him away

with such force that he staggered against the bed, falling backward to lie sprawled full length across the coverlet.

"Well, think again, my Lord Sedgemoor! You will find yourself at checkmate, if you try any such thing!" she called from the doorway, pausing there only long enough to push her gown back up over her shoulders until she was decently covered, before she slammed out.

Sedgemoor was left hot and aroused and monumentally frustrated, both physically and emotionally. He had been on the point of winning her, winning her body and bending her to his will. Why had he been so unwise as to let her know what he was thinking? He should just have made love to her.

He turned over onto his stomach and pushed himself up off the bed. He arose to pace barefoot around the room, running a hand through his damp hair until it was thoroughly disheveled, almost standing on end.

He stopped his pacing and grinned wickedly. An audacious idea occurred to him.

He would tame his little wretch in the bedroom! Next time he would whisper only sweet words of love during their play, and convince her to do his bidding only *after* they were both fully sated.

Now why did that thought give him so much pleasure? he wondered with an anticipatory grin.

Georgie was stunned. For the first time in her life, she had lost control of herself and been ready to bend to another's will.

What in the world had happened to her?

Her husband's body and his kisses had sent her mindlessly whirling, spiraling down into a place filled with warm liquid and shimmering light. Everything had been centered on the hot aching she had felt in her breasts, between her thighs, and deep in her womb.

She had sagged against him, her legs turning to water when he kissed her and touched her and caressed her so thoroughly ... so passionately ... so expertly! ... flooding her with an ache that was as compelling as it was undreamed of.

Heavens! And there had been more to come! She had almost become his wife indeed, but he had ruined everything by giving away his game. He had not been as carried away as she. He had planned the whole thing to seduce her into doing his bidding.

Oh! He didn't play fair, the wicked seducer! But how could she resist him?

Well, if he sought to use that gambit, he would see that two could play at that game, she decided with a devilish laugh.

Sedgemoor was feeling relaxed. He and Georgie had enjoyed a truce over a late afternoon tea in the drawing room. She had chattered away, as usual, but there had been a heightened awareness between them. Every time they had looked at one another, or touched, sensation seemed to sizzle up his skin. He thought she felt the same way. He was confident that his plan to seduce her into submission was going well.

Wilkins assisted Sedgemoor as he dressed for the

evening. After dinner, he was taking Georgie to see a revival of Sir George Etherege's Restoration comedy *The Man of Mode* at Drury Lane Theatre. The play depicted a scintillating battle of wits between the sexes—a fittingly apropos entertainment, he thought.

Although as a married woman, Georgie no longer required the services of a chaperone, the party was to include Charlotte and her mother, Lady Widecombe, since the arrangements had been made long before their abrupt marriage, even before their temporary falling out over her friendship with Cunningham.

Mention had been made of the plans to attend the production at the wedding breakfast, and Henry had asked if Sedgemoor would mind if he came along. Sedge had grinned and replied jestingly, "Not at all. Is it Sir George Etherege's wit that attracts you, or a bit of female pulchritude?"

Henry had blushed scarlet and stammered that he always enjoyed the theatre.

The viscount had clapped his friend on the shoulder and said, "No need to fly up into the boughs, old man. It is no surprise that you and the little Fraser chit seem to have hit it off. You are both of a retiring nature."

Sedge had asked Max to join them, as well, to make up the numbers and serve as unofficial escort to Lavinia, Lady Widecombe.

This would be his and Georgie's first public appearance together as a married couple. Since Georgie would not leave town yet, Sedge had reluctantly decided it would be best to face the storm of gossip and talk about the marriage head on. If their marriage was to be a nine-day's wonder, then it was as well to appear together, surrounded by a number of their friends. Should deflect some of the talk, he hoped optimistically as he dismissed his valet and prepared to walk through his dressing room into his wife's chamber next door.

Intending to escort Georgie downstairs for dinner, Sedge put his hand on the handle of the door, tapped lightly and asked in a low voice if he could enter. He could hear humming in a cheery, off-key voice. She had not heard him. He smiled slightly and cracked the door open without knocking after all.

He rocked back on his heels at the sight that met his eyes, his breath quite suspended.

Just emerging from her bath, Georgie had no maid to assist her as she stood up dripping wet and totally naked in the hip tub. She stepped out onto a mat and reached for a towel.

Her bright red hair shone like a fiery nimbus against the whiteness of her skin.

Her skin glowed rosily from the heat of her bath when she rubbed herself dry. To his absorbed gaze, her large, full breasts lifted and stretched taut as she reached up to rub the towel under her hair at the back of her neck, shaking out water droplets from her curly hair like a puppy.

Completely unaware that he was watching her through the partially open door, Georgie continued to hum happily while she wiped away the moisture, drawing the towel over her shoulders and arms, her back, her stomach, bending over to dry her legs and feet.

He swallowed awkwardly.

The sight of her rounded hips, flaring out from her waist sent his pulses thrumming and desire surging through his loins. He wanted to cup them with his hands, wanted to press her up to himself. He had never before considered her figure particularly attractive, but seeing her unclothed, he was overcome with hot, pulsing desire. He longed to slake his desire in her ripe body.

He was reminded of a painting he had once seen of a gloriously full-bodied nude, all rosy and glowing and enticing, lying languidly in a bed of roses, satisfied after an arduous tumble, waiting for her lover to return to worship her body once more. An enigmatic half smile had curled up the beauty's mouth as she reclined in her flowery bower, one leg bent up at the knee and her head resting on one bent arm, her hair tumbling over it.

Sedge's breath caught in his throat. He fought for air. His reaction to her that afternoon was multiplied ten-fold now. The ache in his loins was too strong to be denied. He was fully aroused, wanting her with an urgency that caught him off-guard.

Why wait until tonight, he thought through a haze of blazing passion, his heart pounding madly. He wanted to join them *now*.

He had intended to start making love to her in the carriage on the way home. He would kiss her gently at first, then more urgently, letting his hands, his lips, his mouth, his tongue roam over her delightfully responsive body until they would both be so hot and eager to satisfy their desires that they would find it difficult to refrain from joining their bodies together there on the seat of the swaying carriage.

Drinking in the sight of her, wanting her as a parched man longs for water, he lifted his hand to knock on the partially open door, but stopped as his knuckles grazed the wood, suddenly aware of his own ragged breathing thundering in his ears. He shut his eyes and pulled the door shut quietly, then leaned back against the wall, trying to impose some calm on his aroused body and his shattered nerves.

No, he must not go in there now. If he went in there now, he would ravish her, not seduce her.

Even an intrepid female like Georgie would be frightened and upset if her husband suddenly rushed into her room, threw her down on the bed and made love to her before he had had time to prepare her. She was an innocent, after all.

Sedge bowed his head, his eyes still closed, drawing deep, calming breaths through his nostrils. He clenched his fists, fighting his desire. She was driving him insane, his little wretch.

Chapter 14

"Oh, Gus, who is that striking woman sitting over there?" Georgie pointed with her fan toward a beautiful blond woman who sat across from them in the brightly lit theatre. She and Sedgemoor sat shoulder to shoulder in the second row of the viscount's box at Drury Lane, behind Max, Lady Widecombe, Charlotte, and Henry.

"Whom do you mean, my dear?" Leaning close to speak into her ear, Sedge's arm came round her waist to pull her nearer. His fingers played against the silk of her gown at her waist, sliding around to the small of her back, over the top of her hips, then down over the curve of her thigh.

His breath brushed softly against her cheek, stirring her curls and her blood. Georgie tried to conceal the fluttering of her pulses and the delicious quiver that invaded her body at his every touch, at the very *nearness* of him. After the incident in his dressing room, she had felt this tingling awareness of him all afternoon and evening. He looked at her with eyes full of desire. Eyes full of the promise of things to come later.

She swallowed with difficulty and repeated her question. "See. Over there. The rather regal-looking creature with the lovely silvery-blond hair falling in a long curl over her left shoulder. The one in the very decolleté green silk gown whom everyone is staring at, sitting almost directly across from us."

She leaned against his shoulder, speaking into his ear to make herself heard over the din in the crowded theatre. Even that brief contact was sending delicious shivers coursing down her spine. And his strong, slender fingers were tightening on her waist, sliding up her bodice to the underside of her breast, stroking her surreptitiously, one long finger brushing across the material at the low neckline of her gown, whispering over the bare skin exposed there, exciting her unbearably, his brazen actions shielded from view by their two arms.

"I see no one but you tonight," he murmured. "I congratulate you on your gown, my dear. This luminescent pearl color sets off your hair and your eyes and your glowing skin to perfection."

Georgie was inordinately pleased. Her plan to seduce her husband tonight very much on her mind, she had taken special pains with her toilette, choosing to wear her modish gown of Nakara-colored silk, cut daringly low at the bosom. The creamy, rounded tops of her full breasts were exposed to his view.

She let her blue eyes dwell on him. He looked immaculate, as always, in black pantaloons and a maroon velvet evening jacket over a white waistcoat shot through with silver threads.

Was he looking even more handsome than usual? Or was it just her heightened physical awareness of him since their interlude in his dressing room that afternoon?

She moved closer to him, leaning her knee against his, feeling the hardness of his muscular thigh pressing back against her soft flesh.

He raised her ungloved hand to his lips, surreptitiously nipping the tip of her little finger with his teeth, touching it with his tongue, sucking on it for the barest moment before releasing it.

Her breath quickened at his daring action. She felt gloriously sinful. She smiled at him, indicating with her eyes the others sitting in front of them, signalling him to have a care.

His eyes held hers. Something hot and fiery smouldered in their gray depths. His heated gaze was like a touch of fire on her skin, turning her insides to molten liquid.

Georgie felt the heat rise in her own face as she gazed back at him. She moistened her lips with the tip of her tongue, and saw the flames leap higher in his eyes.

Her gaze dropped to his mouth, focusing on his lips.

She wished they were somewhere private so he would kiss her . . . so she could kiss him back . . . so that she could touch him, run her hands over his bare flesh, tangle her fingers in the tawny golden fleece that covered his chest . . . so that she could experience again that glorious pulsing excitement she had first known that afternoon.

It seemed an unbearably long time to wait until

they could be alone together. Perhaps when they were in the privacy of his carriage on the way home . . .

She shivered in anticipation.

Sedge lifted heavy-lidded eyes from Georgie's inviting mouth and flushed face and gazed unseeingly in the direction she had indicated. His heart was pounding furiously from their stealthy little interplay.

He was cursing the devil that it would be impossible to get up and leave before the play even started, as he violently wished to do. However everyone in the damned theatre would know why they had left. Lewd jokes about newlyweds would undoubtedly begin to circulate even before they had stepped outside the theatre.

His eyes finally focused on the woman Georgie had pointed out. He sat up with a jerk, his hand falling from Georgie's waist.

"Do you know her, Gus?" Georgie's eyes never left him. She saw the look of shock that came over his face when he recognized the woman.

"Goddamn it to hell!" he cursed under his breath.

The woman was fanning herself slowly and chatting to her companion. Diamonds sparkled at her throat, in her ears, and on her wrist when she plied her fan. The simple purity of the green silk gown with its deep décolletage had been chosen as the perfect foil for her unusually pale hair and white skin. Without any effort, she seemed to hold the attention of everyone. Her large, luminous eyes lifted and briefly touched on their box, locking with the viscount's gaze for a fraction of a second, almost as though she knew herself observed by him.

Her perfect countenance, still and cool and serene,

showed no emotion. Her gaze did not linger, but moved on after the briefest, most infinitesimal of pauses, to sweep around the theatre. A gentleman in a nearby box rose to his feet and bowed to her. In almost regal fashion, she took no notice, but continued to fan herself languidly and resumed her low-voiced conversation with her companion, a wraithlike woman dressed in a high-necked gown of dark gray silk.

"Who is she, Gus? One of your old flames?" Georgie asked lightly, but acutely.

Sedge turned to look down at her, a frown creasing his brow. His gaze was opaque, unfocused.

To judge from her husband's reaction, Georgie was struck by the unwelcome thought that her flippant remark was accurate.

"Sedge, do you see that Diana Carstairs is here tonight?" Max asked loudly enough for Georgie to hear.

Georgie gulped. Diana Carstairs! Her heart gave a painful jerk.

"I see her, Max," Sedge said, his voice superbly controlled.

"Isn't she the woman who was at your friend Left—" Georgie began incautiously.

"Yes, I believe you may be right," Sedge spoke quickly to quiet her. No word of his time with Georgie in Little Bickton must ever leak out. After all, he had married her to prevent any such thing.

"I have not seen her in years. She is looking magnificent, I must say! Queenly almost ... I wonder what brings her to town?" Max asked, turning in his seat and leaning his arm on the back of his chair to speak to them.

"I have no idea," Sedgemoor answered coolly, giving Max a hard stare over Georgie's head.

Max had the good grace to look somewhat abashed, realizing that perhaps he should not have mentioned the woman's name in Georgie's hearing, or be discussing the widowed Lady Carstairs's' motives for coming to London in front of his friend's wife. The interest between the viscount and Carstairs's lovely widow was rumored to have been strong. No one knew for certain what their past relationship had been, but the gossip had circulated that they had been lovers. Sedgemoor was close-mouthed about his amorous affairs and Max did not know if there were any substance to the rumors or not.

Max had always been intrigued by the lovely Diana, even before she had become Lady Carstairs. He had remembered dancing with her when she made her come-out some ten years ago. She was one of the few women who was tall enough to partner him without making him feel a giant.

She had not been so coolly composed then, he recalled. She had been a laughing girl, ready to poke fun at her own gawkiness. Max had been fascinated by her, and had almost decided to court her himself, but he was young, only twenty-two at the time, and a bit unsure of himself with women. Also he had been about to embark on a military career. It had not been the time to think about forming a permanent attachment.

But he recalled fondly that they had always spent time together when they found themselves at the same entertainments, danced together when there was dancing, and shared several pleasant conversations, discovering that their feelings and ideas were in accord on many subjects. But no promises had been made. None had been expected, he was certain.

Max had left for his regiment before the end of that season, and Diana had gone on to marry Baron Carstairs at the end of the summer. He had been unhappy for weeks afterward, when he had learned of it.

It had surprised no one at the time that the tall, green-eyed, blond Diana Astridge, of no particular pedigree and with nothing to speak of in the way of a dowry, had married the rather dull Lord Carstairs. He must have been twenty years her senior at the time. The marriage had lasted for five years before Carstairs was found dead in mysterious circumstances. There had been no children from the union.

After her year of mourning, Diana had reappeared in London, resembling the laughing, somewhat gauche girl she had been not in the least.

Strikingly tall and graceful and always exquisitely garbed, she was soon hailed as one of the most beautiful and sophisticated women in London. No one knew anything of her past life with Carstairs. She was all the more intriguing for that. With her aura of mystery and her regal beauty, gentlemen by the score laid siege to her. But the gossips said she was an iceberg. No one had ever succeeded in storming the citadel—until she met Viscount Sedgemoor. It was whispered that he was the only man who had ever melted her icy reserve.

They had first been introduced at a house party some two or three years previously. One wag who had been present at the time said he had been scorched by the sparks flying through the air between them whenever they looked at one another.

Max had no idea if they had indeed been lovers. If so, the affair had been conducted in the utmost secrecy. Why had his friend not married her, if he *had* taken her to bed? Max wondered in bewilderment.

Max knew he would have had no such hesitation. What could a man desire more in a woman than the exquisite Diana Carstairs?

And now here was his former flame come to London only two days after Sedgemoor had made Georgiana Carteret his viscountess. Wondering uncomfortably if there would be any unfortunate repercussions from Diana's presence in London, Max decided the situation would bear watching.

The play began.

At the first interval, Georgie could no longer keep still. She was anxious to take some exercise. It had been most uncomfortable sitting beside Sedgemoor for the past hour. He had been stiff and unmoving, not even allowing his shoulder to touch hers, though she had leaned toward him several times during the play to whisper a comment or two. He had returned abrupt answers. All their earlier intimacy had evaporated.

Lady Carstairs's presence had had a most profound effect on her husband. How on earth was she ever to seduce him if he would not pay the slightest heed to her? Georgie wondered.

"Shall we take a turn in the corridor, my dear?" Sedge turned to ask. Acutely sensible of the fact that it was important for them to be seen together as a newly married couple, he was determined to act the

devoted husband. He shook off his disturbance at seeing Diana across the crowded theatre.

"Oh, that would be lovely, Gus!" Georgie exclaimed, giving him a brilliant smile. She arose with
alacrity and allowed him to lead her from the box. "I
could do with some exercise after sitting still for so
long."

Max stayed behind to entertain Lavinia, while
Henry and Charlotte joined Sedgemoor and Georgie.

Seeing that many of the people milling about in the
corridor hailed the viscount and his new viscountess
in order to congratulate them on their recent marriage, Henry and Charlotte wandered off, talking quietly together, sharing their impressions of the play.

Those who sought to learn why the Sedgemoor's
marriage had taken place so expeditiously and in
such secrecy were summarily dealt with by the viscount. He quelled all such queries with a haughty
look, often accompanied by a dampening comment. It
was left to Georgie to charm any who took offense
with her friendly smile and gracious thanks for their
best wishes on her marriage.

"Lady Sedgemoor, I congratulate you on your recent marriage. I must say, you took us all by surprise," Ann Forester said. She had walked a little
away from her aunt who was chaperoning her that
night in order to greet Georgie.

Rather tall and angular, with her light brown hair
wound tightly in braids around her head, Ann did not
make the most of her appearance, Georgie noted,
clucking her tongue. The color of her rather plain
pink muslin gown was unsuited to Ann's dark looks,

sitting unhappily against her smooth olive skin and
dimming the luster in her warm amber eyes.

"Oh, Ann, call me Georgie, do. I shall not know to
whom you are speaking, if you address me as 'Lady
Sedgemoor.' I doubt if I shall ever recognize myself
by that name."

Ann lost her habitual serious look as both girls
laughed. Sedgemoor had become involved in a polit-
ical discussion with two current Members of Parlia-
ment and a government minister, so Georgie stepped
aside, pulling Ann with her. She wished to say a few
private words to her friend.

"I hope you will soon find it in your heart to forgive Robin, Ann," Georgie said boldly, coming
straight to the point. "I have had the whole story of
the misunderstanding that occurred between the two
of you last Christmas from the poor boy, and he really does regret the incident that led to your estrange-
ment most sincerely."

"Georgie, it is all over and done with now. No
need to open old wounds. I'm sure we have both
gone on with our normal pursuits and have put the
incident behind us," Ann said somewhat primly.

"Oh, Ann. I am sorry you feel so, my dear. Come,
can you not forgive him? He *is* suffering, you know.
And I think you are, too . . . I do hate to see my
friends suffering."

Ann did not deny it. "Georgie, my dear, you have
too kind a heart," she said instead. "I—I saw them
together you know. He was holding her. Kissing
her—I think."

"But perhaps he never intended to seduce the
woman. He was just holding her to console her, not

wanting to embarrass her too much by rejecting her out of hand."

Ann laughed mirthlessly. "Oh, Georgie. You would defend the devil himself, I believe."

"It was not Robin's fault, you know."

"It *was* his fault. Even if he weren't trying to seduce Mrs.—ah, the woman in question, such activities are not unknown to him. He is a famous rake," Ann explained as though Georgie were a slightly backward child.

"He loves you, you know."

"Do you think so? I doubt he knows what love is."

Georgie looked at her, using her expressive eyes to plead Lord Robert's case in his stead.

Ann gave an exasperated sigh. "Georgie, Georgie. I am a plain woman. There are so many beauties to catch his eye."

"You are not! Or, you wouldn't be," Georgie amended candidly, "if you changed your hairstyle and wore more modish gowns. Your eyes have quite an unusual almond shape and their warm amber color is glorious. Striking, with your smooth olive skin."

"It is kind of you to take an interest, but it's really of no use. Even if I were as pretty as you, my—my personality is rather dull."

"Me, pretty! No, I am not in the least." Georgie laughed at the notion. "Will you not speak with him? Be friends with him again?"

Ann shook her head. "How could I ever trust him? Could you trust a man who had been a notorious lover of so many women? Who might continue to pursue his rakish proclivities even after you had become his wife?"

"But, my dear Ann, that is exactly what I have done," Georgie answered, her eyes gleaming with a touch of humor and a touch of something else.

"Oh, Georgie, forgive me!" Ann said, her sensitive eyes full of contrition.

Georgie hugged her. "Never mind, my dear. I can handle Gus. His philandering days are over, believe me."

"Thank you for your concern, Georgie. I quite thought that perhaps you and Robin—"

Georgie looked back at her wide-eyed, shaking her head.

"Well, no. I suppose I was being overly fanciful. For all he is so charming, so appealing—and I do not mean just because he is so heart-stoppingly handsome—I can never allow myself to fall completely in love with Robin. I cannot risk a broken heart. We are from such very different worlds . . . our ideas, our values are so very different, you know, my dear," Ann said sincerely, trying to make Georgie see that a match between Lord Robert Lyndhurst and her would never come to pass. "You do understand, Georgie? And you will not continue to press me?"

Georgie assured Ann that she understood and expressed her concern for Ann's future welfare. "I will only press you to one thing. Will you not promise to come to the party Gus and I are giving to celebrate our recent marriage with all our friends?"

Ann could not refuse such a charmingly phrased invitation.

* * *

"I say, there's the bell for the next act," Henry said, coming up to rejoin Sedgemoor. "Think we should return to the box?"

"Yes, let us rejoin Mama," Charlotte whispered, holding tightly to Henry's arm, and gazing at him with stars in her eyes.

"Why do you not take Charlotte back now, Henry? Georgie and I will follow," Sedge said, seeing Georgie and Ann Forester standing talking with their heads together. What was his little wretch up to now? Plotting more mischief? Nothing could be more likely. A smile twitched at the corner of his mouth.

He sauntered slowly toward his wife, skirting the edge of the corridor that bordered the boxes. He stopped in his tracks when the snatch of a conversation being carried on behind one of the curtained boxes reached his ears. It concerned Georgie and it was not at all pleasant.

Sedge didn't move a muscle while he listened to the low-voiced discussion. It seemed Norman Mayhew had spread word all over town that the new viscountess had had an assignation with Lord Robert Lyndhurst that very day. Mayhew had been in Chandler Street that afternoon and with his own eyes had seen Viscountess Sedgemoor entering Lyndhurst's rooms unaccompanied by so much as a maidservant. According to Mayhew, she had arrived on foot, and left the same way, some three-quarters of an hour later.

One of the speakers behind the curtain snickered knowingly, "That little Carteret chit ain't got a grain of sense in her red-haired noddle."

"She has more hair than wit," rejoined the other sneeringly, "and not too much of that!"

The first speaker said spitefully that the toplofty Sedgemoor would look a real fool now, with horns on his head before he had been married a week.

Murderous fury gripped Sedgemoor. It was all he could do to prevent himself from charging through the curtain and choking the life out of the damned scurrilous scandalmongers.

If it had been difficult for Georgie to sit beside her taut, unbending husband during the first part of the play, the second was even more distressful.

Whereas before he had been stiff and distant, now there was an anger radiating from him toward her that was almost tangible. Georgie was at a loss to understand it. She could not imagine what *he* had to be angry about. She was the one who should be angry!

She had glimpsed him coming toward her out of the corner of her eye when she was speaking with Ann. Then he had stopped suddenly as though something had caught his attention. She had looked up and seen that Lady Carstairs stood not far away.

Georgie had watched as her husband stared stony-faced for a long while before bowing his head a fraction of an inch to acknowledge the lady. Lady Carstairs had returned his greeting coolly, lifting one exquisitely arched brow briefly before turning away.

When he had come up to take her back to the box, Sedgemoor had looked at her with a hard glint in his eyes Georgie had never seen there before. His arm had been rigid under hers as they made their way quickly back to the box. He had maintained a stony silence, frowning ferociously and limping heavily.

As he hurried her along, Georgie abandoned her strategy of trying to seduce him, and merely tried to tease him into a better humor. But he had not responded to her merry jokes about Dorimant and Harriet, the play's heartless rake and the witty woman who entrances and tames him. He had seated her without ceremony in the box and, without a word, had turned his head toward the stage where the action had already started.

Not one to engage in subtleties, Georgie decided to face the problem that plagued them head on. She intended to maneuver Gus into introducing her to the formidable Lady Carstairs and see if she could judge what had been between them in the past so that she could better know how to deal with the new situation.

Or, if Sedgemoor would not cooperate, perhaps Max was the man for the job. He had as much as said that he was acquainted with the lady, hadn't he?

Yes, it would probably be better if she asked Max to introduce her. Wasting no time in putting her plan into action, Georgie rose quickly from her seat as soon as the second interval began, saying, "Max, be a dear and take me out into the corridor for a breath of air. I declare, it is warm in here, is it not?"

"Georgiana?" Sedge began, but she waved to him as she placed her hand on Max's arm.

"I shall return soon, my dear. You stay here and bear Lavinia company and rest your leg."

As soon as they had passed through the curtain to their box into the corridor, Georgie said, "Max, I want to meet Lady Carstairs. Will you take me to her and introduce me?"

"Good Lord! Have you run mad, Georgie?"

"She was involved with Gus?"

"Deuce take it, my girl, you shouldn't ask questions like that!"

"Max . . ." Georgie looked at him coaxingly.

He was uncomfortable under that pleading look from those usually twinkling blue eyes. "How would I know?" He shrugged his shoulders and would have protested further, but he was forestalled. Lady Carstairs and her companion were just emerging into the same corridor and stood not five feet away.

"Damnation!" he muttered sotto voce. "Of all the devilish luck!"

"Lady Carstairs?" Max said, trying to look nonchalant, while wondering if she would even remember him.

"Oh!" Diana looked startled for a moment. She recovered almost instantly and said in her smooth, throaty voice, "Captain Templeton. Good evening. It is many years since we have met."

"Indeed, my lady. May I say that you look even lovelier with the passage of years than I remembered you?"

"Thank you, you are very kind. I seem to have survived the years in a reasonable state of preservation, I hope," she replied dryly.

Max looked somewhat nonplussed. He certainly had not meant any disparagement of her looks. Quite the contrary. She would think him a clumsy oaf, trying to offer a compliment and bungling it so badly.

Georgie nudged him with her elbow as she stood

by his side, giving the woman a friendly smile, assessing her all the while.

Max recovered himself shortly, saying, "Lady Carstairs, allow me to present Georgiana, Lady Sedgemoor." Try as he might, it was impossible to be nonchalant about introducing Sedge's wife to her.

"How do you do, Lady Sedgemoor," Diana said, extending her gloved fingers. She took Georgie's outstretched hand in a firm grip.

Georgie was surprised. She had expected Lady Carstairs to merely touch her hand lightly with her fingertips, as was the custom among many of the high-nosed grande dames of society.

"Lady Sedgemoor, Captain Templeton, allow me to present my cousin, Cecilia Gregson," Lady Carstairs introduced her small, bird-like companion. The woman was of indeterminate age, her small, pale face concealed behind a pair of large spectacles. "Cecilia has been kind enough to keep me company this season."

"I understand you are a friend of my husband, Lady Carstairs," Georgie said in a friendly way, catching herself just in time to prevent herself from saying "an *old* friend."

"Yes, I have met Lord Sedgemoor," Diana replied cautiously, her face closed. She held her head stiffly, at an awkward angle, and clenched her fingers on her fan.

Not sure what Georgie might take it into her head to say or do, and disliking the charged situation he found himself in, Max broke in, asking Diana where she was staying and how long she planned to be in town. To his considerable relief, the conversation became mundane for several moments.

The bell rang for the final act.

"We must go back to the box, Georgie," Max said, not bothering to hide his relief that the uncomfortable meeting was at an end.

With Max dragging on her arm, Georgie said in a rush, "You must join us next Thursday, Lady Carstairs. My husband and I are giving our first entertainment. You know the address? Thirty-three Brook Street. at eight-thirty."

"Thank you, Lady Sedgemoor," Diana said coolly, not giving an indication of whether or not she would accept the hurried invitation.

"Oh, *do* call me Georgie. Everyone does. I'm afraid that I am an informal sort of person, you see." Georgie's freckled face broke into a large grin, and her blue eyes twinkled as she smiled disarmingly at the regal woman.

Diana looked somewhat taken aback at this forthright admission, but she recovered in a moment. "Thank you, Georgie." She smiled back, a little more warmly than was her custom. "You will call me, Diana, won't you?"

"Well, I will, if you truly wish it, Diana."

"Of course," Diana said, turning away to rejoin her companion and make her way back to her box.

Meet the enemy head on and charge, was Georgie's motto. Except that she did not in the least feel that Lady Carstairs—Diana—was her enemy. She had secrets to hide and Georgie wished to know what they were. She would dearly love to learn all about the exquisitely beautiful, utterly reserved woman and what had been between her and Sedgemoor.

Max and Georgie stood looking after Lady Carstairs for a moment, both curious about her, but for vastly different reasons.

Chapter 15

Georgie sat opposite her husband, all alone on the velvet seat of his luxurious town carriage as they made their way home after the play.

It was not where she had planned to be, not where she wanted to be at all. She wanted to be beside her husband, with her hand in his, or perhaps with his arm about her waist and her head resting on his shoulder. She wanted to be putting into action her plan to seduce him. Instead of which, they sat apart. Cold and lonely.

She had tried every tactic to soothe away his angry mood. Not even her deliberately provocative teasing was enough to overcome her husband's coldness tonight. She stifled a sigh.

"Well, Gus, what did you think of the way the wicked Mr. Dorimant met his comeuppance at the hands of Harriet in Sir George Etherege's play? 'In men who have been long hardened in sin we have reason to mistrust the first signs of repentance,' Harriet said to him when Dorimant tried to protest that he truly loved her. . . . I was vastly amused by her wit. I believe I shall always consider her one of my heroines."

"You enjoyed the comedy, did you, Georgiana?" Sedge answered tightly. "I must confess, my mind was otherwise occupied. I'm afraid I took in little of the play tonight."

He was in the devil's own temper. The anger had been eating away at him all evening, ever since he had overheard those malicious gossipmongers accusing Georgie of the scandalous indiscretion of visiting Lyndhurst's lodgings.

He was furious at the gossipmongers. Furious at Mayhew. Furious at Lyndhurst. Furious at Georgie for being such an indiscreet little wretch . . . and, most of all, furious at himself for being so foolish as to marry her for in the first place.

All his plans to begin making love to her on the way home were overset, put paid to by the ugly rumor he had overheard. He well knew his heedless little imp was capable of the monumentally scandalous indiscretion of which she had been accused.

She was *capable* of indiscreet behavior, yes, but he also knew, deep down, that she was too innocent to actually have had any criminal connection with Lyndhurst. Georgie was still a virgin. He would swear to it.

Mayhew may well have seen her entering Lyndhurst's house, but there had to be an innocent reason behind her extremely imprudent visit, Sedge was certain.

Mayhew, he could deal with. He *would* deal with him.

However, he was too angry now to try to deal

with his wife, to find out what had prompted her to act so foolishly—so *typically* foolishly. No doubt she would consider her motives for her actions quite unexceptional and would wonder that anyone would find fault with her.

The situation put him forcibly in mind of his first meeting with her in the King's Head Inn where she had been in company with those two unsuitable farm laborers in the taproom. She would no doubt laugh at him now, as she had at the inn when he had pointed out her improper behavior in talking and laughing with the pair of yokels.

"Come, Gus. Whatever is the matter that you are snapping at me in that fashion? Is it something to do with Lady Carstairs?"

"What?" he replied, completely at sea. He hardly recollected Diana's presence at the theatre, although when he had first glimpsed her it had given him quite a jolt.

"You certainly looked as though you had seen a ghost, or something, when you acknowledged her in the corridor."

"I really don't recall what you are referring to, Georgiana." He had only the vaguest memory that he had indeed seen Diana at a distance and nodded to her. He had been standing stunned by what he had just overheard concerning Georgie, a cold fury freezing him to the marrow of his bones. It had been all it could do not to rush through the curtain and take the two gossipmongers by their throats and squeeze the life out of them. Through the red haze of his anger, he must have glimpsed Diana for a moment.

"I have invited her to our entertainment next week."

"What? Who? I have not the least idea what you are talking about, Georgiana."

"Lady Carstairs. I gather that you are very well acquainted with her. I promised I would invite all your friends, as well as my own, to our entertainment."

"Invited her to our entertainment? How came you to do such a thing? You have never met the lady ... have you?" he asked in confusion.

"Oh, yes, indeed, I met her tonight. Max introduced me when we went out for a breath of air before the last act."

"What! *Max* introduced you to Diana?" Sedge's thoughts were in turmoil. What had Georgie compelled Max to do? And what devilish piece of mischief was she up to now? He could not deal with one scandal without her creating two or three others right under his nose. Confound it all to hell, but he needed to get her out of London and home to Gloucestershire before they should find themselves a byword among the *ton* for outrageous behavior. They would provide enough scandalbroth to keep society amused for a twelfth month!

"Here we are, home so quickly," she exclaimed brightly, as the driver pulled the carriage up before the Brook Street house.

Damnation, he thought, curling his hands into fists. Here they were at home. And he had not even so much as *touched* Georgie during the ride, much less seduced her.

* * *

"Goodnight, Georgiana," Sedge said somewhat abruptly as they reached the second floor landing and prepared to part outside their separate bedrooms. He was favoring his leg, the events of the night weighing heavily on him.

"Goodnight, Gus. Oh ... I did want to mention that I appreciate your decision not to assume marital relations. I would not want to find myself with child before the season ends," she said clearly and deliberately. "I have more freedom this way."

"Freedom?" he exclaimed, thunderstruck. "Freedom to do what?" he shouted. "And what makes you think I do not plan to assume, ah, marital relations, madam wife? You may expect me in your bedchamber tonight." He stormed into his own room, a volley of curses issuing forth from behind his closed door.

Georgie smiled secretly, highly pleased at the success of her ploy.

She skipped into her bedroom, thankful that she did not as yet have an abigail to pester her with questions while she helped her undress. The presence of a servant would have been distinctly in the way at the moment.

Hopping on one foot and then the other, she quickly removed her shoes and stockings. She hurriedly stepped out of her gown and underthings, leaving them in an untidy pile on the floor, and drew her nightdress over her head.

Smiling with tingling anticipation, she doused the candles and slipped between the sheets of her bed. Her stomach was churning with excitement when she heard the door to her room open abruptly. She peeped over the bedclothes she had drawn up to her chin and smiled out into the darkened room.

As her husband neared the bed, Georgie could see that he did not return her smile.

Sedge was still seething from Georgie's remark. He entered her room almost immediately, without bothering to knock. Taunt him about not wanting to assume marital relations, would she? The devilish little wretch!

He had thought he was being considerate, had planned to ease into their "marital relations," slowly seducing her, introducing her to the delights of love-making in gradual stages. He would have done so earlier tonight, if events at the theatre had not intruded to overset his careful plans.

But no. Georgie evidently did not see it that way. She seemed to think him a slowtop, a backward boy, in waiting to claim his husbandly rights.

Well, she would learn that he was man enough to master her. Now. Tonight.

Images of Georgie emerging from her bath flashed through his mind. Desire pounded through him.

His breathing ragged, he quickly shrugged out of his dressing gown. Lifting the sheets, he joined her in bed, sliding right up next to her. Desperately, urgently wanting her, he lifted her nightgown without a word, pushed her legs apart, and positioned himself between her thighs.

His leg hurt like the very devil as he moved atop her. But another more urgent ache in his loins demanded to be assuaged. He took her with no preparation, felt the resistance of her maidenhead, but did not stop. He could not stop.

Georgie gave a startled squeak, then reached up and clasped his shoulders, holding him as he moved over her, biting her lips against the pain.

It was over in a minute. Collapsing over her with a suppressed groan, he was mortified at how quickly he had finished.

His leg was hurting but he thanked God he had managed to consummate the marriage before he noticed the pain. He breathed one sigh of relief, following by two or three others of distress and irritation at himself for his behavior—letting his raging desire overtake him, acting like an unfledged schoolboy at his first sexual encounter with a woman—letting Georgie's provoking comments spur him on to act like such an inexperienced stripling.

"Gus," she murmured softly, ruffling his hair with one hand, savoring the feel of his warm flesh under the other, soothing over the muscles of his shoulders, his back, his waist, down over his lean hips. "Gus."

He did not answer, suddenly ashamed at the way he had treated her, impersonally, with no preparation—as though she were a thing, simply a vessel for his pleasure. He had been more gentle, taken more care with Polly, his favorite mistress, than he had with his wife.

And he had just taken her virginity.

It had been so quick, almost impersonal, Georgie thought in disappointment. She had expected more after that afternoon in his dressing room and the tingling excitement of his stealthy play at the theatre. She had expected something absolutely earth shattering.

He had not even kissed her, or touched her at all—except there—with that part of himself.

It had been uncomfortable, and even painful at first. She had not expected that.

He was still joined with her, with all his weight resting on her. He was squashing her to a pulp, but she did not mind. She was his wife now indeed, she thought with a small, satisfied smile.

She noticed he was gritting his teeth. Oh, dear, his poor leg must be aching from his recent exertions.

"Your leg is paining you, is it not, Gus?" she asked in that same soft tone. "Is there not a way it—this, would be more comfortable for you?"

Comfortable for him? She was worried about *his* comfort when he had just treated her so abominably, used her so badly? Used her shamefully, with clumsy lust. His actions were indefensible, unworthy of him. This was his wife! What kind of gentleman was he to treat her so?

He would apologize. Hold her and apologize—kiss her awhile to make up for his unkindness.

"A different position would help, perhaps?" she whispered, not knowing if such a thing were possible.

"What!" How did she know about different positions? Only women of the demimonde knew about a variety of positions. Surely she did not mean something like that? "What on earth do you mean?"

"I—I do not know, Gus," she admitted in a small

voice. "I do not know anything about it—this," she amended.

He moved off her. "I hope that was not too uncomfortable for you," he offered grudgingly, knowing that he had hurt her.

"I was not prepared, did not expect . . ."

"Devil take it, Georgie, what did you expect?"

"Well, you are a bit *large,*" she murmured with the devastating candor that characterized her.

"Most women would not complain about that," he fired back as he raised up above her, displeased and upset by her criticism.

"Oh, now you are throwing your other women in my face, are you?" she said, her voice trembling with anger or tears or hurt, or all three.

"*No!* That is not what I meant at all! Oh, the hell with it!" he ground out, lifting himself off the bed with a stifled curse and limping out of the room. "Goodnight, Georgie," he called, finding his way in the dark to the door connecting with his dressing room.

He was ashamed, mortified by his actions. The calm, cool, rational behavior that characterized him had deserted him. He had been unnecessarily curt, almost brutal with Georgie. He had taken her virginity with no care for her. He knew he should apologize, should hold her and soothe her, but he was in such a state of emotional turmoil, he could not think straight, did not know what to do for the best. His masculine pride was at stake.

* * *

After Sedge left, Georgie rolled over onto her side with a sniff. It had not been what she had expected at all.

Gus had been so detached, dispassionate. It had been more a physical act and less the emotional encounter she had expected, had wanted. It had been a joining of two bodies, rather than two selves, two souls. She needed something more intimate and warm to feel completely satisfied.

All the excitement of that afternoon had completely disappeared. Perhaps he had only bedded her out of a sense of duty and felt no real desire for her at all, she thought, despite that wonderful embrace they had shared in his dressing room earlier and his delicious play at the theatre before the performance. Of course, it was to be expected that he would find her inexperienced, but she was afraid he had found her lacking in any physical appeal, too. Not beautiful enough for him. Not feminine enough.

Oh, do not be such a watering pot, my girl, she chided herself. Stifling her disappointment, she sat up in bed and reached for her handkerchief on the bedside table and blew her nose determinedly.

You are a woman. He is a man. And now you are truly his wife. Your gambit worked tonight, she congratulated herself. More of the same was called for, she decided with a determined glint in her eyes as she settled herself for sleep.

Well, she had married Gus, hoping for the best, knowing her reasons were pure.

Firstly, the happiness of Susan and Tom was at stake. Now that she was married to someone else, Tom would see that she could not marry him. He *must* turn to Susan. Georgie would do her best to see to it.

Secondly, there was unfinished business between Robin and Ann. Robin had had no business proposing to *her* when he was still in love with Ann. She swiped at her eyes and grinned suddenly. Well, it just went to show that Robin was ready to settle down and reform his wild ways. He was more than ready for the commitment of marriage if he had been desperate enough to propose to *her.*

Thirdly . . . well, thirdly, and most importantly, she had married Sedgemoor for a reason other than to smooth the way for the other two couples. That reason was something she preferred to hold secret in her heart for yet awhile.

"A word with you, Mayhew," Sedge drawled, sauntering up to the man where he sat with a group of his cronies in a corner of White's, regaling them with the latest gossip.

Mayhew turned an interesting shade of purple when he recognized the viscount looming over him. "Not now, Sedgemoor," he blustered. "Can't you see I'm engaged with my friends?"

"No, I see no one," Sedgemoor said disdainfully, lifting his quizzing glass to gaze over the motley collection of riff-raff and hangers-on, fops and fribbles, court cards, and jumped-up mushrooms who were gathered around Mayhew.

Mayhew got stiffly to his feet. "Don't know what can be so urgent," he mumbled.

"I am about to inform you. In private. Come with me," Sedge commanded.

Mayhew preceded the viscount out of the large, open gathering room.

"Well, Mayhew!" Sedge said in a voice as cold and hard as steel as he closed the door to the unoccupied private dining chamber. "What is your excuse for spreading damnable lies about my wife!" He fixed Mayhew with a glare full of deadly menace.

"I don't know what you're talking about."

Sedgemoor walked over to the cowering man, reached out and grabbed him by the collar, pressing him up against the wall. "You damn well *do* know what I'm talking about. You have been busy, haven't you, you bloody little viper, reporting all over town that you saw my wife coming from the rooms of a certain infamous bachelor. It's a damn lie, Mayhew! And now you're going to tell everyone it's a bloody damn lie!"

He shook Mayhew once. Hard.

"But, my lord, I did see her—"

The viscount raised his fist and tightened his hold on Mayhew's collar. By God, but he wanted to kill the bastard.

"No, Mayhew," Sedgemoor spoke from between his teeth. "You did not. You mistook *someone else* for Lady Sedgemoor. Do you understand? Or will you force me to kill you?"

Mayhew's complexion went bright red, then purple. "You're choking me, my lord," he managed to gasp out.

Sedgemoor loosened his grip a fraction. "Well?"

"You are quite right, my lord," Mayhew answered

in a shaking voice, sweat pouring from his brow. "I mistook the woman. A taller woman, it was. A brunette. Don't know how I came to make such a damnable mistake. I have not seen Geor—your wife in quite some time, my lord. My most abject apologies, my lord, to you and to Lady Sedgemoor."

"You will tell the world of your 'damnable mistake,' starting with those toads out there when I leave this room, do you understand? I expect this matter to be cleared up before nightfall. I do not think either of us wishes to renew this delightful conversation on the morrow, is that not right, Mayhew?"

"Y-yes, my lord. As you say, my lord. I made a terrible error. Will tell everyone. Never intended to cause her ladyship any harm."

"You will never mention her name again after today, understood?"

"Of course not, my lord. I wouldn't dream of it. You have my word on it."

"Good. This will help you to remember your promise, your word as a man of *honor*," Sedge said sarcastically, drawing back his fist and sending it crashing into Mayhew's face.

The viscount did not wait to see his adversary hit the wall behind him and slowly sag down, collapsing on the floor.

Sedgemoor had already left the room. He had another pressing call to make.

"But, my lord, my master ain't at home," Samuels, Lord Robert's man, tried to block the viscount's entrance to his master's house in Chandler Street, but

Sedgemoor had got his foot wedged in the door and thrust forward with all his weight. He was inside within a few seconds.

"I believe you will find that you are mistaken. Call Lyndhurst. Now."

"No need to call me. Behold me at your service," Lord Robert said from the top of the staircase that led to his first floor bedroom. "You must not blame Samuels, Sedgemoor. I neglected to inform him that I had returned home not long ago."

Sedgemoor saw that Lyndhurst still sported the evidence of the blow he had delivered three days previously. There was a purple bruise under his bloodshot eye and over the top of his nose, while the top of his cheekbone was yellow and swollen still.

"Come into my library, Sedgemoor, such as it is," Robin invited easily, his hands in his pockets as he walked casually down the stairs to join the viscount in the entryway. "I assume you wish a few moments of my time?"

"How prescient of you, Lyndhurst. I am all admiration."

Tension crackled between them, electrifying the air.

Robin gave a half smile and opened the door to the same small room where he had received Georgie on the previous day. He invited the viscount to precede him into the room, then closed the door behind them, leaning his shoulders against it as he stared across at his glowering visitor.

"You know why I am here?" the viscount said.

"At a wild guess, something to do with Georgie—ah, Lady Sedgemoor, that is?"

"Right again, Lyndhurst."

"You look as though you are going to slap a glove in my face at any moment, Sedgemoor. Can you relieve my suspense and tell me why you are wearing that warlike aspect?"

"Cut line, Lyndhurst. You know it's all over town that Georgie called here yesterday and was inside this house for the best part of an hour?"

"No. Georgie never called here. Who is saying that she did?" Robin asked, his eyes narrowed dangerously.

"Mayhew."

"The damned mawworm is a bold-faced liar. It never happened. If you haven't called him out, Sedgemoor, I will."

"That would serve no good purpose. Georgiana's reputation would suffer even further, were you to do such a thing."

"I daresay you are right, old man."

They stared at one another assessingly for a moment, each looking as dangerous and forbidding as the other.

"You are saying she did not come here?" Sedgemoor demanded harshly, a steely glint in his eyes piercing his opponent.

"Disbelieve me, if you will. Go ahead, issue the challenge that is hovering on your lips, Sedgemoor. Is it to be swords or pistols at dawn? You would do well not to underestimate me. I believe I am your equal with a smallsword, and I spend as much time shooting wafers at Manton's as the next man. Shall we take our chances on the field of honor?" Robin folded his arms over his chest and gave the viscount back glare for glare.

Sedgemoor wavered. Could he believe Lyndhurst? Or, more to the point, could he assume that Lord Robert would continue to deny Georgie's indiscretion and defend her honor. Would it not be better for Georgie's reputation, if he could be certain that Lyndhurst would keep his mouth shut?

"My wife's honor is at stake."

"Your wife's honor is precious to me, too."

"By God, Lyndhurst, how dare you say so!" Sedgemoor raised his fists and stepped nearer.

Not intimidated by Sedgemoor's bloodthirsty threats, Lord Robert lifted his hands, curled into fists, and assumed a wide stance. "Try to hit me again, if you can, Sedgemoor. You will not take me by surprise this time. I daresay that flawless mug of yours will take some punishment, too." He actually grinned at the viscount.

Breathing heavily, Sedge imposed an iron calm on his temper and stepped back, his chin still jutting out threateningly. "I know Georgiana came here for what she thought was a good reason. She is imprudent enough to—Let me have the truth with the bark off, Lyndhurst, so that I may know what to do for the best to protect Georgie."

Robin sighed and moved to the sideboard to pour them both a glass of brandy. "Look, Sedgemoor, Georgie delivered a note to my door, informing me of her marriage to you. I never saw her. . . . It was quite a shock when my man gave me the news."

"If that were all, she could have sent a servant with the message."

Robin handed him a glass. "You know Georgie, Sedgemoor. She doesn't think about what people will say of her, she just does whatever pops into her head on the spur of the moment. She's such a kind-hearted little thing, and she felt she owed me the courtesy of a word or two. I *had* asked her to marry me, and you interrupted us that night before she could give me her answer. My man denied her seeing me, of course. I do not receive respectable females at my door for all the world to see," Robin insisted, not so much as moving a muscle as he looked the viscount straight in the eye.

Sedgemoor narrowed his eyes and stared hard at his opponent for a moment or two, before taking a deep breath and saying, "What I do not understand is why you proposed to her in the first place."

"Well, you see, Sedgemoor . . .," Robin curled his hand and looked down at his fingernails for a long moment before lifting his battered face to answer Georgie's husband, "I happen to love her."

"You love *Georgie?*"

"Yes. why else would I ask her to marry me? Do you?"

"That's none of your damned concern, Lyndhurst." Sedge answered coldly, his jaw hardening.

"No, but if I ever find that she is unhappy with you, I might make it my concern," Robin returned pugnaciously. He was no coward to be frightened or intimidated by Sedgemoor. They were equals. Each formidable in his own right.

"Indeed! Then I recommend that you continue to frequent Manton's Shooting Gallery to perfect your aim with a pistol and Angelo's Room in the Haymarket to practice your fencing skills. For if you should ever decide to interfere with my wife, you can be sure that you *will* find a glove slapped in your face."

"Sedgemoor," Robin said, his glinting smile radiating a threat of his own, "I believe you will take good care that it never comes to that." Then seeing the fury in the viscount's eyes, he laughed shortly. "Why, I do believe you are head over heels for her. . . . Well, that should come as no surprise. No man could live with Georgie and not love her to distraction. I'm convinced of that. She is such an irresistibly charming little piece of mischief, one can not help but love her!"

The viscount did not answer. His feelings for Georgie were private. He did not fully understand them himself, but he knew that whatever it was he felt for her, he could not tolerate another man near her.

Lyndhurst seemed to have a genuine care for her. Deciding that even if Lyndhurst were lying to him about whether Georgie had actually entered the house, he could trust the man to uphold Georgie's honor.

Sedgemoor lifted his glass and took a sip of the brandy, assessing his rival over the rim of his glass.

Lord Robert did the same.

Grudgingly satisfied with the interview, the viscount took his leave.

Chapter 16

"Oh, Gus, you are finally home. How happy I am! I have just been wanting you to—wanting to discuss a few things with you about our entertainment—," Georgie began in an excited voice, bursting in on her husband as he sat in his study that afternoon, glancing through a newspaper.

"May I ask, madam wife, why you went to see Lyndhurst yesterday?" Sedge asked without preamble.

She was looking as cheerful as all bedamned, he noted irritably, but without surprise. With her bright smile lighting up her face and her blue eyes twinkling at him, she looked very happy, indeed almost overjoyed, to see him.

It was the first time they had met since he had left her room the previous night.

After he had left Lyndhurst, he had met Max and Henry for a late luncheon at Offley's, the hotel in Henrietta Street, Covent Garden, where members of the sporting fraternity often gathered. He had enjoyed a rare beefsteak, one of the establishment's specialties, and quenched some of his leftover ire in several pints of the excellent ale served there. Now he felt calm enough to confront his wife about her improper behavior.

"Oh!" She put a hand up to her cheek. "You found out!"

Throwing his paper down, Sedge got up from his chair and walked up to her.

"Georgiana, the whole town has found out," he ground out, all his newfound calm completely deserting him.

"What! No! How in the world! Oh dear!"

" 'Oh dear!' is not the half of it. Someone saw you and spread the juicy scandal."

"Oh!"

" 'Oh!' Is that all you can say, madam? You make a laughingstock of yourself, of me, and all you can say is 'oh!'?"

"Well, you see, Gus, I—"

"Devil take it, Georgie, you little fool, what did you think you were about, calling alone at a man's lodgings like that?"

"Well, I just had to see Robin for a few minutes to explain that I could not marry him—that I had married *you* instead," she replied ingenuously.

Unable to stop himself, Sedge reached out and took her by the shoulders, gripping her hard. "Deuce take it, woman, did you think to make a cuckold of me?"

"Oh no, Gus. Never." She looked up at him solemnly, contrition writ large in her wide blue eyes.

She looked about ten years old, he thought, disconcerted. Some of his anger dissipated.

"People will say so, if you go calling on other men."

"I shall not do it again, I promise . . . unless it is absolutely necessary."

"Devil take it, Georgie!" he thundered, giving her shoulders a little shake. "You will *not* go to another man's establishment under *any* circumstances. Ever. Is that understood?"

"Oh, do not get angry, Gus . . . I will ask you to take me, if it's necessary," she said brightly, thinking he could find no fault with this compromise.

"Georgie, Georgie," he groaned, closing his eyes. Letting go of her shoulders, he lifted one hand to cover his eyes, rubbing his aching temples with his thumb and forefinger. "Whatever am I to do with you?"

Seeing his distress, she stood up on tiptoe and kissed his cheek softly, resting her hands against his chest. "Well, Gus, I have an idea."

He lifted a brow and looked down at her inquiringly, determined not to let her put him to the blush. She was so innocent, she undoubtedly did not know what she was implying.

"You can play chess with me."

"Play chess? Why?"

"I want to best you again at *something.*"

"Have I bested you at everything, then?"

"Well . . . in some things," she said archly, seeing that she had succeeded in charming him out of his bad mood.

"It does not seem that way to me—why are we still in London, if so? In any case, I find it very doubtful that you will beat me again."

"I will certainly try. . . . Please."

"Hmm. You think to turn me up sweet. What mischief are you plotting now?"

"Nothing. Only I want you in a good mood for our entertainment." She stepped closer still and played with the folds of his neckcloth, creasing his valet's careful arrangement.

"I will be in a good mood. You have promised we can leave for the Oaks, once the blasted thing is over."

She looked up at him, her blue eyes twinkling provocatively.

His arms circled her waist comfortably and he lowered his head to kiss her.

The butler entered the room to announce the arrival of Miss Susan Tennyson.

"Hell's teeth!" Sedge muttered under his breath, wishing for the hundredth time that Georgie had agreed to go into the country with him. Home to the Oaks, where he could keep her under his eye, where she could not get up to mischief, where they would not have a hectic round of social activities to distract them.

Home, where they would not be constantly interrupted . . . where they would be alone.

Georgie cancelled her plans to go with Susan and Mrs. Tennyson and Tom to a musicale that evening. Tom was to have been her escort to the entertainment, but when she had sent him word of her recent marriage, she had cancelled all their prearranged social engagements at the same time. Susan had told her that afternoon that Tom was still in the boughs over Georgie's sudden marriage.

"All the better that he is, Sukey, dear. You can soothe his poor broken heart—not that I think for a moment there is even the tinest crack in his heart. He was more in love with my acres than he ever was with me."

Susan had sighed and said that she would *try* to comfort him, but she did not know if he would accept her solicitude.

"Oh, he will accept it, my dear, never you fear. He is a man whose confidence in his own worth has been dented ever so slightly. His vanity is wounded, not his heart. If you sympathize with him, letting him know you think he is wonderful, he will turn to you in a minute."

Susan had looked doubtful, but had gone away with Georgie's advice and encouragement ringing in her ears, persuaded to try to flirt with her old childhood friend without making herself foolish in the attempt.

Instead of accepting one of her other invitations, Georgie elected to stay at home with her husband, intending to coax him into playing chess with her again. She had a new gambit she wished to try.

They had a quiet dinner, during which all Sedge's residual anger and irritation at Georgie's most recent indiscretion subsided.

Feeling more relaxed than he had in days, he teased and joked with his viscountess during their meal.

"Oh, Gus, I do like the pattern on this china service," she told him at one point. "It reminds of a Chinese vase that I had in my bedroom at Chitterne St. Mary's."

It amused him that she was still inclined to exclaim over every little thing that caught her attention, from the silver to the china to the paintings on the wall to the serving's maid cough, for which she recommended a mixture of honey and Scotch whiskey, advising the girl to take a glass full every hour.

Sedgemoor laughed at her and poured her more champagne. "I think it should be a *tablespoon* full, not a glass full, my dear. If the poor girl takes a glass full of whiskey every hour, she will be dead to the world in a very short amount of time."

"Well, perhaps when she wakes again after a good night's rest, her cough will be gone," Georgie replied artlessly, her blue eyes twinkling at him.

Remembering Georgie's wish at Little Bickton that she would like to drink champagne every night when she was in London, Sedge had directed his butler to bring up several bottles of the bubbly wine.

She had insisted on sitting to his right, instead of at the end of the table where she was entitled to take her place as the mistress of his establishment. And now as she sat at his elbow, drinking yet another glass of champagne, she was beginning to get a little bosky.

Sedge encouraged her, enjoying her merry high spirits, and not realizing that he was drinking two or three glasses to every one she had.

"Have I told you that I have decided to make our entertainment a masquerade?" she asked, smiling at him sweetly.

"Have you?" He sat up more stiffly in his chair.

"Yes. I think everyone will enjoy the chance to dress up like some historical or fanciful character. I know I shall."

"I had envisioned nothing quite so—so risque." He waved his hand airily. "I had thought something, ah, quiet and dignified, perhaps, for our first party?"

"Oh, nothing stuffy or formal will do for me, you know, Gus. I'm afraid I am not a formal kind of person, as you should know very well by now." She reached over and covered his hand with hers and looked right into his eyes, a smile lurking in hers. "You are the distinguished, *dignified* partner in this marriage."

"Hmm. You mean you are not prepared to put on a stiff, stately gown embroidered with heavy golden threads and encrusted with jewels, weighing you down to the floor, and preside over the solemn, dignified at-home I had envisioned? Where we would stand quietly, nodding loftily, extending our gloved hands briefly to each person who passed through the receiving line?" he asked, one brow lifted quizzically. "I am surprised at you, my dear Viscountess Sedgemoor!" he said, a light gleaming in his eyes as he gazed at her.

"Oh, you are roasting me, Gus!" Georgie laughed merrily, her blue eyes crinkling up at him.

A lazy smile curved his lips as he lifted his glass and sipped at his champagne.

Realizing vaguely that they had been sitting at the dinner table for over two hours, he arose to accompany Georgie when she decided it was time to retire to the drawing room.

"With your permission, lady wife, I shall take my

brandy with you instead of sitting here in lonely state."

"Oh, good. And you will play chess with me, too?" she asked, resting both her hands on his arm and leaning against him as he escorted her from the room.

"If you wish. But it is quite late. I do not know where the time has flown away to this evening. . . . May I suggest that we retire to your sitting room rather than the drawing room? I have a chess set in my room. I shall fetch it."

"Oh, yes! That will be lovely."

"Be warned, Georgie. I do not intend to lose to you again."

"We shall see about that, my lord husband," she teased, arguing lightly with him over the best tactics to employ in the game while they walked upstairs together and went to his room to locate his chess set. When they reached her sitting room, she watched somewhat groggily, but happily, while he set up the board and arranged the opposing chess pieces.

Georgie chose white and moved first. She bit her lip in concentration while they played, trying to outmaneuver Sedgemoor and get him to fall into her clever trap. But her strategy failed.

Sedgemoor took her king with his remaining knight.

"How in the world did you manage that, Gus?" she asked, looking down with a puzzled expression at the configuration of pieces still on the board.

"Skill and forethought, my dear." Seeing the look of consternation on her piquant little face, he reached out and flicked her soft cheek with a long finger.

When she looked up, he grinned lopsidedly. "That, and you have had too much champagne and were too ambitious. You signaled your plan to me from your opening move. Though, I grant you, a less experienced player may well have fallen for your clever ruse."

"Oh, how odiously superior you sound, my lord Sedgemoor."

"Aim straight for the heart of the enemy's strength. You may be wounded in the process, lose some of your pieces, but they can be spared, if you are truly prepared to risk all in order to win the game."

"Well, that sounds a warlike strategy, indeed. . . . Another game?"

"Yes, and to make it more interesting, let us agree to play for stakes."

"Oh, yes! That will be fun. What do you propose?"

They were sitting opposite one another at a small Sheraton card table. Moving his chair nearer the table, he pressed his knee against hers under the table.

"Hmm." He looked at her mouth, noting the fullness of her lips, the soft curve of her freckled cheek, the deep blue of her eyes and the rich red of her hair framing her animated face. Remembering again his voluptuous Venus rising from her bath, his body blazed into flame.

It was on the tip of his tongue to demand a kiss if he won—a kiss that would lead to other delights. But retaining some hold on sanity, and remembering that he must tame his little wretch soon, or she would continue to lead him a most uncomfortable dance, he said instead, "If I win, I want a promise from you, Georgiana."

She looked at him almost pleadingly. "Oh, Gus,

when you call me *Georgiana* in that stiff, arrogant way, I know you are not pleased with me. Now what have I done?"

"It is not what you have done, but rather what you might do in the future."

She sighed when she saw the sober look on his face. Excitement had begun to churn in her and she had been hoping he was going to propose something suitably exciting, like the loser kissing the winner silly. Instead he was going to lecture her, she saw with disappointment. "What is it you wish me to promise."

"That you will behave with the utmost propriety in future. Remember, you are my viscountess now. You must act according to your station."

"You may as well wish for the moon, Gus! As I told you before we were married, I am not a very proper person. I cannot remember all the rigid rules and codes of behavior you seem to think proper. I could not abide to be so hedged about. Why, I would—I would likely burst!" she exclaimed, jumping to her feet and throwing her arms wide.

"Calm yourself, my dear. You are too emotional."

"Yes, I am emotional. And if I win this match, I want a promise from you, my lord husband."

Watching her warily, his eyes bored into hers. "And what is that, my dear?" he asked, his fingers tightening on his chair arm.

He wanted her, but on his own terms. He had intended to seduce her tonight *before* he began bending her to his will, but his cursed impatience had forestalled that move. He was weary, still feeling upset, angry with her over the Lyndhurst incident, and had likely had too much champagne to think clearly. He was wary of hurting her again, afraid he had given her a distaste for him.

She lifted her chin and said, "You will not be offended with me, continually taking me to task for all my faults. Agreed?"

"I do not—"

"You do. You knew you would have to take me with all my faults and imperfections. Just as I have taken you with your precious dignity and uncertain temper and endless lectures."

Oh, the evening was not going at all as she had planned it, Georgie thought, wanting to bite her ungoverned tongue. She had planned to seduce him into making love to her again, but she was still feeling delicate and unsure of herself after last night's encounter. Rejection would hurt.

Watching her carefully, Sedge saw the hurt look on her face and heard the note of pain in her voice.

"Oh, good God, I never meant to hurt you, Georgie," he cried, jumping up from his chair and folding her in his arms and rocking her, his hand coming up to press her head against his shoulder.

"Oh, Gus, just kiss me." She lifted her face for his kiss and when their mouths met, a dam broke, unleashing a rush of desire. Heat rose between them, cresting and spilling over, filling them with an aching hunger.

Georgie wound her arms about her husband's neck at the same time that he lifted her off her feet, up against him, wrapping his arms about her, crushing her to him, wanting to take her into himself.

His tongue pushed against her yielding lips, meeting moist welcoming warmth within.

This time she was ready and waiting to receive him, her tongue meeting his in a dance of desire, nipping, tasting, devouring him, as he was doing her. They could not get enough of one another.

"Oh, Gus, please!"

"Yes, Georgie, yes," he murmured against the hollow of her neck, his breath coming short.

Letting her slide down his body to touch the floor, he tugged the bodice of her gown down to her waist, freeing her breasts.

Helping him, she shrugged the material off her shoulders.

His hands were on her breasts, lifting them, caressing them, all the while his tongue was pushing between her lips rhythmically, promising other delights.

Pulling away his jacket and his neckcloth, she opened his shirt at the neck. He helped her push the shirt up over his head to land in a heap on the floor.

Running the palms of her hands over the hard muscles of his shoulders and arms, she twined her fingers in the hairs of his chest, following the rough texture down over his flat stomach as it trailed off into the waistband of his pantaloons.

"God! Georgie!"

Half carrying her to the long chaise longue set against one wall, he collapsed on it with her.

"So lovely, so sweet, let me kiss you, let me love you," he rasped, touching her breast with his lips, tasting, devouring her, his fingers stroking her thigh in a swirling motion, reaching ever higher.

"Oh heavens, Gus! I did not know men did such things to women."

He lifted his head and gave a husky laugh. "Funny little love!"

"No, no, do not stop. I like it. But it makes me feel so strange. I can't breathe properly and I think my legs have gone all wobbly, and oh dear, there is something funny happening in my stomach."

She did say the funniest things, he thought with a rumbling laugh against her stomach as he went back to work pleasuring her, pleasuring himself.

"Oh I—Gus! I feel so—Oh, please—do something to take away this ache. I can't bear it. Oh, what is it?"

Ridding himself of his pantaloons, he dragged her gown and underthings back up and off over her head. She arched into him, all warm and soft and alluring woman.

"Dear Lord, woman!" He was at the limit of his control, but he gritted his teeth, vowing not to behave as he had done the previous night. Lying side by side as they were, he did not think he could manage with his still stiff leg to balance his weight over her on the narrow chaise. Reaching for her hips, he lifted her so that she was astride him.

"Gus! What are you doing? Is this not all wrong?"

"No, no. It is just as good this way, you will see."

And soon she did see, as he made love to her slowly, lovingly, putting her pleasure above his own.

"Go carefully," he told himself. "Do not hurt her. Make it good for her." Holding his breath, he watched in the flickering candlelight as he carefully joined them. He pulled out again slowly, to plunge in

again just as slowly. She moved down on him and he
was completely inside her. He began to move faster,
reach deeper, taking them to the ultimate pleasure.

"Oh! Oh, yes. This is—is ... oh ... *Gus!*" she
wailed.

He released his breath in a woosh, calling out her
name. "Ahh, *Georgie,* my love!"

His love? No. She *couldn't* be that.

He had never loved a woman. . . .

God! His love.

Her head rested in the crook of his neck and shoulder. Closing his eyes, he turned his face toward her
and buried his lips in her hair. "Georgie," he whispered, swallowing awkwardly against the unfamiliar
emotion tightening his throat.

"Umm, that was lovely, Gus," she murmured
dreamily.

They lay warmly and snugly together for several
long minutes while Georgie murmured soft endear-
ments and expressions of her pleasure into Sedge's
ear. A last soft sigh of contentment faded away and
Sedge realized she had drifted off to sleep. Reluctantly but carefully, he disentangled himself and carried her through into her bedchamber. She was light
as a feather, despite her generous curves. He cradled
her to him, cherishing her as he carried her. Although
she roused enough to murmur an endearment against
his neck and rest her lips there warmly for several
moments, he managed to put her to bed without waking her completely.

Brushing a final kiss on her soft hair as he drew

the bedclothes up to her chin, he collected his clothing and limped through to his own room. Though she was not a heavy burden, he had taxed his leg carrying her.

Wearily he collapsed onto his own bed. Resting his arm over his forehead, he tried to sort out his confused feelings. He had never loved a woman before. Enjoyed them, yes. Pleasured them. Even liked one or two.

Was he in love with Georgie? He did not know. She was his wife. He bore her some affection. He desired her. Did not think he could stay away from her now.

But love?

Loving Georgie would be foolhardy, perilous even. It would leave him vulnerable. Could he risk the hurt, if she did not love him back?

He did not know what the devil he felt.

He lay awake long, pondering the question, trying to understand his own emotions and wondering what difficulties lay ahead.

Chapter 17

Arising with the sun the following morning, Georgie hopped out of bed to find herself completely naked.

"Oh!" she put a hand up to her mouth and hopped back into bed, laughing with pure delight, realizing that Gus must have put her to bed after their joyous lovemaking in her dressing room.

"Oh dear. What a pickle!" she said aloud, thinking that it would be very awkward to ring for one of the house servants to bring her her morning chocolate and lay out her clothes, as she had done the previous two days when she had been decently clad in her nightgown. "I really shall have to do something about hiring a proper lady's maid soon."

She leaned back against her mound of pillows, cushioning her head on her arms behind her, and smiled at nothing at all in particular.

Their lovemaking last night had been all that she could ever have imagined, ever have wanted! ... More even. It had been ... earth shattering.

She luxuriated in the feeling that she was desired

by her husband. Vividly recalling the feel of his strong body loving hers, she blushed. She had had no idea really. It had been so different from the first time when he had been quick and impersonal, when he had not even kissed her.

She smiled. Her gambit had worked. Beyond her wildest dreams. "Georgie, my girl," she said to herself, "you really must take more care in future what you are about when you decide to make one of these bold moves."

He was going to make a more than satisfactory lover . . . a more than satisfactory *husband!*

Oh, but she did love him so.

Love him?

Did she really?

Yes, her mind said. Yes, her body concurred, delicious warmth coursing through her womb at the thought of him. The vague soreness she felt in her breasts, between her thighs, the slight swelling of her lips, was a small price to pay for the great pleasure he had given her.

Did she really, *really* love him?

Yes, her heart cried.

Filled with joy and boundless energy, she jumped out of bed, pulling a sheet with her and twirled around, doing a little dance. She loved him so much, she thought she would burst with it.

He was almost perfect . . . almost all she could desire in a man. An innate strength of character emanated from him, despite the languid manner he sometimes adopted. He was decent, honorable, generous. And she did not mind the quite beautiful package, both of face and form, that housed all that masculine perfection, either!

Well, he *would* be all she could desire in a man, she laughed with a determined gleam in her eyes, once she taught him to treat her as an equal, not as a young girl to do his every bidding, bending her knee to him, meekly obeying his every command— once she had completely eradicated that streak of stubborn arrogance that was still evident on occasion, and checked his unhappy tendency to lecture her as though she were a child.

He would have to learn that he could not change her unreserved, sociable personality. She would never become a quiet little mouse of a viscountess, never putting a foot wrong.

Yes, he would be a more than satisfactory husband . . . once she made him love her as much as she loved him.

"Good morrow, to you, Mr. Stillman. Is it not a lovely day! I'm starved," Georgie proclaimed, coming into the breakfast room to find the butler just bringing in a pot of coffee and a rack of toast. She had dressed herself in haste and danced downstairs in high good spirits.

"Oh, that looks lovely, thank you, Mr. Stillman. I wish to take Rufus out for a walk in the park as soon as may be. Please tell Eugene to have him ready to go in half an hour."

"As you wish, your ladyship," the butler replied.

"Is the viscount up yet?"

"No, my lady, he's still abed."

"Oh." An unholy grin crossed Georgie's face. "Thank you, Mr. Stillman."

Dashing out of the room as quickly as she had come in, Georgie ran up the stairs to her husband's room.

A smile twitched at Stillman's mouth, quite transforming his habitually dour expression. He was the last of Sedgemoor's servants to hold out against the new viscountess's charm, having given it as his opinion that she was an untamed hoyden, getting above her station. But he was in more danger of succumbing than he knew.

"Gus," Georgie whispered, poking her head in his door to see that his room was still in darkness.

Smiling, she tiptoed into the room, up to the bed, thinking to wake him with a kiss. Thinking possibly to join him in the wide bed.

She stopped when she reached his bedside. He was asleep. His golden hair, tousled boyishly, was spread out over his pillow, and his features, relaxed in sleep, had lost their usual austere aspect. He looked younger, more vulnerable.

Her smile changed from one of humor to one of tenderness. He looked too peaceful to disturb. She bent over carefully and just brushed the top of his head with her lips, then quietly tiptoed out.

When Sedge descended the stairs to the breakfast room some hour and a half later and asked for his wife, he was informed that Lady Sedgemoor had gone out to take her dog for a walk in the park, accompanied by Eugene, the underfootman.

Still unsettled about his feelings toward her, but for some unaccountable reason wishing to set eyes on Georgie again as soon as could be, Sedge did not pause for even so much as a cup of coffee before he headed out to the mews to have his hack saddled.

More thankful than he could say that he could get his leg over a horse's back at last, he mounted his horse and headed for the park, intending to intercept Georgie. Perhaps he would swing her up before him on the saddle for the ride back to Brook Street, he thought with a wicked gleam in his eyes.

He had ridden halfway through the park when he spotted Rufus running off his lead, chasing a smaller dog with Eugene chasing after Rufus. His lips tightened. It was a minor point, but he did not want Georgie's animal causing trouble. He would tell her she would have to be more careful when she took the dog out in future.

Now, if they had been at the Oaks, it would not have mattered a scrap if the animal ran wild over his whole estate, he thought with a spurt of irritation.

He looked away from the chaotic chase and scanned the park for Georgie. He saw her immediately.

She was standing on an open piece of ground near the Serpentine—with Lyndhurst.

Through a red haze, he watched as the rogue lifted her hand and pressed it to his lips.

She was smiling and chattering happily, accepting Lyndhurst's attentions for her husband and all the world to see.

"Bloody hell!" he cursed through stiff lips. Overcome with an odd feeling, as though all the blood had drained from his head, he swayed giddily on his horse's back, grabbing the animal's mane to steady himself. He closed his eyes and lowered his head for a moment to regain his equilibrium.

Then, cursing violently, he kicked his horse and they charged over the remaining distance to where Georgie was conducting her scandalous flirtation.

He pulled up near the pair, leapt off his horse, starting forward toward them with murder in his eyes.

"What the devil do you think you are doing here with my wife, Lyndhurst?" he demanded.

Seeing the light of battle in her husband's eyes, Georgie threw herself against his chest, winding her arms tightly round his waist to prevent him from taking her companion by the throat.

"Gus!" she cried. "Gus! It's not what you think. Listen to me, my dear, before you do something foolish."

He lifted his hands to her shoulders to put her away from him, but Lyndhurst's amused remark stopped him.

"Sedgemoor. You look like a knight of old, riding to rescue his fair damsel in distress," Lord Robert said by way of greeting. Seeing the ferocious look of fury on the viscount's face, he added, "I hope you do not plan to knock me to the ground so that we may roll about in all this dirt. That would be most detrimental to my tailoring. I had this jacket from Weston only a sennight ago."

"Gus, Gus. I had no idea Robin would be riding here at this hour. It was pure coincidence," Georgie said urgently to her husband. "When I waved to him, he did not want to stop and speak to me, saying you would not quite like it. But I told him not to be so foolish. Such a nonsensical thing, not to be able to speak to me because I am married now. I was inviting him to our masquerade next week, but he does not believe you would approve. I told him that was absurd, but he will not hear of accepting until you have been consulted."

She was looking up at him coaxingly, trying to look seductive, but only succeeding in looking outrageously youthful and utterly adorable instead, Sedge thought, unwillingly distracted from his just anger.

Vastly amused at the way Georgie was grasping her husband by the collar and speaking earnestly up into his face, and at the way she was leaning against him most improperly in public, Robin said, "I told Lady Sedgemoor I believed it would be politic to consult your wishes in this matter first, Sedgemoor, before I responded to her kind invitation."

"Gus," Georgie whispered in her husband's ear, "Please do not forbid Robin to come. I have hopes, made plans ... you know, with regard to Ann Forester. She would be perfect for him. And he loves her, I am certain of it."

Robin hid his smile at the way the viscount's face softened as he bent his head slightly to catch what Georgie was saying. It was as good as a play, he thought, with only a little ache tugging at his heart to see that they had indeed made a love match, and that there had never been a chance for him at all.

Georgie's pleading tone softened the viscount's anger.

Feeling somewhat foolish for showing his jealousy so openly, but not entirely convinced of the innocence of the meeting, Sedge replied with ill-concealed hostility, "My wife has issued the invitation. You may feel free to respond as you wish, Lyndhurst. . . . One word of warning, however. I expect you to toe the line in my house, and not just in respect to Georgie. I will not have any females offended by your conduct while you are under my roof."

Torn by feelings of affection for Georgie and insult at the viscount's tone, Robin responded belligerently, "Do you think to order me, Sedgemoor—"

Georgie intervened hastily. "Oh, Robin, you will come, won't you? I shall convince Gus that you are a model of propriety these days." Still holding to her husband, she gave Lord Robert a conspiratorial smile, turning her head to look at him over her shoulder.

Chewing on a grin, Robin said that he would look in for a brief while, adding outrageously that he should be able to hold his lecherous inclinations in check for a suitably short period of time. "I shall not turn *your* house into a den of iniquity, my dear Viscountess Sedgemoor."

With that Parthian shot, he sauntered away to his horse, that was tied to a nearby bush.

Sedge watched through narrowed eyes while his rival rode off. He was not happy. It had not been pleasant to see his wife for the first time since their lovemaking of the previous night engaged in conversation with Lyndhurst, of all people.

* * *

After the incident, Georgie and Sedge went their separate ways. The viscount felt wary of his wife, his feelings toward her more confused than ever.

Deciding he needed to take a long ride to shake off his still simmering anger, Sedge rode off alone, leaving Georgie to walk back home with her dog and the footman.

They did not see one another again until the evening when he was to take her to a gala night at Vauxhall Gardens where they were engaged to meet a party of friends.

The viscount dined alone. Georgie had decided to skip dinner, since they were to have one of the famous Vauxhall suppers in their box when they reached the Gardens.

She was looking forward to seeing the fascinating Gardens for the first time on her husband's arm, and longed to try all the unique, outrageously expensive treats she had heard about, tiny chickens no larger than pigeons and tongue and shavings of ham said to be so thin they were transparent, and fruits and biscuits and assorted cheesecakes—and especially the sweet, fruity arrack punch.

When she was dressed in a long-sleeved gown of pale yellow lustring, a warmer garment than she would have worn for an indoor entertainment, Georgie smiled at herself in the looking glass, deciding she would persuade Gus to take her for a stroll down one of the shadowy lovers' lanes that crisscrossed the park after they finished their supper. The narrow, notorious Dark Walk had long been known as a favorite spot for lovers' trysts. She would express her longing to see it and convince him to stroll with her there. She shivered with delight at the expectation of a daring, passionate interlude.

Yes, she would have a lovers' tryst of her very own before the night was over, both there, and here in her room—or his—when they returned home. She couldn't wait.

Sedge was edgy. All day he had been fighting the urge to go to Georgie and take her in his arms and kiss her. But after the morning's incident he had not acted on his desires.

He was not at all sure he could trust her.

He wished he had not given in to his wife's pleadings that morning and allowed Lyndhurst to attend their entertainment. She had used her wiles on him, wound him round her finger that morning. He had been like putty in her small hands. He did not like the feeling that she could manipulate him. He should have taken a stronger line with Lyndhurst, should have forbidden him the house under any circumstances.

And he had been too easy with Georgie. But it had been hard to remain severe, to think clearly, when she had been pressing herself against him, sending waves of desire coursing through his body while his anger had been hot and he had been trying to concentrate on dealing with Lyndhurst's possibly scandalous attentions.

Georgie prattled excitedly to Sedgemoor all the way to Vauxhall. Listening indulgently to her lively chatter in amusement and growing relaxation as they sat side by side in his carriage, he propped his foot against the opposite seat and tucked his wife's arm snugly through his. Lifting his other hand over hers, he played with her fingers, smiling down at her in the dark as she talked on.

When they arrived at the famous pleasure gardens, Georgie, being her usual bubbling, unreserved self, exclaimed over each new wonder as they made their way through the maze of walks until they arrived at the edge of the area known as the Grove. Spotting Max and Henry with Charlotte and Lady Widecombe awaiting them in their supper box across the way, Georgie waved gaily to them. She and Sedgemoor began to walk toward the box.

Starting with surprise, Sedgemoor jerked her to a halt several feet from their destination. Georgie looked inquiringly in the direction in which he stared, and recognized Lady Carstairs sitting in the box next to theirs. Miss Gregson, her little companion was with her, as well as an elderly couple, the gentleman of military bearing. Diana's head was turned away from them. She was talking with Max.

Georgie saw at a glance that she looked absolutely breathtaking in a confection of white gauze, with a satin silver ribbon at her neck and another binding up her hair.

Breaking off her conversation with Max, Diana looked up and saw Georgie on Sedgemoor's arm. Her brows rose in surprise, before a mask of stillness came over her features, concealing all emotion.

Without a second's hesitation, Georgie walked for-

ward and greeted Diana in a friendly manner, compli-
menting her unaffectedly on her appearance. "How I
envy you, Diana! You are so beautiful tonight in your
silver and white. You must come to our masquerade
as your namesake—Diana, goddess of the moon."

Diana thanked the viscountess and returned the
compliment, then with cool poise presented her companions, her uncle, Colonel Malcolm Astridge and
his wife. Georgie's friendly nature smoothed away
any awkwardness attending on the unlucky meeting
and soon she was chatting away to Colonel and Mrs.
Astridge, and even managed to extract a word or two
from Miss Gregson, Diana's self-effacing companion.

It was only natural for the occupants of the two
boxes to join their parties and share their suppers
while they listened to the orchestral concert. After
some time, the music changed, and the orchestra began to play a waltz. The strains of the compelling
music soon echoed through the trees and many couples descended from their boxes to dance in the open
space of the Grove. Finishing her third glass of arrack punch, Georgie hummed and swayed to the
lovely music and looked at her husband, wondering if
his leg were yet up to the exercise.

"Good evening, *Lady Sedgemoor,*" Tom Cunningham said, taking her by surprise. He was standing
below their box, glaring up at her with anger flashing
in his eyes. "How do you like Vauxhall? I recall we
were to come here together, but you cancelled the engagement."

He had arrived on the scene abruptly and greeted
the others in the party in a brusk manner before turning to Georgie once more and asking her to dance.

"Oh, Tom, do ask Charlotte, instead." Georgie tried to beg off. But when she turned to look at her friend, she saw that Henry was just soliciting her hand. She glanced at Sedgemoor, but he was speaking quietly with Diana.

"No, Georgie. I wish to speak to you."

She met his smouldering gaze with a resigned look and stepped down from the box to the ground. She set her hand in his and he swung her into the dance.

"Now, Tom, I wish you would stop looking at me as though you would like to stick a dagger through my heart. You are dying to ring a peal over my head. You have my permission to get it out of your system."

"Not here, Georgie, my girl. What I wish to say to you requires a bit of privacy." He stopped dancing abruptly and pulled her along at a fast clip down one of the darkened paths, complaining vehemently about the dashed trick she had served him.

In trying to calm him, Georgie reached out and put her hand on his arm. "We would never have suited, you know, Tommy dear. You want someone a little less forceful and managing than I am. And then, too, I am not beautiful. You will want a beauty for a wife. Just think what gorgeous children you would have if you married someone like Susan." Georgie stopped and raised her hand to cover her mouth.

"Oh, not Susan! No, I am afraid you have missed your chance there. Her eyes are turned in quite another direction. I am sorry I mentioned our Sukey. I'm afraid there is no hope for you in that quarter."

To Georgie's secret satisfaction, Tom's brows drew together in consternation. "What are you talking about? Who is pursuing Sukey? Not that rogue Lyndhurst?"

"Oh, as to that, I should not say anything to you. There are any number of eligible men who are interested in her. It is not quite clear which one Sukey will choose."

"The devil she will!" Tom exclaimed. "You will tell me the name of the blackguard who has captured Sukey's attention. Now, Georgie. Out with it, or I will give you a good shaking, my girl." Tom put his hands up to clasp Georgie's shoulders.

Sedge had been conversing with Diana, trying to smooth over the awkwardness of this unexpected meeting between them when he realized his wife was no longer on the dance floor.

Swallowing an extremely vulgar expletive, he left the box without a word to anyone and went in search of her.

It was not long before he came upon her down the Dark Walk, the most infamous of the badly lit walks that criss-crossed the Gardens. He stood for a moment as though turned to stone.

She was locked in an embrace with young Cunningham. Searing pain shot through him.

It was too much for a man of his pride.

"Ah, Georgiana, I came to see if you required my assistance," he said in a voice that cut through the stillness like a whiplash. "But I see that you are enjoying yourself *again* today, without any aid from me whatsoever."

He turned on his heel, and strode back the way he

had come, not conscious of taxing his leg, not conscious of anything but the blazing pain, aching hurt piercing through him.

He *knew* he should never have begun to trust a woman. Having married her for reasons of honor, he should have left it at that. He should never have let himself develop any feelings for her. He had been drawn to her light and warmth, to the flame of her hair and the warmth of her engaging personality. And he had got burned.

Twice in one day, she had met other men, flirted with them, laughed up at them, touched them ... promising, sharing who-knew-what favors with them.

Well, two could play at that game, he decided grimly.

He had planned to ask Georgie to waltz that night. His leg was feeling strong enough for the exercise. Now he would ask Diana instead.

"Gus!" Georgie called after her husband in an agonized voice as he disappeared from view. She had been giving Tom a brief hug after she had convinced him that they should cry friends again and get on with their separate lives. She had just released him when she suddenly saw her husband standing at the edge of the pathway, not ten yards away.

Sedgemoor had been looking at her, not with exasperation or the fury she had come to expect when he was angry with her, but with an entirely different expression. He was looking through her, as though she were nothing to him, as though he had blotted her from his life in the space of a heart beat.

Wordlessly, Tom escorted a silent Georgie back to the boxes. When they arrived it was to see that Sedgemoor was waltzing with Diana Carstairs, their tall, well-matched figures drawing all eyes as they moved slowly to the bewitching music.

Georgie turned unseeing eyes toward the others in their box, the hurt look on her face visible for any who had the wit to look. Her foot missed the first step that led up to the box.

Max came to her rescue at once, intercepting her. "Let us walk for a while, Georgie, my dear."

"Max." She reached for him blindly.

"I know, my dear. Lean on me a little."

"They are waltzing together."

"Well, there's nothing in that. All the other men have waltzed with Diana—Henry, her uncle Colonel Astridge. Why, even I have danced with her. It would seem odd if Sedge did not. He is only being polite."

"He is not only being polite," she said from between clenched teeth, clenched to prevent herself from shaking. "He has not danced since . . . since he broke his leg. And the way they are looking at one another is enough to—oh dear, Max, forgive me, but I fear I am going to cry."

They had reached one of the sheltered walks, so Max stopped and took her gently in his arms and let her cry against his shoulder. It was an uncomfortable experience. He was furious enough to plant Sedgemoor a facer himself for treating darling little Georgie this way.

He had never thought he would see Georgie cry. He felt a little choked up himself, and not only at her pain, but because of an ache in his own heart at the sight that had disturbed her so greatly.

Georgie went home knowing that all her plotting, all the moves in the lighthearted game she had been playing to win her husband's love had gone for naught. One impetuous moment with her childhood friend had caused a misunderstanding that had driven Sedge away from her into the arms of another woman.

Her light heart became heavy. She had lost the game, and more, much more, had been at stake than she realized.

The viscount had been so angry that he had not even accompanied her home, sending her on alone in his carriage.

She lay in her bed, listening for sounds of him moving about in the room next door, but all was silent. He had not yet returned. Had he accompanied Lady Carstairs home and been invited to stay?

Georgie turned over and closed her eyes, a single tear sliding down her cheek in the lonely darkness.

Chapter 18

Sedge and Georgie spent an uncomfortable week, seeing little of one another. Georgie tried to speak to her husband several times, but he did not respond to her overtures. He either looked at her through cold, narrowed eyes and issued freezing setdowns, or assumed a look of haughty detachment, as though he did not hear her, as though she were not even there, and then walked away. Mostly he avoided her, staying away from the house much of the day, only returning to Brook Street in the evening when she was out with friends at some social function or other.

Livermore, Sedgemoor's man of business, called on Georgie during that time to give her the details of the generous settlement her husband had provided for her. She had been amazed at Sedgemoor's generosity and thoughtfulness ... after she had recovered from her shock. For when the servants had told her Mr. Livermore was below and wished private speech with her, Georgie had been afraid that the viscount was going to try to put her aside, try to send her into exile somewhere away from him. *That* was something she would not have stood for. Not for a minute.

It was sultry and warm outside on the evening of the Viscount and Viscountess Sedgemoor's festive masquerade.

"It be so 'ot tunnight, me lady, I dunno as how ye'll bear wearin' all the layers of yer costume," Madge, Georgie's cheeky new lady's maid, said in her thick Cockney accent. She was helping her mistress dress for the masquerade. "If'n it were me, yer ladyship, I wouldn't wear nothin' but this 'ere gauze overdress." Madge laughed as she fingered the spun-gold, spangled material Georgie had chosen to wear over her silk undergown.

"Well, Madge, perhaps you are right," Georgie said innocently.

"Lawks a mercy, me lady! I ain't serious!"

Georgie laughed. "No, no. I do not mean that I shall be completely bare underneath. But perhaps we can get rid of some of the bits and pieces, pare the costume down to the bare essentials, shall we say?"

The maid winked at her mistress and they began to refashion the costume.

Georgie had decided to dress as Titania, the queen of the fairies in Shakespeare's *Midsummer Night's Dream.* She had conspired with Wilkins, Sedgemoor's valet, who was as susceptible to his mistress's charm as all the viscount's other servants, with the possible exception of Mr. Stillman. Wilkins agreed to change his master's costume from the simple black domino and mask the viscount had planned to wear, to one suitable for Oberon, Titania's sometimes imperiously overbearing consort. The garment was sewn up to Georgie's specifications by the seamstress who made her own costume.

Despite her husband's stubborn failure to make peace, Georgie's spirits had bounced back over the course of the week. He had not accompanied her out in the evenings, but when she returned home each night she found that he had already retired to bed. She had also learned that he had *not* turned to Lady Carstairs for comfort. Max had made it his business to find out and had told her so. Once that worry was over, her natural cheerfulness and optimism had reasserted itself and she formed a new plan to win her husband. He could not stay angry forever, could he? she asked herself. Perhaps if she provided enough temptation, she could lure him back to her bed and place herself in his heart.

Tonight she would enchant him, as Oberon had enchanted Titania in the play, though she would refrain from using some of Oberon's nastier tricks, she thought with a laugh, envisioning Gus enamored of a Miss Bottomley, a female with an ass's head!

Even if her gambit did not work, they were to leave for the country in a day or two. She would have him all alone and at her mercy, she thought with a warm gleam in her eyes, remembering how passionately he had responded to her on those other occasions.

Georgie was mindful, too, of the other players in her game. Tonight Tom would find himself captivated by Susan, of that she was certain. Like Oberon's servant, Puck, she would anoint the recalcitrant lover's eyelids with a magic potion.

Her potion would be Susan's costume—a long white silk chiton, fastened over one shoulder with a golden pin, softly belted with a golden cord. A thin circlet of gold would crown Susan's long, midnight black hair worn loose, flowing over her shoulders.

When she tried on the costume, Susan's dark eyes had glittered like stars through her golden mask. Georgie had laughed and told her she was the goddess Venus incarnate.

Susan had almost rebelled at such an idea. She had no wish to resemble that wanton deity. Only the thought of winning Tom, and a hitherto suppressed streak of adventure, had persuaded her to dress in the almost indecently revealing costume.

Georgie had had less luck with Ann. She failed to talk that sensible lady into dressing as a wild maenad, a follower of the god Dionysus.

Ann said she would dress as a prioress and told Georgie to abandon her plans to reconcile her with Lord Robert. Georgie had looked mischievous and said if Ann wanted to dress as a holy nun, perhaps she should dress as Heloise.

"And I suppose Lord Robert is to be Abelard. Well, you know what happened to him!" Ann had riposted.

Georgie had been disappointed, but did not dwell on it. She could do only so much to try to reconcile Ann and Robin. She would sprinkle her magic dust and hope that love would bloom.

Georgie took a quick peek at herself in the looking glass before she left her room. Yes, it had been a good idea to cut off the arms of her gown and arrange the shimmering blue and green silk shift over just one shoulder, she thought, twirling around to let the sparkling gold gauze she wore over the wispy garment catch the candlelight.

Hemming the shift up another three inches as Madge had suggested gave her more freedom to run and skip and dance about, too. She glanced down, pleased to see that the soft, flesh-colored kid slippers she wore made her stockingless feet look almost bare. The effect was just as she had envisioned.

The wreath of pale green leaves nestling against her copper curls gave her the appearance of a roguish sprite. Her mask, fashioned of blue and green feathers tickled her nose. She sneezed once, then readjusted it. Humming happily, she danced from the room, feeling indeed like a magical creature of the enchanted forest. She had a recalcitrant lover of her own to enchant that night.

Sedge moved among his colorfully garbed, cheerfully reveling guests with a frown on his masked face, knocking aside one of the low-hanging garlands festooning his ballroom as he walked through the partially lit room, out through the open doors to the darkened garden beyond. It was late, almost midnight and time for the unmasking.

A couple standing in the shadows hastily broke apart when they heard his foot fall on the stone pathway.

Why the devil had Georgie not had more candles

lit inside and hung some Chinese lanterns out here? he wondered irritably.

He longed for the infernal party to be over. He would take Georgie to the Oaks by the end of the week, will she or nil she.

Perhaps there he could find some peace. Perhaps there they could come to some better understanding with one another.

It had not been a pleasant week. He had not been happy after the disastrous trip to Vauxhall Gardens, either with Georgie's behavior, or with his own. She had tried again and again to smooth things over. But he had coldly rebuffed all her attempts at reconciliation. He berated himself for being so unreasonable.

Max had had a few choice words to say to him concerning his callous behavior, taking him to task for his ill-treatment of his warm-hearted, lively little wife.

Well, he knew he had acted badly, knew they must reach some sort of accommodation with one another. He had married her. She was his viscountess now. He must make the best of the situation. Perhaps to do that, he must remove her from proximity to other men.

Yes, he would take her to the country, keep her closely confined, so that only he could see her, talk with her, hold her, kiss her. . . .

Kiss her! Aye, there was the root of the problem. His desire to kiss her, to love her with his body was so strong, he was in danger of abandoning his iron-willed decision to stay away from her. Why he acted so obstinately against his own wishes and desires, he did not know. He cursed under his breath.

Jealousy was the reason. There! He had admitted it. He was insanely jealous. He had allowed himself to be captivated by the managing little baggage and now he was in grave danger of allowing her to invade his heart the way she had invaded his life.

A day or two after the evening at Vauxhall, he had calmed down enough to realize that Georgie's meeting with Cunningham had been relatively harmless. If she had wanted the boy, she had had ample opportunity to engage herself to him. No, she was just embracing him as she would have done anyone. And there was a great part of the trouble.

Georgie gave her affection, her love, freely to almost any and all comers. With her friendly, open, confiding manners, everyone was charmed by her, loved her even. Just look at that scoundrel Lyndhurst, proposing marriage to her of all things!

He had come out here to the garden to look for Georgie. He had lost track of her some quarter of an hour ago when he had been talking with Diana, who was dressed very fetchingly, if somewhat incongruously, as Sir Francis Drake, complete with a curling black mustache and dark wig covering her own pale tresses. He had admired her long, shapely legs, exposed as they had been in the doublet and hose she wore. He had been exchanging a few pleasantries with her when Max had happened by, dressed as a dashing pirate.

"Good evening, my lusty buccaneer," Diana had hailed him in a deep, gravelly voice. "You look like a sailor who would be useful on one of my long voyages. Have you any experience on a privateer, sir?"

Max had grinned devilishly, his teeth gleaming

white amidst the full black beard he sported. He had made the most of his scar painting it a bright vermillion. The red scar, together with the midnight black mask covering his eyes and the razor-sharp cutlass hooked in his sash, gave him a suitably bloodthirsty appearance.

"You are looking very dashing, Max," Diana had added in her own normal throaty tones.

"Sir Francis? I must say, I applaud your daring, Diana," Max had answered, regarding her with an appreciative gleam in his masked eyes, while he twirled the ends of his fake mustache roguishly.

She had responded in kind and Sedge had walked away, leaving the two to their flirtatious badinage. Out of the corner of his eye he had seen someone garbed in white from head to toe disappear behind the curtains drawn across one of the deep window embrasures at the side of the room. He had walked on, taking no further notice of this bit of impropriety as he continued his search for his wife.

"Let me go, my lord. It is not at all proper that you have pulled me back here behind this curtain with you."

After she had refused all his attempts to converse with her that evening, Lord Robert had boldly reached out and grabbed Miss Ann Forester by the wrist, pulling her into the concealed window embrasure with him.

"Ho! Miss Prim and Proper, are you? Dressed as a holy nun ... that's a bit rich after last Christmas,

Ann," he drawled sardonically, his green eyes glittering at her through the slits in his mask.

"How dare you!"

He caught her hand as it flashed toward his cheek and held it in a strong grip. "No. You shall not hit me again. I carried the imprint of your hand for days last time."

"Let me go, Lord Robert, or I shall call out."

"Promise you will not hit me."

She nodded warily, the coif of her nun's headdress dipping down low over the white mask covering her eyes.

He flicked the headdress with a long finger. "Why have you covered all your glorious hair with this monstrosity, Ann?"

"My hair is not 'glorious' in the least."

"It *is* glorious. When it's all loose and spread about your shoulders, Ann."

She took two steps back from him. "What do you want?"

"A few words. A few *kind* words, perhaps?" One side of his mouth quirked up in a half smile under his plain mask. The costume, complete with cape flipped over one shoulder and the long curled wig he wore, proclaimed him a cavalier from the court of King Charles II.

"There is nothing more to be said, my lord."

All evening, Ann had desperately been avoiding him, had been trying to banish the thought that he was the most dashing man in the room. Now, in such close proximity to him, she found it difficult to breathe properly.

"There are volumes more to be said." He reached

out and took her hand and held it gently, playing with
her fingers.

Ann looked up at him and saw the soft look in his
eyes as he gazed down at her. They stood speechless
for a long moment.

"Forgive me," he whispered, looking directly into
her wavering amber eyes.

"I—," Ann began.

Someone pushed the curtain back, exposing the
tableau to the view of the whole room. "Oh, ho!
What have we here? A lover's tryst? A naughty nun
and the Earl of Rochester, if I mistake not," the in-
truder exclaimed. "How intriguing!"

Ann pulled her hand from Robin's and fled.

Sedge pulled off his mask and walked on down
into the darkened garden, looking for Georgie. He
would spot her soon enough, for she was dressed
quite unmistakably as Titania, the queen of the fairies, in a shimmering, sparkling slip of a costume.

He had had an unpleasant surprise earlier that evening when his valet arrived to help him dress. There
was no plain domino and mask set out, but a green
and gold and brown and red patterned knee-length
chiton. There were golden sandals for his feet, with
long leather thongs to bind round the calves of his
legs. A crown of green leaves, interspersed with
some winking golden stars was provided for him to
wear over his hair. And his mask was fashioned of
some sparkling gold material.

Sedge had stood speechless with shock. "What the
hell is this?" he had thundered finally, a blistering

setdown for Wilkins trembling on the tip of his tongue.

"A costume for Oberon, my lord. The king of the fairies."

"I know who Oberon is, but I do not plan to impersonate him tonight, or ever!"

Wilkins had sniffed and said it was her ladyship's wish that he wear the garment.

Closing his eyes and clenching his fists to prevent himself from giving in to the urge to shout for Georgie to present herself in his room immediately so that he could ring a peal over her head that would make her ears sting for weeks, he had taken several steadying breaths through his nose before saying that he would wear the ridiculous thing, but he would be damned if he would enjoy making a bloody fool of himself by doing so.

When he had greeted his guests earlier and observed the motley collection of costumes they had chosen to wear, he had realized that he was in good company. He would not be the only one making a damned fool of himself, or herself, that evening.

Sedge walked on down the darkened pathway, his heart hammering in his chest as he searched his garden. He feared to find his wife locked in an embrace, platonic or otherwise, with another man. This time, he knew he would commit murder and mayhem.

She was nowhere in sight. And, he remembered grimly, Lyndhurst, dressed as the Earl of Rochester, the most infamous cavalier at the court of Charles II, had been talking with Georgie earlier in the evening. Were they together now?

He heard a rustling in the small rose arbor off to

his right. He quietly made his way there, catching sight of something ahead of him twinkling and gleaming in the moonlight. It could be Georgie—but it might be anyone. Many costumes had incorporated spangles and sequins and sparkling jewels.

The shimmering gauze overdress Georgie wore over her shift caught in the light breeze and billowed out behind her.

Sedge reached out a hand and grabbed Georgie's arm. He swung her about forcefully, a low growl issuing from his throat as he did so.

He frowned down into his wife's eyes and opened his mouth to demand an explanation of why she was skulking about in the garden. But before he could begin shouting at her, he found Georgie's hand covering his mouth, pressing hard against his lips.

"Hush!" She commanded in a fierce whisper. "Don't make a sound, Gus, or you will ruin everything."

She removed her hand.

"Georgie! *You*—," he began in a furious undertone, but she clamped her hand over his mouth once more and pointed out into the center of the arbor where a couple were seated on a stone bench.

Absorbed in eavesdropping on their conversation, she dropped her hand from his mouth and reached for his hand instead, linking her fingers in his, clasping his hand tightly in hers.

As his eyes adjusted to the light, Sedge could see Susan Tennyson, dressed in a very revealing Greek costume, sitting with Cunningham. He was holding her hands and speaking to her earnestly. Both were unmasked.

Their words were not quite distinguishable to the onlookers, but the gist of the conversation was evident enough. They were speaking words of love to one another.

Miss Tennyson had been looking down at her lap while Cunningham was speaking to her, but when she finally looked up at him, the brilliant smile on her face was enough to outshine the moon, Sedge saw. The couple leaned toward one another and kissed. Then Cunningham put his arms around the girl and enveloped her in a crushing embrace.

How painful the sight was to Georgie, how much she cared for Cunningham, Sedge did not know. What she had seen may have broken her heart.

Georgie squeezed his hand more tightly at the sight, unconsciously raising it and pressing it to her breast. Then she turned and gave him a brilliant smile of her own.

Sedge looked down at her in the moonlight, seeing that her mask was gone and that her eyes were shining up at him not with tears, but with a glad light.

His heart gave an odd little jerk. He looked down at her lips and began to lower his head toward hers, but she tugged on his hand, drawing him farther away from the new lovers, leaving them to their privacy.

"Oh, I am so pleased!" she exclaimed in a low voice.

"You are pleased?"

"Susan has been in love with Tommy *forever,* you know, and I have been trying to convince that thick-skulled, slowtop of a Thomas Cunningham that she is the only woman in the world who is just right for him."

"So you have been playing matchmaker again, have you, my little Lady Mischief?"

She heard the smile in his voice and continued, "Well, if I have, it's only for their own good. Oh, Gus. People can be so obstinate and thickheaded when it comes to admitting they are in love with one another."

"Henry and Miss Fraser managed to pair themselves off without any help from you," he reminded her teasingly.

"Yes, it was wonderful to read of their engagement in the papers yesterday. But just look at Robin and Ann."

His brows drew together at the mention of Lyndhurst.

"I have been working to bring them together for weeks now. He told me earlier tonight that Ann has given him no hope. He loves her, but she will not give him a second chance—after the incident last Christmas, you know. I believe he has already gone home, too discouraged to stay and enjoy himself here. . . . It is really too bad. I think Ann would be perfect for him. She is brilliant—some men would be frightened of her wit, you know. But she is kind and fun to be with, too. It is too bad she is afraid that Robin would break her heart."

"But he proposed to you. I believe he loves *you.*"

"Oh, well. He may feel some affection for me—as a friend, you know."

"Loves you like a sister, does he?"

"Umm. Something like that. He just enjoys being

around me. On the rebound from Ann, you know. And his proposing to me just goes to show that he is ready to marry, to settle down, reform his wicked ways and become a model husband."

"Georgie, your logic defeats me."

She gave him an impish smile. "Well, Robin may be ready to give up, but I am not. It's like moving the pieces around on a chessboard, as you taught me. If there are still a few pieces left, there is hope one can turn things around and win the game, if one plays carefully. I shall invite them both to—"

"No!" Sedge interrupted fiercely. "I do not want you interfering in any way whatsoever." What he wanted to say was that he did not want her to have anything further to do with Lyndhurst, but he feared to act too much the jealous husband just now when they had reached this fragile peace.

"Oh, well, there are other couples who need a helping hand."

"Are there indeed? Do you have anyone specific in mind? Come, let me know the worst."

"I have some hopes for Max and Diana."

"Max and *Diana!*"

"Yes. I hope you do not mind too terribly, Gus."

"Mind? Why should I mind?"

"Well, you and she—you were in love with her, weren't you?"

"In love with Diana? Never!"

"But how could you not love her? She is so beautiful and poised and mysterious and—"

He hushed her. "I may have been fascinated by her at one time, but she never had my heart."

"You were lovers."

"No, Georgie. We never were. I have only ever loved one woman."

Surprising him, Georgie put her hands up to ears. "No! Please do not tell me about it, Gus. I had rather not know."

"But—"

"No. Come, my dear, let us return inside for the unmasking." She grabbed his hand.

He stopped her, grasping her shoulders. "No. It's already after midnight. The guests have probably already unmasked, revealing what everyone undoubtedly knew beforehand. I have had enough of this party."

"Have you, my dear?"

"Yes. Definitely. Though I must congratulate you on the success of your theme."

"Thank you, Gus." She reached up on tiptoe to plant a kiss on his cheek.

He accepted her affectionate gesture with a slight smile, folding his arms around her waist and hugging her to him, burying his lips in her bright hair for a moment.

"Although I was not best pleased when I first saw this costume, I have come to see it has definite advantages," he said, pressing his bare knee between her thighs, rubbing gently against her silk-covered legs.

"What do you have on underneath there, anyway?" she asked with a chuckle. "I never thought to provide for that detail."

"Come closer and find out."

"I can't get any closer, Gus."

Her eyes gleamed brightly in the moonlight and he

could see the mischievous smile curving up her lips. He raised one of his hands and tipped up her chin with his fingers.

"You know, there is another couple who is crying out for your attention to see that all comes to rights with them."

"Oh? Who is that?" she asked, trying to fight the breathless feeling of being held so tightly against his body, with only his short tunic and her whisper of a gown between them.

"Us, Georgie," he murmured, his breath whispering along her skin, his lips only inches from her mouth.

"Oh," she breathed.

He touched his lips softly to hers on her inhaled breath. He lifted his head slightly to look down at her, then kissed her again, as lightly as a butterfly alighting on her lips.

"Gus," she wailed, throwing her arms up around his neck and lifting her mouth to his, "kiss me properly!"

"I think you mean improperly," he said on the breath of a laugh. "Always ready to oblige my lady wife," he whispered, covering her lips with his, sliding his tongue into her mouth, at the same time sliding his hand down her bare shoulder under the filmsy material of the slinky shift to caress her bare flesh, letting his fingers play over the sensitive tip of her breast, teasing it until he felt the moan rise in her throat.

He raised the skirt of her wispy costume so that their bare thighs met and rubbed together, smooth skin meeting rough.

"Oh, Gus . . . please . . . oh, yes. I—oh dear, we really ought to go inside and see to our guests," she said breathlessly some time later, sagging against him, her arms holding on around his neck her only support.

"I think not, my dear," he responded huskily.

"Gus, what on earth are you doing?" Georgie protested as he lifted her up in his arms and began to carry her back to the house.

"You are tired. I am carrying you up to bed."

"But I am not at all tired."

"All the better then."

"Better for what?"

"You will see."

"Oh dear, Gus, put me down. I am too heavy for you. Think of your poor leg . . ."

"My leg is much better, thank you."

"Oh! Oh, good . . . but everyone will be expecting us at the unmasking . . . they will think we have run mad."

"They will forgive us, if we don't appear. We are newlyweds—still on our honeymoon, or had you forgotten? All sorts of moonstruck behavior can be expected from us."

Georgie continued to argue, pointing out the madness of his behavior, until she remembered this was just what she wanted.

He paid no attention to her protests, his superior strength for once overcoming her indomitable will. He carried her upstairs over her laughing protests—up the stairs into his room where Wilkins had turned down the sheets of his bed and was warming them with a long-handled copper warming pan.

314   *Meg-Lynn Roberts*

On seeing the servant in Sedgemoor's room, Georgie hid her scarlet face against her husband's shoulder.

"Leave us, please," Sedge ordered impatiently.

Seeing his master standing in the doorway, holding the viscountess in his arms, both clad in their scanty woodland masquerade costumes, Wilkins was rendered speechless. He scurried from the room, taking the warming pan with him.

"Oh, Gus, really! Having your sheets warmed on such a hot night?" Georgie said teasingly, tickling his ear with her breath.

"I shall dispense with the warming pan in future. From now on, my dear viscountess, I shall expect *you* to warm my sheets for me. Every night."

Sedge used his foot to slam the door behind the retreating figure of his surprised valet.

He walked over to the bed and deposited Georgie on the coverlet. "Now, my girl, you will stay in this room until you agree to go home with me to the Oaks tomorrow."

"Oh?" she grinned up at him. "How do you plan to make me agree to that?"

"By making love to you until you give in."

"Oh. In that case, I think I may need a lot of persuading."

"We have got all night."

"If you do that, we will be too tired tomorrow. But I will promise to go with you the next day instead, if you like."

Her saucy reply was too much for him. "You provoking little wretch," he growled. Drawing his ridiculous costume over his head even before he finished speaking, he threw it to the floor, and joined her on the bed.

Pulling her gauze scarf off in one jerk and lifting the silk shift off over her head, he went to work on her, kissing her all over her delightfully curved body. Not slow to respond, Georgie urged him on, letting her hands and her lips play over the every inch of his wonderful, hard, lean, masculine body, eliciting as many moans of pleasure from him as he was extracting from her.

He loved her slowly, tenderly, teaching her her own pleasure and his own. He loved her with his body and with his heart, taking her to new heights of passion, of pleasure, as he joined their bodies, losing himself in her, as she lost herself in him.

Lying happily exhausted in one another's arms after they had sated their desires, he murmured wickedly in her ear, "Well, madam wife, do you still think I'm too large?"

"Well, you certainly did not look *that* way in Little Bickton."

"My God! You saw—" He was speechless.

"Yes, of course, when I was helping the doctor. Remember, he thought I was your wife. But it did not seem the same. It was not quite so—"

He stopped her mouth with a brief kiss. "You certainly know how to put me to the blush, my dear little wretch."

"Are you blushing, Gus? I did not know you were capable of such a thing."

"Assuredly I am. And now, madam, let us see if I can put *you* to the blush," he said, running his hands slowly, lovingly down her body from her neck to her toes, beginning their play all over again.

"It is all right you do not love me. This is good enough," she whispered as she lay cuddled snugly under his damp body after they had made love to one another again.

"Who said I don't love you, goose?" Sedge raised up on his elbows and nipped her chin, then her bare breast with his teeth.

"Oh, Gus, no need to try and bamboozle me. I know you cannot love me, with all my faults and imperfections."

"You have no more faults than the rest of us, little goose, certainly fewer than I have," he assured her tenderly. "You are my wife, Georgie. You will be the mother of my children, I hope. I love you. All right?"

"Oh, you love me because we are now related. I see."

"Georgie!" He was shaking with laughter, sending delightful sensations coursing through both of them. "I certainly hope I don't love any of my other relations the way I love you!"

Georgie laughed, too. "No. And you had better not love anyone else this way, or I will pinch you black and blue!" she threatened jokingly, but jealously, nipping the bare flesh of his lean, muscular hips with her fingers.

He rolled off her, gathered her in his arms and kissed her lingeringly for a long while. "I have never loved any woman but you, Georgie."

"Gus!" she wailed. "Please don't tell me such a clanker. I can't bear it!"

Seeing that she still doubted him, he kissed the top of her curly head tenderly and whispered earnestly, "My dearest Lady Mischief, I love you dearly, utterly, completely! I can't eat, I can't sleep, I can't think straight, you enchanting, provoking, utterly adorable little imp, and unless you plan to have my insanity, if not my death, on your conscience, you will tell me you love me as much as I love you and that you will always, *always* share my bed all this night and every other night for the rest of our lives!"

"Oh, Sedgemoor!" Georgie wailed, moved more than she could say.

"What happened to Gus?" He grinned lopsidedly.

"Gus, I love you. I have loved you almost from the first moment I saw you. From the moment I saw you lying all covered with mud in that ditch, anyway."

He chuckled. "Well, there's no need to cry about it," he said, wiping away the tears streaming down her cheeks with his fingertips.

"No," she said, wiping away the last of her tears with her small, fisted hand. "My gambit has finally worked!" she exclaimed happily.

"What gambit was that, my dearest love?"

"Why to seduce you into loving me, of course."

He shouted with laughter. "Well, Georgie, I believe we may have to declare it a draw," he said when he could speak again, wiping away tears of mirth. "You see, I used a gambit, too. I planned to entice you into my bed so that I could seduce you into loving *me!*"

"Oh, Gus, you didn't!" She gave a soft chuckle. "And I thought I had won the game!"

"I concede the game to you, my darling love. My dearest queen, my Titania, behold your king, your Oberon, at your—ah, feet."

"Feet?" She teased him.

"In a manner of speaking. You do indeed hold me in check, my love. I cannot get away now. Nor will I ever wish to."

He kissed her, and she kissed him back, savoring the feel of him, cherishing his words.

"Your love gambit worked, my dearest love." He kissed the hollow in her shoulder, his lips warm on her skin.

"'Twas a love gambit, indeed, then!" Georgie laughed huskily, her warm languor dissipating and excitement beginning to churn in her stomach yet again.

"Umm." He nuzzled her neck. Kissing her ear, he whispered, "Should you wish to engage in any more love games, I will let you take my king any day, dearest queen of my heart."

Meg-Lynn Roberts welcomes comments from her readers.

You can write to her c/o Kensington Publishing Corp., 850 Third Avenue, New York, NY 10022-6222.

For a reply, please include SASE.

ZEBRA'S REGENCY ROMANCES
DAZZLE AND DELIGHT

A BEGUILING INTRIGUE   (4441, $3.99)
by Olivia Sumner

Pretty as a picture Justine Riggs cared nothing for propriety. She dressed as a boy, sat on her horse like a jockey, and pondered the stars like a scientist. But when she tried to best the handsome Quenton Fletcher, Marquess of Devon, by proving that she was the better equestrian, he would try to prove Justine's antics were pure folly. The game he had in mind was seduction — never imagining that he might lose his heart in the process!

AN INCONVENIENT ENGAGEMENT   (4442, $3.99)
by Joy Reed

Rebecca Wentworth was furious when she saw her betrothed waltzing with another. So she decides to make him jealous by flirting with the handsomest man at the ball, John Collinwood, Earl of Stanford. The "wicked" nobleman knew exactly what the enticing miss was up to — and he was only too happy to play along. But as Rebecca gazed into his magnificent eyes, her errant fiancé was soon utterly forgotten!

SCANDAL'S LADY   (4472, $3.99)
by Mary Kingsley

Cassandra was shocked to learn that the new Earl of Lynton was her childhood friend, Nicholas St. John. After years at sea and mixed feelings Nicholas had come home to take the family title. And although Cassandra knew her place as a governess, she could not help the thrill that went through her each time he was near. Nicholas was pleased to find that his old friend Cassandra was his new next door neighbor, but after being near her, he wondered if mere friendship would be enough . . .

HIS LORDSHIP'S REWARD   (4473, $3.99)
by Carola Dunn

As the daughter of a seasoned soldier, Fanny Ingram was accustomed to the vagaries of military life and cared not a whit about matters of rank and social standing. So she certainly never foresaw her *tendre* for handsome Viscount Roworth of Kent with whom she was forced to share lodgings, while he carried out his clandestine activities on behalf of the British Army. And though good sense told Roworth to keep his distance, he couldn't stop from taking Fanny in his arms for a kiss that made all hearts equal!

Available wherever paperbacks are sold, or order direct from the Publisher. Send cover price plus 50¢ per copy for mailing and handling to Penguin USA, P.O. Box 999, c/o Dept. 17109, Bergenfield, NJ 07621. Residents of New York and Tennessee must include sales tax. DO NOT SEND CASH.